EARTHRISE

Earthbound
Book 3

Aprilynne Pike

EARTHRISE

Copyright © 2015 by Aprilynne Pike

All rights reserved.

Cover design by Saundra Mitchell /
SaundraMitchell.com

This book is a work of fiction. Names, characters,
places, and incidents are either products of the
author's imagination or are used fictitiously. Any
resemblance to actual persons, living or dead,
events, or locales is purely coincidental.

Written in the United States of America.

ISBN-13
978-1-941855-02-7

Also by Aprilynne Pike

Glitter (Forthcoming 2016)

Life After Theft
One Day More: A Life After Theft Prequel

The Wings Series
Wings
Spells
Illusions
Destined

The Earthbound Series
Earthbound
Earthquake
Earthrise

The Charlotte Westing Chronicles
Sleep No More
Sleep of Death

Anthologies
Dear Bully
Defy the Dark
Altered Perceptions

Visit Aprilynne online at AprilynnePike.com

To Benson and Evelyn,

Scott and Ashley's Happily Ever After.

CHAPTER ONE

"We'll find him."

She turns her tear-streaked face away. "It's been so long," she says, almost in argument. "I'm as weak as I've ever been. Some days I may as well be human."

The wind blows across the hillside where we sit, side-by-side in our velvet gowns, our knees pulled close to our chests. A silver circlet rests on her forehead, holding back strands of long hair—prematurely streaked with gray in a stark contrast to her smooth, unlined skin. I reach out an arm to drape across her shoulders and, though she leans in, still she does not look at me.

"We have a ship," I say softly. "Jovan is a great and wealthy lord and his entire force will be at your command."

"Sometimes…sometimes I think maybe it would be better if I had never gotten my memories back. Perhaps ignorance was preferable."

I sit straighter and meet her downcast expression with a hard stare. "Ignorance is never better. You've said so to me many times. Ignorance leaves one's future to accidents of fate, and fate is a fickle mistress."

But she says nothing.

"*Mariana.*" *I circle around to crouch in front of her, but she won't meet my gaze.* "*You are hardly helpless. Jovan and I can assist you in ways no human can. We will travel and look everywhere. We'll find him.*"

"*Your lover doesn't like mine. Never has. Why should he help?*"

"*He will help if I ask him. And you know I will.*"

"*I've almost forgotten what he looks like. Do you remember?*" *Her eyes lift and lock with mine at last, and something in them, unexpected, inexplicable, frightens me.*

Do I remember? *It has been ages. Dozens of lifetimes; each just a little shadier than the last. It's hard enough to find one's* diligo, *never mind one's friends.* "*It doesn't matter whether I remember or not,*" *I pronounce, sounding more glib than I feel.* "*What matters is that you remember. And I know that you could never forget. Not truly.*"

A horse's whinny catches my ear and I turn toward my lord and his knights in the tiltyard of Ruinwell Castle. From this small rise I can't hear his voice as he calls out to his men, but I can see the sun glinting off his tousled gold hair and the sight—as always—makes me smile. It has been a glorious three years since the handsome Lord Jovan Williams came riding through my tiny township, past my parents' filthy hovel, and spied me. I tried to hide my bare feet and dirty face, but the mighty lord would have none of it. He bounded from his horse and came to me. I thought my heart would stop beating as he loomed over where I hunkered, preparing shriveled vegetables.

"*Come be my bride,*" *he said simply. As though such a thing could ever truly happen. I was mortified. I gasped in shock and wondered who had put him up to such a jape. The shame of my filth and poverty overwhelmed me and I wept in agony at his cruelty. He swept me up in his arms and lifted me onto his enormous warhorse, then swung into the saddle behind me, holding me tight against his chest.*

A crowd had gathered by that point and I dreaded the mockery I would suffer on the morrow when I was dumped back into my miserable existence. My mother and father came out to protest—not the loss of their daughter, I would daresay, but of my able, working hands. Lord Williams removed one arm from about me, dug into his saddlebags, and drew out something I could not see. It was only when he upended it and I heard the clink of gold hitting the ground that I realized what it was.

"For your loss," he said, and I gaped at the price he had paid for me. My parents did not look in my direction again; their attention was riveted on the coins. Not that I blamed them—it was more than they could earn in a lifetime.

They would not miss me.

I still could not believe it for myself though. Not when I was taken to Rainwell Castle and scrubbed and dressed in a fine gown. Not when more food than I had ever seen in one place was set before me on a banquet table that night. Not even when Lord Williams came to me on bended knee and begged my hand.

But when he slipped an old, tarnished ring onto my finger, I believed. Because then, at last, I remembered who I really was.

We were wed the next morning in the church. Since his tenants would expect a formal joining, we gave it them. They could never understand just how joined our souls already were. A mortal wedding seemed almost farcical after the eternity we had already been as one. Jovan—as he is known in this life—had been looking for me for nearly five years, ever since his Earthbound memories were restored when he happened upon an ancient wrist cuff in the castle treasury. He had sought me relentlessly from that day forward.

This is what we could do for Mariana. But I had to restore her hope. In the span of millennia I'd known her—though I hadn't seen her in centuries now—I had never seen her so desperate. We could help. With our creationist powers we could make a difficult journey easier. We could pay for information and sail to distant lands, scanning face after face for Mariana's long-lost love.

But I could not find him for her.

She was right—I couldn't remember what he looked like.

CHAPTER TWO

"Tave, it's time." I gasp at the sound of Benson's voice close to my ear, his heart a slow thump that counters my own racing pulse. His fingers are clasped in mine and as I float to awareness I realize I'm squeezing so tightly I've cut off circulation to two of my fingers.

But I can't let go. Benson is my lifeline.

The last few days have been so full of grief and fear and surfacing memories that at times it's difficult to tell the difference between reality and the maze of my own damaged mind. Grasping onto Benson's hand means I'm myself—at least for now.

What happened? I try to assemble the fading shards of a dream—a dream that wasn't a dream. A memory.

A glint of gold curls in the sunlight—Logan. Not then, though. *Jovan*, she called him. Yet another lifetime when we were together. I squeeze my eyes shut at that. I made my decision, and I don't question it. But that doesn't mean it's easy. It doesn't mean I don't miss him.

And to Benson's dismay, it doesn't mean I haven't cried myself to sleep over him for the last three nights.

But he holds me anyway, and doesn't say a word.

There was more. There was a woman. *Mariana.*

My eyes fly open and I sit up, hitting my head on the—luckily, soft—barrier above me. With my palms pressed against my eyes I try to draw back details, remembering the dream with an artist's eye. The velvet gowns, the circlet on her head. The one on *my* head. The armor Logan was wearing, the architecture of the castle in the background.

Medieval Europe for sure—early Renaissance at the latest. Almost a *thousand* years ago. We were friends, though, at that point.

Or were we? How far back does Mariana's deception reach?

"You okay?" Benson asks. His hands slide over my arms. He's used to seeing me upset. Not just since we left the destroyed Curatoria headquarters, but all the way back to when we first met in Portsmouth. I rub my forehead into the crook of his neck and feel his lips against my hair. Confidence seeps into me along with his radiant warmth. I dream of the two of us being able to live together without disaster looming over our heads, but it seems so far-fetched as to be impossible. A childish wish, especially as whole world is coming unraveled around us.

Still, I wish it.

EARTHRISE

"A memory," I mumble. "Again." Sometimes they're clear, sometimes fuzzy, but they've been coming every night in my dreams since we left Las Vegas. I want to believe it's a good sign, but with the extent of my brain injury it could simply be a sign that I'm shaking things up in there. *Something* is bound to rise to the surface.

"We have to get dressed," Benson whispers. "We'll talk it out later."

Reality slams back into me and I remember why Benson's waking me up in the middle of the night. It's time for some breaking and entering, and not the kind we did a few months ago in Portsmouth—breaking into my aunt's office via a lock-picked door. This is high-security, multi-million dollar medical facility breaking and entering.

It's a little difficult to approach the clinic without being seen—an imposing concrete monolith jutting skyward from a plain of parking asphalt and desert landscaping. The whole expanse is visible all the way to the 101, which is busy enough even in the dead of night. We could circle around and approach from the back, but the clinic operates around the clock and it's less likely that we'll look like we're sneaking in if we come through the front doors, even at four in the morning.

"The best disguise," Thomas said when we made the plan, "is simply to look like you know exactly where you're going, and have every reason to go there."

7

The trick is to avoid cameras, to avoid anything that might tip off our whereabouts to anyone powerful who might happen to be looking for us. We can't just traipse about, making phone calls and setting appointments, hoping for the best. We're in a hurry and we have to stay hidden—not a great combination.

It feels weird to be using my powers for illicit activities, but in the end, it's to help people. I try to focus on that. I'm *helping* people. Even if, at the moment, that means trespassing, with a side of B & E. The actual hospital part of the clinic will be bustling—even at this time of night—but the offices should be empty. I create a wrapped gift in Alanna's hands and a *GET WELL* balloon in my own. We look almost like a family and the thought makes me vaguely uncomfortable.

"One there," Thomas whispers, indicating a translucent dome over the entrance. It vanishes, leaving only a hole and a cleanly-severed coaxial cable as evidence that a security camera was ever there at all. Thomas glances at me, but I shake my head. The hope was to have Alanna wreck the wires, or have me recreate the cameras once we'd passed by—possibly even in working condition, a feat beyond Thomas' power. But with the domes covering them, Alanna can't see what needs to be destroyed and I can't see what I need to create. Benson foresaw the eventuality, though, and it doesn't slow us down; the disappearance of cameras is sure to attract security's attention at some point, but as long as we stay ahead of them, we should be fine.

The glass doors slide open automatically and we never even glance toward the woman sitting at the front desk—like we've been here before and need neither permission nor directions. I hold my breath, but she doesn't stop us, barely even glances up. Thomas was right. Without slowing our purposeful strides, we take a quick left, then right, and duck into an elevator.

I take away all of our props and as soon as the doors open Alanna glances around for surveillance, eliminating two more cameras before we emerge from the elevator. We make it to Dr. Martin's door without any trouble, and Alanna erases the middle of the deadbolt from existence.

"Careful as you open it," Thomas whispers. "Watch for sensors."

But there are none. There simply isn't much up here to steal. Thank goodness we aren't trying to break into their laboratories—probably tighter security down there. At least I *hope* they have tighter security in the labs. Phase two of our plan is to make use of them.

Not that there's a security system in the world that could realistically stop an Earthbound. Maybe I'm judging this one too harshly.

Thomas restores the deadbolt in the lock and we stand huddled in Dr. Martin's office, straining our ears in the silence. After about fifteen minutes, footsteps sound in the hallway and someone tries the handles of a few office doors—including the one we're standing behind. But gradually the people move away, accompanied by a chorus of muttered bewilderment.

Since it's summer in the desert, the sun is already starting to rise, but it'll be a few hours before the office's owner arrives, so Thomas and I create small bedrolls and we all curl up for a bit more sleep.

Not that I expect to actually get any; not even when I feel Benson's breathing deepen and slow on the back of my neck. I'm too nervous. This is the part where everything could go wrong. The part where I have to tell the truth.

Some of the truth.

Once I'm sure Benson's all the way asleep, I slip out from under his arm and create a simple Cheval mirror in one corner of the office. The sun is just high enough that I can see myself clearly without additional light—good. I need to be presentable. Credible, if such a look can be said to exist in such a circumstance. I add a few touches of color—especially on my cheeks, which are still a bit pale from blood loss. Even though I removed all outer signs of damage, my stomach is still incredibly sore from the stabbing and the surgery, so I replace my black yoga pants with a soft gray cotton dress that doesn't press on my abdomen. I add black tights and the red chucks that I loved so much back in Michigan, then a jean jacket for the cool room.

I considered a nice suit. Even a formal dress that would make me look more like a goddess. But none of those are *me*, and this is my crusade, now.

I arrange a few chairs right in front of the desk. Then I sit in the center one and wait for Dr. Martin.

At 8:27 in the morning we're all awake and in position when I hear the doorknob jiggle. In my mind's eye I can see Dr. Martin entering the code on the small keypad. I glance over at Thomas, sitting with the others just behind me.

We have to get this right. Because it doesn't matter that I have the vaccine if I can't get it to people. We need a respectable name behind the new vaccine and a means of worldwide distribution…and we need it two months ago.

Dr. Martin walks into her office and closes the door behind her, her eyes fixed on a smartphone in her right hand, her thumb working furiously at the simulated keypad. Alanna puts one hand over her mouth, likely stifling an inappropriate giggle. Dr. Martin drops her briefcase beside the door before looking up to finally see us.

She stands frozen for a moment. "Can I help you?" she asks at last, pushing brown waves behind her ear.

"I certainly hope so." I don't rise, hardly even move. The truth is I'm still too sore from surgery to jump to my feet—will be for at least another week, I suspect—but she doesn't need to know that.

She looks at the four of us—hardly a menacing bunch—and her eyes come back to me, the formation of the chairs marking me as the one in charge, despite her doubting expression. "Do we have an appointment?"

"No, but we think you'll want to hear what we have to say. About the virus."

She looks like she's wondering if she should call security, but she doesn't. She doesn't sit behind her desk, either—she remains standing, tall for a woman, and taller still on three-inch heels, looking for all the world like she's ready to bolt. I don't blame her. "Which, uh, virus would that be?"

"*The* virus," I say. "We're here to make you the most important physician of the century, and to save a hell of a lot of lives." I lean forward, cringing when it hurts my stomach. "What would you do if you had a vaccine for the virus?"

"You're talking about the Kentucky virus?" Distantly I remember that the first cases were in a small town in Kentucky—I've been secluded from news for long enough that I'd forgotten the virus had a name. Or, at least, humans have a name for it. "If I had a vaccine for that, I'd get it into mass production right away. Anyone would."

I look up at her, hoping that I appear serious, that in her eyes I don't just look young and crazy. "And if someone—a very powerful someone—tried to kill you to prevent you from doing just that? Would you risk your life to save the world?"

She looks behind me at Benson, Thomas, and Alanna. "Why are you asking me this?"

"Dr. Martin, I need to know if we've come to the right place. The right *person*. So tell me, would you risk your life to protect the world from this virus?"

"Of course," she says, confidence edging into her voice as she turns slightly back toward the door. "But we're very likely years from developing such a thing, if it can ever be done. Now—"

"Good," I interrupt. "Because that's exactly what we need you to do. I have a working, tested vaccine but I also have very determined, powerful enemies. I need you to take credit for the vaccine, and use every resource in your power to get it out into the world before it can be destroyed."

She regards me skeptically, but the hand that was reaching for the door handle stops. "You...really believe that?"

"We're in your office, and we got here without anyone catching us. Seems a bit complicated for a prank, don't you think? And not a very funny one, I might add."

"Indeed not," she replies, and her hand goes to the doorknob again. I know I have only seconds before she has security chasing us out of the building.

I hold up my hand, and at a thought, a tube of milky colored serum fills it. Dr. Martin's eyes widen.

"Doctor, do you believe in magic?"

CHAPTER THREE

"Would you mind sitting down, Dr. Martin? You're making me nervous," I say as calmly as I can.

"I'm making *you* nervous?" she mutters.

"If you refuse to help us it's possible that everyone in the world will be dead before we can find someone else. So yes, you clinging to that doorknob is making me *very* nervous. Will you please sit down?"

I see her gulp in a breath to shout, but I'm too fast. A thick gag covers her mouth and when her hands fly to it, I transform the door and doorframe into a solid piece. Dr. Martin whips around, but I'm not done. Cords of rope wrap around her hands and legs and as she thrashes she begins to fall.

"Thomas," I whisper-hiss and Thomas jumps up to catch Dr. Martin. He drags her across the room and sets her softly down in her chair. Dr. Martin continues to thrash; I create cords binding her to the chair, but I'm a little afraid she'd going to hurt herself and I don't know what to do about it.

Alanna finally stands and leans forward, fingers splayed across the desk.

"Katherine Martin!" she says softly, but with a sharp edge.

She's struck momentarily still at the sound of her own name.

"We'll put you in a full-body cast, if we must. You have to listen. You're obviously not going anywhere for a while so I suggest you calm the hell down."

Alanna's entire speech comes out in a calm, near monotone, but the directness of it somehow worms its way through and the doctor stills. Even so, a tear slips down her cheek and I ache inside, knowing she must expect to be murdered at any moment.

"I need your undivided attention," I say softly, taking up Alanna's place right in front of Dr. Martin's field of vision. "So please do remain calm. I'll do what I can to make you comfortable." As a show of good faith I remove the gag. When she doesn't scream, I conjure up a series of poster board illustrations, and though *that* makes Dr. Martin's eyes bulge, I immediately launch into a scientific lecture similar to the one Daniel gave me when introducing me to the virus. Science—something familiar and hopefully comforting. The first several minutes must be review, but it not only helps her to calm down, it tells her I have actual knowledge about the virus.

I continue on with more poster boards, pointing to strands of DNA and explaining the work I did in Daniel's laboratories. The wild panic has left Dr. Martin's eyes and I'm not sure she even realizes it when the ropes binding her to her chair melt away. First I explain my failures. She nods along silently—likely she's tried some of the same methods.

"The real breakthrough came from Dr. Ryder here," I say, gesturing at Thomas and hoping he doesn't mind that I'm applying his former profession to his current incarnation. I suspect it'll put Dr. Martin further at ease to know that there's another medical professional here—even if not technically in this life. I remove the last of Dr. Martin's fetters, and this time she does notice—but simply leans forward on her desk, peering at my poster boards.

I explain Thomas' theory about using proteins to fight the virus. "Last week I was able to successfully isolate such a protein. We had one-hundred percent effectiveness in our lab tests."

I lace my fingers in front of me. All four of us peer at Dr. Martin—it's her turn now.

"And…someone is trying to kill you over it," Dr. Martin says slowly.

"Yes," I answer, not wanting to go into detail—for her own safety, and maybe mine as well. "They are."

"You've skipped a step," she says after a moment, her hands rising to straighten her mussed hair, then setting to rights the lapels of her jacket. "How did you find this protein? And once you did, how did you synthesize it into the virus?

I'm uncertain of what kind of technology would even be—"

"I've tried to make it obvious that I can do things you can't explain, Dr. Martin," I interrupt. "Under other circumstances we might talk more about that but, well, the clock is ticking."

"You know, I haven't seen a clock that ticks in years," she says, smiling wanly. Her fingers are shaking where she clasps them together on top of her desk. "I can't deny that you've piqued my interest. But you have to understand how…difficult…this is for me. To believe, I mean."

"I have proof, of course."

She raises her eyebrows in interest, but I'm a little worried that she's going into shock.

"Let me introduce my friends," I say with a small gesture, trying to maintain the formality that seems to be holding Dr. Martin's panic at bay. Only Thomas reaches forward to shake the pale woman's hand when I introduce him as *Dr. Ryder*. Probably for the best.

"I inoculated the three of us a few days ago," Thomas explains. "Consider us your willing test-subjects. Blood samples, expose us to the virus, whatever you need to convince yourself that we have a true vaccine."

She purses her lips. "Who would want to stop you from saving millions—billions—of lives?"

"The same people who created the virus to begin with," I respond.

A red flush colors her face and her hands are still shaking as she grabs a tissue and blots it across her forehead. "I'll take you to the lab. I don't like all this cloak-and-dagger stuff, but if it stands to save lives, I'm willing to look at whatever material you have." She pauses. "Besides, I don't get the impression you're giving me a choice."

"We won't force you to help," Alanna says in her soft, calm voice, her hand on my arm silently entreating me not to speak. "We're already sorry that circumstances left us with little choice but to compel you to listen."

Benson steps up beside me and I cling to his hand. Soon I can let the lab results speak for themselves.

I loose the door from its frame and we follow Dr. Martin out into the reception area. The secretary's face lights in surprise as five people exit an office she saw only one person enter. "Clear my schedule for the day," Dr. Martin says, not slowing as we stride by. "*Everything.*"

The elevator ride is tense and silent and I'm grateful for Benson's warm, comforting presence. When the doors open, I see Thomas and Alanna consult one another silently before Alanna peeks into the foyer, then gives us a thumbs up so we can follow Dr. Martin before she notices we're holding back a bit. It's probably overkill, destroying the cameras wherever we go, but if it's not…better safe than sorry.

We enter a reception area marked as the entrance to lab

number three, and through a large window along one wall I can look into a laboratory itself, so much like Daniel's that it crimps my stomach with fear. *Surely his influence doesn't reach this far*, I tell myself. *He despises humans. He'd never willingly work with them. Surely.* Still, shivers of doubt work their way up my spine.

Dr. Martin leans over the counter and whispers something to the receptionist, who nods and picks up a phone. A few moments later a tall, slim young man in dark blue scrubs enters through a swinging door near the back of the room, pulling latex gloves off his hands as he walks.

"Blood draws," Dr. Martin instructs him when he reaches us. "At least half a unit from each. This takes precedence over everything else you're doing today. In fact, let's bring them back right now. I'll get the samples directly to the lab."

The tech's eyebrows knit together for a moment as he visibly weighs the price of asking a superior to explain her unusual—possibly policy-violating—demands. Eventually he decides against it and turns to us with a tentative smile. "Right this way."

We follow him through the swinging door and down a very short hallway into a room that looks like every check-up room in every doctor's office I've ever visited, right down to the vinyl-upholstered table overlaid with crinkly white butcher paper.

"I'm Michael," the technician says as he jots something

down on a clipboard. "Who's first?"

Thomas volunteers and Michael swabs his inner elbow with alcohol. I turn away, not wanting to see the needle—I've simply been stuck with too many in the last two years to be comfortable seeing them, even when they're going into someone else. Irrational? Yes, but it reminds me of all the ways in which I really am still human.

The lab tech is efficient, moving on to Alanna and then Benson. Soon he's tugging at my arm. "It's your turn. It's okay. I'm good, and I'm fast."

In a gesture that ends up looking far more dramatic than I intend, I jerk my arm out of his grasp and cradle it against my chest. "Not mine. You can't have mine."

"Just the three of us, as I said," Thomas hastily covers when Dr. Martin gives me a puzzled frown.

She nods, but continues frowning as she addresses her subordinate. "Be absolutely sure they're correctly labeled. I'll take them and let you get on with your work."

Michael edges an odd look at me, but turns and begins writing on labels, which he affixes to the vials before slipping them into a small rack. When all fifteen are labeled and nestled in place, he slips the rack into a plastic container, clicks the hinged lid shut, and hands it to Dr. Martin. "Now it's a blood vessel," he says, gesturing to the container and cracking a smile at Alanna. She gives him a pity smile for his terrible pun, but I can hardly blame him for trying to lighten the mood. With a grim as we are, he must feel like he accidentally wandered into a funeral.

If he only knew.

Dr. Martin cradles the container in her hands and we follow her back into the waiting area. "I'm going to need a few vials of your vaccine as well, of course," she says, then seems to hold her breath as though she doesn't quite believe I'll give it to her.

I glance at the secretary, but she's on the phone, facing away from us, so I angle myself a few more inches out of her line of sight and create four vials of the vaccine in my hand. "Is this enough?"

I look up and see a bead of sweat trickle down Dr. Martin's temple. I force myself to continue holding out my hand, proffering the vials. Dr. Martin swallows hard, but reaches out to take them. "It should be enough, yes. Depending on how concentrated the protein is in the medium…thank you," she whispers. Then she clears her throat and resumes her business-like demeanor. "The four of you are welcome to remain here, or just down the hall—there's a cafeteria." She retrieves a white keycard from a pocket and hands it to me. "This will cover your meals. Unlike most hospitals, we actually have decent food," she says with a chuckle that doesn't reach her eyes.

"You're not letting us come with you?" I ask. "We could help."

"No. I need clean tests without any chance of contamination or—" she hesitates, "—sabotage."

I hear Thomas' offended intake of breath, but he grasps her reasoning as quickly as I do and says nothing.

"We'll be as quick as possible," the doctor says by way of apology. "I want this as much as you seem to." She meets each of our eyes for just a second before turning and swiping an access card to let herself through a set of doors that hiss with a vacuum release as they open.

"It's all we can do for now," Alanna says.

"So we just *wait*?" I ask, breathless as the cyclone of a panic attack starts to build in my chest. "Wait for the Reduciates to come find us?"

Benson steps close, angling an arm around me and across my chest, holding me tight against him, but without putting any pressure on my still-healing stomach.

"Or the Curatoria," Thomas adds dryly.

"We should probably stop using those names altogether," Alanna says. "They've become meaningless. It's simply the Earthbound."

"Agreed." Thomas crossed his arms over his chest, his expression determined. "We're not helpless. And we have no reason to assume they have any idea where we are. Yet. May as well make ourselves comfortable until the tests are done." He looks over at me. "As your personal physician," he adds with a quirk of a smile, "I'd like you to take it easy and stay lying down as much as possible to give your stomach muscles a better chance of healing properly."

There's a couch in the small room, but after a glance at the secretary, Thomas hides it with his back and I see him creating a soft blanket and extra pillows.

I hate feeling weak, but after several hours of remaining upright my stomach muscles are throbbing, so I don't protest when Thomas points at the now pillow-bedecked couch, mock-sternness furrowing his brow. I lie carefully on my back and, with a sigh, relax all the muscles in my body I hadn't realized I was clenching.

There's a rustle at my feet and Benson lifts my legs, settling them on his lap. I look up and meet his eyes as his fingers stroke my shins, and my stomach flutters in a way that has nothing to do with my stab-wound. Benson and I haven't been alone since we all escaped the Curatoria headquarters.

Since I chose him.

And my body is near busting with wanting: wanting to pull him close and relearn his body, this time with no secrets between us. Even sleeping next to him at night, my back spooned with him, barely touches my craving. But we're still traveling with two adults, one of whom is his *father*. There have been stolen kisses and subtle caresses, but I ache to have him to myself and simply can't predict when that might happen.

If that might happen. The world needs a future if Benson is to be in mine.

Thomas and Alanna have done their best to not make us feel like they're babysitting, but the world is at stake and I'm still very injured, so I don't blame them for keeping me close.

The feather-light touch of Benson's fingertips on my skin sends shivers up my legs. I close my eyes, enjoying the sensation. I wish there was room for him to lie beside me, but even if there were, it would feel odd in front of the secretary who's now darting confused glances at us. I turn my head away and nestle my face against a pillow, wondering how I can feel so much safer just having Benson near. It's not as though he's in a position to protect me, not from the kind of enemies I have. But somehow, with his warm hands on my legs and the quiet of the room around me, I'm able to relax and my eyelids grow heavy. I hear Alanna and Thomas conversing quietly, and Benson is humming absentmindedly under his breath.

The fate of the world hangs in the balance in a laboratory on the other side of one flimsy wall.

I drift into a dreamless sleep.

CHAPTER FOUR

"Tave."

For the second time in twelve hours, I awake to Benson calling my name.

"Dr. Martin wants to talk to us."

Thomas and Alanna are already on their feet—I assume Dr. Martin had to pass us to get back to her office, but she didn't wait around.

"What time is it?" I ask.

"About 2:30," Benson answers.

"Man, I'm never going to be able to sleep tonight."

"I have a feeling none of us are going to have anything resembling a normal sleep schedule for a long time," Thomas says darkly. "Better go see if she's on our side or not." He takes two steps toward Michael—ostensibly sent to fetch us—then stops, turns, and beckons us all close. "I hope, like we all do, that the tests have gone well, and that she's willing to believe us. But remember the escape plan."

Dr. Martin is sitting behind her desk, typing away at her

computer keyboard when we enter. She nods in the direction of the chairs I created in front of her desk this morning, but continues to type until Thomas closes the door behind us and we all sit.

I have no idea what she's going to say next.

"Do you know," she asks, "how long it takes to develop a vaccine, test it, and manufacture it for use?"

"Years," I answer automatically. "Decades, maybe."

"Just so," she says, letting her eyes find mine for a second or two. "Even in dire emergencies, government approval alone takes months—weeks, if you can get the right politician to throw their weight around. And that's not even the scientific part. What percentage of people will have an adverse reaction to a new vaccine? What are the possible side effects? Human trials take *years* to conduct. No matter how amazing your product is, you can't just hand it out like so much Halloween candy."

Tears burn my eyes. She's going to turn us down. We're going to have to find another way, another clinic…and we're going to have to do it fast.

"You came here because my clinic is one of the most reputable research facilities in the world. You wanted to use that reputation to distribute your treatment, and conceal your activities from the…bioterrorists…who created the Kentucky virus."

I close my eyes and nod.

"Can you tell me…are you religious?"

I open my eyes and look into Dr. Martin's face. Confusion must show in my expression, because she gives me a crooked, self-deprecating grin.

"Well, I'm not. At least, I haven't been lately. Grew up Catholic, though. Are you familiar with the phrase 'creation *ex nihilo*?'"

Creation from nothing. I nod.

"Tradition says that's how God created the world, and the laws of conservation of mass and energy prove it can't be so. But that's the power you've shown me, several times today. For all you've come to me, hat in hand, asking me to do this impossible favor, it's obvious that I'm powerless before you. I don't know what you are—some kind of holy emanation, or angel, or—"

"I'm just a person," I say, "who's trying to save the world."

"And I'm a scientist who has just had her faith in the most inviolable laws of physics stripped away by a girl who looks no older than my daughter. At any other time in history, I'd be begging for a chance to speak with you, follow you, work with you, study what you do and who you are."

I don't know how to respond to that.

Quietly, almost to herself, she continues. "Maybe that's why you didn't reveal yourself before."

The room descends into awkward silence.

Thomas clears his throat, and Dr. Martin's chin snaps up as if she'd just been caught napping. "Your vaccine—is there a way to manufacture it?"

The question gives me a glimmer of hope. "I imagine there is, but I couldn't tell you how. At least for now, I *am* the vaccine."

She nods slowly. "How much can you make?"

"I honestly don't know. Lots?"

"Timing is on our side; before you showed up we'd been running trials on an experimental flu vaccine—an attempt to replace seasonal forecasts with comprehensive immunity. Under ordinary circumstances I'd estimate FDA approval within a year. But I can create a false report that it's generating immunity to the Kentucky virus. That should clear the deck for distribution; it was mostly down to administrative hurdles anyway. We can find a point in the distribution process to just swap it with the serum you…make."

A grin pulls at the corner of my mouth as I realize that we definitely came to the right person. *She's going to help us.*

"It's not a perfect plan," Dr. Martin continues. "There are a lot of people involved in manufacturing and distribution. There are researchers who will be asking after our process—to test it for themselves and deploy it in their countries. I won't be able to keep a lid on any of this for very long. Best-case scenario, it's the end of my career as a researcher and a scholar."

"Surely people will understand—" I begin, but she shakes her head.

"No, successful science is all about sharing and trust. Dishonesty, even when it's for the best possible reasons, is the end of science and the beginning of…something else."

I'd expected this "discovery" to make her career. Not break it.

"I'll get to the point," Dr. Martin continues, her voice only a little shaky. "Yes, I will help you save the world. I will do everything in my power to aid your cause, and I will keep your secrets whatever the cost."

"That could get quite high," Thomas cuts in. "We should be able to get a lot done initially. But eventually we're going to have to get sneaky. Like you said, dishonest. The organization that's determined to kill as many people as possible with this virus won't give up simply because we've created a vaccine. They'll hunt for us, they'll kill people lining up to receive the vaccine. They have powers of their own, and they have greater numbers as well. Don't mistake this vaccine for a magical solution. We're in the midst of a war for humanity and there *will* be casualties."

Dr. Martin nods soberly. "I have some friends at the CDC—I'm sure they'll be anxious to help, and they have experience mixing medicine with military action."

She seems to know just what to say to maximize my feelings of apprehension and anxiety. "When do we start?" I ask, as much to change the subject as to hurry the process along.

After a couple of owlish blinks, she smiles. "Now."

***

The problem with keeping my involvement a secret, even from the staff that are helping to run the operation, is that I have to tag along constantly and feel completely in the way. Thomas is in his element, answering questions and giving orders in his odd capacity as unofficial second-in-command. Benson has stepped into the role of Thomas' assistant, and Alanna is the calming voice of reason when one of the staff starts to have a meltdown. I just stand there.

All afternoon a rounded-up staff of about fifty at the Phoenix Mayo Clinic have been on the phones alerting hospitals all over the nation that they'll be receiving important shipments in advance of a product announcement. They don't seem to get much in the way of pushback—whether because of the state of the world or the reputation of the clinic I couldn't say, but I'm glad.

I'm also worried.

There's Daniel to be concerned about, of course. There's still no way to know if he's alive. But the bigger worry is the Reduciata as a whole. Based on the final phone call I heard Daniel make to Mariana—when he thought I was dead—she knows *everything*. Crippling the Curatoria was, at best, only half the battle. And whether they hear about our efforts through the FDA, the CDC, the delivery sites, or even spies right here in the Mayo Clinic itself, we're can only hope to get a lot of good done before the Reduciates can organize enough to begin attacking our distribution channels.

Or our supply—especially since *I* am our supply.

Despite that, my role at the moment is simply to stand and watch. It occurs to me that Logan would fit in perfectly here. He'd love to be a part of this. I wish I could simply know whether or not he's alive. It's easy to believe that surely, some part of me would know if he were dead…but I think that's a lie.

And I can't look for him. Not now. Because to do so would expose me to anyone searching for *me*. The people I *know* are searching for me. So I can't. He could be lying in the desert bleeding to death right at this moment, and there's not a damn thing I can do about it.

Hard to feel like much of a hero, given that possibility.

During a break in the chaos, Thomas comes to find me. "I need you to spend the next five or six hours resting," he says.

APRILYNNE PIKE

"Sleeping, if you can. Michael has arranged for a room with a cot for your use. I suggest you create yourself a large, high-calorie meal, then turn that cot into something you can *actually* sleep on," he says with a wry grin. "Come midnight we'll be off to Sky Harbor airport—the four of us and Dr. Martin. You'll have ten cargo planes to fill so I want you as fed and rested as possible."

I nod, my insides quivering at the enormity of the task ahead. "Can I—" My voice cuts off and I feel my cheeks flush hot and red. "Can I bring Benson? If you don't need him," I finish, each word quieter than the last, until the final word is whispered at Thomas' shoes.

He's quiet for a few seconds and I'm too embarrassed to look up. "Tavia, I may be Benson's father, but I haven't been his *dad* in many, many years. There's a distinct possibility I've lost that privilege forever. You don't need to think of me that way."

After a pause I shift my feet on the squeaky linoleum and ask, "Is that a yes?"

Thomas snorts and shakes his head, but puts me out of my misery. "Yes, that's a yes."

Both Alanna and Benson have remained close, ready to help with any tasks Thomas might assign to them, but at this point neither of them are particularly necessary. I don't look at Alanna—I try not to draw attention to myself at all—as I twine

32

my fingers through Benson's and pull him off in the direction of the room that has been set aside for us.

For me.

"Thomas says it's okay for us to take a break," I whisper as we weave through moderately crowded hallways.

"Are you okay?" Benson asks as I drag him along, my steps getting faster and faster as we draw nearer to the room. I push the door open tentatively to make sure we're not bursting in on anyone, but Thomas was right; an empty room with a cot on the ground, a small closet on one wall, and a sink and mirror on the other. Probably where doctors sleep when they're on call overnight.

I pull Benson into the room and close the door behind us; a thought seals it shut. A second thought transforms the wobbly cot into a real bed. I smile at the realization that it looks like the bed we shared in the hotel room in Maine.

Before he betrayed me.

After Thomas betrayed *him*.

How far we've come.

Without a word, I grip the front of Benson's shirt and pull him forward. My lips practically hit his, but it's such a relief I scarcely notice the dull pain. "I need you," I whisper against his mouth.

"Tave, we—" But his words are muffled as I lift his shirt, forcing his arms to rise as I drag it over his head. I press myself against his bare chest and I am home.

The world spins around me—around us—as I stand, clutching myself to him, my face pressed into the crook of his neck. His skin warms me and I can feel his heart racing in his chest, only inches from my own.

There hasn't been time to discuss the significance of what happened that day when I came to him in his cell, stabbed and bleeding, and left Logan behind. There was a brief discussion in the hospital, and there are shared whispers at night as we fall asleep, but I'm ready for the kind of conversation that doesn't use words.

His lips tickle my ear as his fingers grip tight against my back. I raise my head and find his mouth again and all the fear and nerves of the last few days melt away in his kiss. I pull him backward with me, toppling us onto the bed. Though Benson is careful with my stomach, he holds me tightly, his mouth exploring mine.

We haven't been able to be together like this since…have we ever been together like this? Even before Mariana caught up with us in Camden, our kisses were always hurried or stolen, or rather rudely interrupted. Even in the hotel room it was almost too dark to see one another, and I know Benson was carrying a terrible weight of guilt.

But today, for just a little while, we can be us. We can be free. We can simply be a boy and a girl in love.

I open my eyes when Benson breaks our kiss and look up into his face. A ray of sunshine from a high window illuminates the golden tips of his light brown eyelashes. It's amazing to be with him and not hiding. Well, not hiding our feelings, anyway.

But even this level of hiding feels normal. Like I, for just a few minutes, have returned to being an average teenage girl, sneaking kisses out of sight of her parents. Or *his* parents, as the case may be.

It feels good.

I know it can't last, but I've learned to take what I can get.

I start to kick off my shoes, but realize that I'll have to lean down and loosen the laces first. I roll my eyes and just make them disappear instead.

I'm supposed to be eating. A big, full meal to prepare me for tonight.

But I have a different hunger to feed first.

CHAPTER FIVE

I actually feel quite refreshed when Thomas knocks on the door several hours later. I raise my head from the pillow and call out, "Ready in five," in a gravelly voice, before snuggling in for one more minute. Benson's arm is heavy across my chest. I wish I had the time to just turn and watch him sleep. Watch his chest rise and fall, and smooth away the wavy lock of hair that always curls over his forehead.

I remind myself that if we win, there'll be a lifetime of that.

I elbow him softly. "Benson. It's midnight."

We're a warm, soft jumble of limbs and blankets and I laugh as we try to untangle ourselves from each other and the bedding. I stand and, with a thought, am dressed in black stretch pants and a light, three-quarter-sleeved fitted black shirt. Black seems appropriate, given that we'll be sneaking around filling planes with crates of vaccine for transport all over the United States.

Benson grabs his T-shirt from where I tossed it onto the floor, rumpled and wrinkly. He looks at it dubiously then starts the turn it right side in.

"Allow, me," I say, and he's instantly wearing dark slacks with a black long-sleeved button-down shirt and a dark gray sweater vest over the top. He looks down and grins at the darker version of the pastel library intern he was when we first met—the person he would have been if he'd had a choice, he once told me in the cells of the Curatoria headquarters.

My smile fades when I remember something else he said. "I'm afraid you're wearing black again," I apologize.

He takes my hand and pulls me forward against the soft cashmere of his sweater vest and the feeling is so familiar I want to rub my face against the fabric like a cat. "For you, I'd wear black every day for the rest of my life," he whispers.

We share a long, lingering kiss before another knock sounds on the door, accompanied by Alanna's voice. "Tavia, we need to go now."

I free the door from its frame and swing it open. "We're ready."

Alanna doesn't meet my eyes, but I can see a smile tugging at her lips.

Outside, a big semi is waiting behind a black sedan with Dr. Martin at the wheel and Thomas beside her.

"What's with the big truck?" I ask as we draw near the car.

"It's a prop," Dr. Martin says. "Dr. Ryder's suggestion." It's funny how Dr. Martin has latched onto Thomas being a doctor—like she needs someone in this crazy, magical group to be a person of science. I don't dare tell her that physician is a career Thomas had in another life, fifty years ago, when his last name wasn't Ryder—not if his being a doctor is making this undertaking more palatable. "No one at Sky Harbor is going to believe us if we show up to load cargo planes with no cargo."

"Good point."

The drive to the airport is uneventful and though Dr. Martin and Thomas chat quietly in the front seat, we're silent in the back. Benson slides his hand into mine and squeezes. In my other hand I create a tall bottle of thick chocolate milk, which I sip through a straw.

I've never created quite this much matter in one night and, though I gorged myself on chicken fettuccine a few hours ago—to the point that I woke up still feeling almost uncomfortably full—I want to be as prepared as possible. That means loading up on sugar and calories.

My stomach is feeling a bit sloshy when Dr. Martin pulls to a stop at a gate with a little booth beside a long, chain-link fence. I worry that someone like TSA is going to want to search us and the truck trailing us, but Dr. Martin just presents her credentials and points at the truck, and the security guard waves us through.

We drive past several large buildings and dark, quiet vehicles, until we reach a concrete slab where ten large-bellied planes await, looking deserted.

"We've done what we can to get you some privacy," Thomas says, turning around to look at me. "No one else is scheduled to arrive for a few hours. The goal is to have all ten planes in the air before sunrise. We're keeping everything as low-profile as possible for the initial distribution, but reports of the vaccine's existence will almost certainly make the evening news. Then the real fight begins."

I try not to think too hard about that. Every time I've ever attempted to take on the Reduciata, I've come out the loser. Do I really think I can do better this time? What are we? Three Earthbound, one former Reduciate, and a handful of humans.

Versus the most powerful beings on Earth, dead set on wiping out the human race.

But we have the vaccine, I remind myself.

They don't. Not even to protect their own members. Which means, I realize, that *all* their efforts won't be simply to destroy the vaccine; they'll have to steal some, too. And I don't care if they do. I'm not out to kill them; I want to save the world. I guess at the heart of everything, that's the difference between us.

The car rolls to a stop. On either side of me, Benson and Alanna scoot out and Benson holds out a hand for me. But I pause as I hear Thomas say, "You've already been through a lot today, Dr. Martin. You can wait for us in the car if you want."

Dr. Martin shakes her head. "I think I need to see this."

The five of us walk toward the first plane. Dr. Martin talks with a man who hands her a clipboard and a flashlight, then the driver of the semi joins them. The clipboard man flashes his beam toward the empty plane, and Thomas whispers something I don't quite hear and puts a large flashlight in each of our hands. "We're all set," he says, louder this time.

The man in uniform looks at Thomas for a second, then nods, turns, and heads back toward a small building with lights shining through long windows. The semi driver goes back to the cab of his truck.

"We're ready," Alanna says. We walk up the ramp with our flashlights and I crouch on the floor. Dr. Martin showed me shipping crates of flu vaccine back at the clinic—plastic lattices filled with individually-marked vials, packed in miniature cooler-chests (also individually bar coded), stacked and divided by cardboard and bubble-wrap. Layers upon layers of complexity that, even had I studied it for days, I probably should not have been able to reproduce perfectly.

But I did, during our practice run at the clinic. Every vial properly coded, every box properly packed—but instead of experimental flu vaccine, each vial ready to immunize against the virus that's tearing the world apart. It's exactly as Daniel said—my power to duplicate things accurately, down to the smallest detail, is far greater than any I've seen exhibited by other Earthbound.

"Stand behind me," I say, taking a deep breath and concentrating on all of the parts of each box. I peer into the plane, trying to memorize the space, and then I hold a mental picture in my head, breathe deeply, and will the picture into reality.

A cry of alarm sounds from behind me and I stand and spin—too fast, losing my balance. I stagger into Benson's chest and have a little trouble focusing. But after a few seconds I figure out that the sound came from Dr. Martin.

I turn my head and see the entire cavity of the plane filled from floor to ceiling with dozens of crates.

"This one's done," I say, pushing away from Benson to find my footing again.

"Are you all right?" Alanna asks, a hand on my arm.

"Yeah. I can tell I'm going to be exhausted before I'm done, but mostly I spun around too fast right as I finished."

"My fault," Dr. Martin says, smiling wanly. "I wasn't quite prepared. I don't know what else I expected but...It won't happen again."

I fill five planes before I have to start chugging orange juice, and by the seventh I've slowed dramatically and switched to milkshakes. The ninth plane I can only fill halfway before slumping against Benson's chest to rest for a few minutes, sipping Mountain Dew from a straw to get a burst of both sugar and caffeine before finishing.

Walking to the final plane I feel like my feet are encased in cement and I lean heavily against Benson. I stand in front of the final empty cargo bay and try to hide how sick my stomach feels, and how shaky my legs are.

Mostly I don't want Dr. Martin to see.

I take several long breaths, trying to soothe the simmering nausea, and with a grunt I manage to fill a third of the space. My legs collapse beneath me and Benson runs forward to scoop me up against his chest.

"It's too much," he says.

"No!" I try to shout, but the sound that actually emerges from my mouth is much quieter than I intended. "I can do it," I insist. "I just need a chair."

I see worried looks pass between the adults and I wonder if I'm slurring my words. Thomas looks meaningfully at Alanna and she nods very slightly and taps Dr. Martin's shoulder to get her attention. As soon as the doctor's face is turned away, Thomas creates a chair for me.

Ah, I see. Thomas is keeping his own abilities a secret. Even from Dr. Martin. It's probably a good idea. He's become the voice of reason for her. A pillar of rationality that she grasps onto. By the time Dr. Martin turns her attention back to me, the chair is in place and Benson is helping to lower me onto it.

Ten minutes pass before I feel strong enough to try again. I get another third of the bay filled and I can barely sit up, even in the chair. Benson is hunkered down beside me, letting me slump over against him, and Alanna's whispered protests are getting louder.

"We have some time yet," Thomas says, just loud enough for me to hear. "Whatever she can do during that time will have to be enough. If we had to stop here, it would be okay."

"Maybe we should stop," Benson says, and the buzz of his voice vibrates against my ear. I shake my head.

"Wait," I whisper. "Just wait."

Time swirls around me and I feel like I'm floating in and out of consciousness as I try to dig up the energy to open my eyes.

"We're finished," Alanna says. "She's done enough."

But I haven't. It *isn't* enough. The numbers have been adding up in my head.

Every empty cubic is one more life in danger. With that motivation burning in my belly I grit my teeth and force my powers to work one more time. A wave of pain rushes through me and I bend over and heave. Nothing's left in my stomach, but my still-healing muscles scream in protest. My eyes flutter for just a second and I see the cargo hold filled right up to where we're standing. A smile touches my lips as the world fades to black.

CHAPTER SIX

Waking feels like regaining consciousness after the plane crash last summer. The association makes me shy away, returning to the darkness and settling back in for a while. It's easier the second time—more like waking up after having taken a sleeping pill. My eyes blink open and I recognize the room I shared with Benson in the clinic. I wonder who carried me back to the car, then up to this room. Part of me hopes it was Benson and, if so, I'm sorry I missed it.

A more reasonable part of me says I should probably be more careful. Unconscious, I'm worse than useless; I'm a liability, a burden for someone to carry.

"There you are," Benson says. "Here." He slips a straw between my teeth and something unfamiliar, though not unpleasant, fills my mouth. It's thick and sweet and tastes about like melted strawberry ice cream. As soon as I take one swallow I feel completely ravenous and gulp the rest down before settling on the pillows and letting my eyes close.

"Go back to sleep if you need to," Benson's voice says, and it seems like such a good idea, I do just that.

The third time I wake I finally feel refreshed, though parched and a little warm. I cringe just before creating a large glass of ice water for myself, half expecting the pain and nausea that accompanied my most recent exercise of power.

It doesn't happen, of course, and I feel a bit silly for having expected it.

"Hey," says a quiet voice from across the room.

I turn my head and find, not Benson, but Dr. Martin sitting on a folding chair a few feet away, looking a bit rumpled. I know she must have gone home to change; she's in a different suit. But her curly hair is pulled back in a plain ponytail with wisps working their way free around her ears, her jacket isn't buttoned, and the shirt beneath isn't ironed. She looks friendlier now, actually.

"I sent Benson to take a walk. Get some fresh air," she says with an apologetic smile. "He'll be back soon."

"It's okay," I say, my voice lower than usual and heavy with sleep. "I should probably have looked around before I...you know," I say, waving at my conjured water glass.

She laughs, but it's a bit strangled.

"What time is it?" I say, as much to break the silence as anything.

"Just after three in the afternoon. You woke briefly at noon, but Benson didn't think you were ready yet."

"He was right." I scrunch my eyebrows together. "He gave

me something. Strawberry. Do you know what it was?"

She brightens. "Did you like it? I'm so glad. You can have more. It's a nutritional drink we developed for patients with eating disorders. It about as many calories as you can squeeze into ten ounces without drinking straight oil."

I wrinkle my nose at the thought, but it *had* been good.

"It's best cold, so I had someone bring up a mini fridge and stock it full of the flavors we have. Thomas told me a little about the relationship between your metabolism and your...abilities," she finishes lamely and I'm amused at how she's treating me like a patient. Trying to solve my problems. It's what she does, I guess.

I don't tell her that now that I've tasted her special drink I can make as much of it as I want. It probably good for her to feel helpful. She reaches into the little fridge and opens a carton before handing it over to me. I subtly make a straw and start drinking. This one's caramel. Also quite tasty.

Dr. Martin glances toward the still-closed door and then watches me drink. I'm just starting to feel uncomfortably self-conscious when she speaks again. "Are you familiar with the laws of thermodynamics?"

I nod. "You can't create something from nothing."

"That's one of them, more or less. But they also apply to energy. You can't get more energy out of something than you put into it. Using your powers obviously requires energy, but not nearly as much energy as it should—the fact that you can create food to energize even bigger creations is clear evidence of the violation."

I try really hard not to laugh at her attempts to explain my abilities with science.

"I had a thought about that, and I'd like to ask you a question. But it might sound a little accusatory, or even ungrateful, and I want to assure you in advance that I don't mean it that way."

I stop drinking and try to decide if I want to hear her question.

"Are your abilities related to the catastrophes around the Pacific rim?"

I blink. I had hoped to avoid her making any connection between us as the disasters.

"Because," Dr. Martin hurries on, "if there were a lot of people like you, and every time they used their abilities, they were actually *channeling* energy, destroying material in one place to create somewhere else—well. It's just a hypothesis, But if there's any chance that we might be saving part of the world by destroying other parts...I guess I just feel like I need to understand how it is that you do what you do."

I pull the straw out of my mouth and the liquid on my tongue tastes a little sour. "It's not like that. And it's not something I can explain, not to anyone. I have powers.

Abilities. Gifts. Whatever you want to call it. I can change matter. Make things appear and take them away. It's as simple and as complicated as that."

"But how long...have you known about this?"

"Not long, actually. Less than a year."

"Then how—"

"Dr. Martin," I interrupt.

"Please, after yesterday I really think you should just call me Kat."

"Kat, then," I say, but I keep my voice firm. "You already know things that people would kill you for, to keep you quiet. And I have to say, you should be terrified."

Her eyes widen, and I'm not sure if my matter-of-fact tone is helping or hurting.

"You're right—the catastrophes in the Pacific and elsewhere are related to what we're doing. But not in the way you're thinking—just the opposite. If we succeed at beating the virus, we'll *also* put a stop to the other disasters. But if I told you everything—and you were willing to believe me—you'd probably have nightmares for the rest of your life." I rush on before she can protest. "I don't want to be patronizing; you're clearly an incredibly intelligent, hard-working woman, and you have done amazing things for us. I understand why you want to know more about what's going on around you. But you have to believe me when I say that it's safer for everyone if you just focus on the task at hand."

Her mouth opens and then closes with a snap. "I suppose that's fair," she whispers. "It's hard, as a scientist, to know that after we've saved the world, I'll still have questions for which I may never have answers."

I nod, unsure how else to respond. I'm beyond grateful when the door handle turns and Benson pokes his head in.

"You're awake!" he says, flinging the door the rest of the way open and rushing toward me. I throw my arms around his neck and kiss his ear and just that moment of physical touch makes me long for a repeat of yesterday afternoon.

Maybe that can be arranged.

"I'll be on my way, then," Dr. Martin says, rising and fastening the top button on her jacket.

"Kat," I say, stopping her just before she exits.

She pauses, and takes one step backward so she can see me.

"I hope you know how much I appreciate everything you've done. We put you in a really tough situation and you've been incredible."

"Thank you," she says, and when she leaves she closes the door behind her.

I grab Benson and pull his face down to me, wanting him so badly it truly does feel like a ravenous hunger. But after only a few seconds he pulls back. "Are you okay?"

"Of course."

"Of course *nothing*. You were messed up last night. Thom—Dad said your pulse was super weak and your face was so white and—" He cuts off and runs his fingers through his hair. "It was scary, Tave. We can't lose you. *I* can't lose you."

"I'm sorry," I say. It's possible I did push a little too hard last night. It never occurred to me to wonder if I can deplete my energy so much it actually damages me. "I promise I feel great now though. Well, hungry. But I feel fine."

"Eat, eat!" Benson says, standing and gesturing at my lap. "Make something. Or I can go get you something. Or—"

"Benson, stop," I say, laughing. "Sit down, I'll make some lunch. Do you want anything?"

But he shakes his head. "They've been bringing sandwiches and chips and stuff into the conference room all day. Although, really, I've been too keyed up to eat much."

"Suit yourself," I say lightly with a grin, but I actually am starving. Hunger is a writhing pit in my stomach and, after a quick thought of what might be a really high-calorie meal, I create a bowl of my mom's homemade baked macaroni and cheese and add an extra layer of melted cheddar over the top. "So fill me in."

"The deliveries arrived safely," Benson says. "The clinic's got some press releases going out. Dr. Martin says she expects to spend the entire evening on the phone." He grins. "There's a betting pool guessing how long it'll be before the White

House calls."

I nod, but it's not politicians that concern me—the Mayo Clinic has a small army of bureaucrats dedicated to navigating regulatory waters, and Kat has personal friends in just about every relevant organization and agency in the country. But within the ranks of some of those organizations will be agents of the Reduciata—how *they* respond will be the real trial.

"So," Benson says slowly once I put my bowl to the side, "don't shoot the messenger or anything, but are you really okay?" His eyes look not only worried, but conflicted.

"I am. Feeling a little lazy, actually. I should get up." I throw the blankets aside and yelp reflexively when I realize I'm wearing my black shirt from last night, but no pants.

"Oh, um, yeah," Benson says as I make a pair of shorts. "Alanna came up with me last night when you were out and thought your pants might be uncomfortable for your stomach, so she made them disappear."

Well, at least it wasn't Thomas. I change my shirt into a dressy tank top and add cute sandals on my feet. "What was the shoot the messenger part?" I ask, pulling my hair back into a loose ponytail.

Benson's face flushes red. "They…they want to know if you're up to making more vaccine. Like a semi-truck's worth," he finishes in a whisper.

"Oh, yeah sure." And I totally am. I'm rested and

exceptionally well fed. I almost feel back to my old self.

"Are you sure?" And the conflicted look is back.

"Oh," I say, understanding. I sit beside him and take his hand. "You're worried about pushing me too hard."

He nods silently, but I can see his jaw clenching. "I seriously thought you were going to burn yourself out last night, Tave. You were so pale you looked dead."

"For the second time in a week," I say sympathetically.

He just nods again. "I don't want to be the one making you do stuff. I wish…I wish I didn't have to be involved. Except that I don't wish that at all." He groans and flops back on the bed. "Does that even make any sense?"

I smile softly and curl up beside him, my head on his shoulder. "It does, actually. It makes total sense." I run my hand up and down his chest, still loving the feeling of him beside me. I wonder if it'll ever get old. I lean against him and he wraps his arms tight around me, holding on to me like a security blanket.

"What's the new big batch of vaccine for?" I ask.

"For Phoenix. All the planes last night went elsewhere."

"Oh, duh."

"Thomas was thinking you could do the empty truck at the airport last night, but obviously, that didn't happen."

"I'm glad he didn't mention it," I say ruefully. "I probably would have tried."

"Stubborn brat," Benson says teasingly.

"Wait, Benson, it's like four in the afternoon now, right?" I push myself upright. "We have to hurry to get it distributed around the city."

"Only if you're ready," Benson says.

"You've got to trust me, Ben. When I tell you I'm fine, I need you to believe me."

"As long as you promise not to push yourself so hard."

I hesitate. "I'll *try*," I finally say. "This is all still new to me, and I'm not used to judging these things. But I have a big job to do, and my life is going to consist of eating, sleeping, and creating vaccine almost exclusively for the next…well, however long it takes."

"Try, then," Benson presses. "Because if you seriously hurt yourself and can't make more vaccine, that doesn't help anyone."

My lips form a sad smile. "You're right." I twine my fingers through his. "Let's go. I have a truck to fill."

CHAPTER SEVEN

"Only eight planes tonight," Dr. Martin says, "And most of them are going to go to the same cities. New York and Los Angeles, especially."

"I wish there was a way to do this faster," I say, frustration heavy in my voice. "Can't we do planes twice a day? I can just sleep and fill, then sleep and fill."

Dr. Martin hesitates. "I can only control schedules for so many planes. We could probably get more, if we asked, but questions are already being raised regarding logistics and suitable oversight. One wrong step and the government is liable to militarize Sky Harbor and the clinic both. Besides, night is probably safest."

"Then what about filling trucks here? And then sending them to the airport."

"We can look into that. That exposes *you*, though. This clinic isn't exactly built to have a dozen semis driving in and out of it every day. I don't want you to be discovered."

"What about a warehouse?" Alanna suggests. "We could drive Tavia out to a warehouse and fill trucks there. In an enclosed garage without prying eyes."

"That's possible. Just understand that the more we make, and the faster we make it, the thinner our cover-stories wear. Someone is going to realize very quickly that we're shipping out wildly more material than we're shipping *in*."

"Maybe it would be better if we weren't living at the clinic," Thomas says. "That way Tavia's not around a Mayo Clinic at all. I mean, the vaccine is inexorably connected with Mayo Clinic as it is. You told me an hour ago that reporters from all over the country have been calling here—I imagine they're doing the same thing with your facilities across the country—it's only a matter of time before they're camped out in front of the building."

A flutter of fear enters my stomach. "I hadn't considered that. Maybe we should leave tonight. We could stay in a hotel somewhere."

"Somewhere close to the airport, maybe. It's an industrial area anyway, isn't it?" Thomas asks Dr. Martin.

"It is. There's got to be dozens of hotels that are decent and non-descript. Perhaps we can go fill planes tonight and then find a hotel for all four of you."

My head is spinning. There are so many aspects of this plan that I didn't think about. Didn't have *time* to think about. And it seems so unfair that the price of saving millions upon millions of lives is endangering everyone who agrees to help.

The next week passes in a blur of eating and sleeping as I discover the exact opposite of every scrap of healthy eating advice in existence—how to cram the maximum amount of fat and calories into every mouthful. After a little research I'm pretty sure the most calorific substance on earth is the peanut butter and chocolate milkshake. I have two of them a day. At least.

We're using a combination of semis and planes now. Every day at noon Benson wakes me up and takes me to a warehouse near the airport—but not too near—and I fill trucks for about an hour. I suck down food on the ride back to the hotel, where I sleep again until almost midnight, when we head to the airport.

Fill planes, more eating, more sleeping. Fill trucks. Eat and sleep again. I want to feel successful, but losing track of the days doesn't mean I can't feel them passing. And worries about what *might* be coming gradually fill me with dread.

"Why hasn't anything happened?" I ask at last.

Thomas is driving us back to the hotel. He looks at least as tired as I feel.

"What do you mean?" Alanna asks, turning in the passenger seat to look at me. "We've been non-stop busy for a week."

Speaking my worries is a bit like talking under water—forcing the words out and struggling to make myself heard.

"Why haven't the Reduciates attacked? They're going to do something. Even if I managed to kill Daniel—which I'm certainly *not* assuming—Mariana is still around. She won't give up, and I think we all know she'll stoop to pretty much anything."

"I think we need to cross that bridge when we come to it, and be grateful for every bit of success we're managing to have," Benson says softly.

I want to believe his words; to accept them and let them wrap around me like a warm blanket. But it's naïve at best. "No, we have to be ready. The fact that they've taken an entire week to gear up for whatever they're going to do only means it's going to be worse than we feared."

"Well, Tavia, at least you haven't lost your optimism in all this," Thomas says dryly. I start to protest but he cuts me off. "I'm not saying you're wrong. But until it happens, how are we supposed to prepare?"

I hate that he's right.

"Sleep for now. Keep doing what we've been doing. We'll move hotels again tomorrow and Dr. Martin has a contact to get us a new warehouse as well. We're doing everything we can to keep you safe." He meets my eyes in the rearview mirror. "Because whatever trick the Reduciata pulls, I guarantee we're going to need you to counter it."

In the end it takes ten days.

The story is on every channel. One small town in Louisiana is the focus of panic—their local drug store received a shipment of the vaccine. Word spread with stereotypical small-town speed and all day inoculations were administered. They even had people coming in from surrounding towns and farms thirty miles away. Every drop of the vaccine gone in twelve hours.

Three days later, everyone who received the vaccine came down with an acute case of the Kentucky virus.

I don't even hear Benson get out of the shower until he takes the remote from my frozen fingers and turns off the TV. "There's no point watching," he says. "We can't change it. Plus, they just keep saying the same things over and over."

"I don't understand." My thoughts feel even more sluggish than usual. "The vaccine is good. It works on *all* the mutations. How could this happen?"

Benson sighs and runs his fingers through his hair. "The media is swinging back and forth between a bad batch of the vaccine and a new strain of the virus."

"It doesn't make any sense—either of those."

"Well, my bet's on this being the work of the Reduciates trying to undermine trust in the vaccine."

I clench my hands to my temples as though I could push away the stabbing headache that started around the time the reporter described a town-wide quarantine. "A whole town. A whole town, Benson! Because they thought they were going to be safe." I flop back on the bed and feel as heavy as if my bones had transformed into lead. "How many of them do you think were children?" I barely whisper it. It hurts to think, and feels even worse to say it out loud. "How many mothers kept their children home from school, from play dates, from everything, to protect them from the virus. And then, took them to get the miraculous vaccine. And it killed them." Because it will. All of those babies will die.

The worst part is that I could go and save them. Save them all. The vaccine can't cure someone—but my blood can. The terrible truth is that I could go and cure every single person in that town.

But then I'd have thousands of newly-immortal Transformist Earthbound to worry about. And I can't do that. It's too much power to unleash into the world.

So I'll let them die.

"Has this been playing all day while I've been *sleeping*?" The accusation is heavy in my tone.

But Benson doesn't wilt. "What could you have done, Tave? What good would it do to wake you up?"

"But—"

"Nothing. No good at all. We can't let this derail us. The most important thing is to keep doing exactly what we're doing. Getting the vaccine out." He straightens and looks down at me. His hands are on his hips but his eyes are soft. "And for that, you need your rest. And food," he adds.

"I'm not sure I can eat," I say as he sits beside me on the bed, placing an arm around my shoulders, holding me close against him. "This whole thing makes me sick to my stomach."

"Try. Milkshakes maybe. Something easy to digest. Because we still have planes to fill tonight."

I heave a sigh that feels like it comes all the way from my toes. I never thought I'd get sick of milkshakes, but I'm definitely getting there. The thought is already making my stomach churn so instead I go for a tried and true comfort food—french fries. I add a big side of fry sauce and drench them in it. No plain ketchup for me these days; every calorie counts.

"We have to find some way to protect the shipments better," I say, thinking out loud.

Benson hesitates. "The shipments may not be the problem. Dr. Martin said that the plane to Louisiana was headed for cities between New Orleans and Baton Rouge. Wilton is up in the northern part, by Shreveport. They aren't scheduled to get their shipment for several few days."

An icy pit forms in my stomach. "Oh, no."

"What?"

"When you said it was probably the Reduciata—I figured it made sense for them to steal a crate for themselves. They need the vaccine as much as anyone, and replacing good vaccine with the virus is just the sort of spiteful thing they would do. But if they aren't swapping out stolen creates of vaccine—if they're just shipping out their own crates—how many infected crates are out there right now? How many of them have *already been used?* This changes everything!"

"It changes nothing."

Benson and I both turn to see Alanna standing in the doorway, her keycard hanging from her fingertips. "Sorry. I knocked, I promise. But I had to make sure you were up and…I heard …"

Tears are starting to burn at the corners of my eyes and I take big gulps of air, trying to force them back. This isn't the time to break into hysterics. "It's awful."

"It's typical," she says. "Something ridiculously cruel and completely unexpected. And just a tiny bit poetic—turning their rivals' weapons around on them. Come with me," she adds, with no hesitation. "Let's have a quick meeting before we head to the airport."

She leads us into the room she shares with Thomas. He looks up from packing for tonight's move and sees our stony faces. "I see you've heard about Louisiana."

I nod. "We have to do something."

"I'm not sure there's anything *to* do," Thomas says. "A warning has been issued to not accept early shipments, and some precautionary quarantines have been put in place. But it seems to me that we just have to keep going."

I'm already shaking my head. "This ploy is terrible and effective, but ultimately, I think it's just distraction."

"Distraction?" Thomas echoes, clearly not convinced.

"We know they're looking for me. No one can make this vaccine except me. Throw in some death and confusion, possibly slow us down, divert our attention, and it buys them time to figure out where I am."

"What do you suggest we do about it?" Benson asks.

"Well, I can't stop making vaccine. The problem the Reduciata always had is that the viral RNA is so complex that they can't just create it, like I can. They have to grow it in a lab. It's only a slight advantage, because it grows ridiculously fast, but not at the rate of truckloads per day. As long as I'm putting out vaccine faster than they're putting out infected serum, they're losing. Which is why their real goal has to be finding us. I suggest we fill planes tonight, and board one ourselves tomorrow."

"Leave here?" Alanna asks, an edge of fear in her tone.

"Better in the air than sitting in one place, waiting to get picked off. I think we've done what we can from here." I look around at all of them. "Not only will we be more effective on an international scale, but..." I spread my hands helplessly. "It's harder to hit a moving target."

CHAPTER EIGHT

"I don't like it." Dr. Martin is pacing the conference room, empty but for myself, Benson, Thomas, and Alanna.

"They're *going* to find us if we stay," I reply. Whether Dr. Martin's reluctance is born of a desire to control the vaccine supply specifically, or her related interest in my abilities generally, she has to let me go. For her own safety, to say nothing of the world's.

"Honestly," Thomas chimes in, "we've been lucky to avoid detection this long."

"Besides, there's still a ton we need you to do." That is the truest truth I've uttered all day. "Without you, we've got no legitimacy. Nobody's going to inject themselves with something on our say-so, and we need your help coordinating distribution on the move. Speed is the only advantage we have against the Reduciata at this point, since they don't have anyone strong enough to just create the virus. They have to grow it in a lab."

"Are you sure about that?"

I eye Dr. Martin for several long moments, my jaw

clenched. "Pretty sure. It's an incredibly complex strand of DNA that had to be created to begin with, in order to affect the immortal lifespan of an Earthbound."

"I've been thinking about that," Alanna chimes in. "If someone made it to begin with, what's to say they can't make it now?"

"I believe that the original virus was created over a century ago." I'm largely speculating here—with the help of vague memories of myself as a hungry, nine-year-old street urchin—but I'm not anxious to give Dr. Martin further details. Especially since I was close enough to Mariana that, for all I know, *I* created the virus. Not that I would ever do such a thing deliberately. I think. But Mariana was my friend; neither she nor Daniel possess the power of creation, and the memories I do have don't seem totally reliable.

It's not a possibility I like to dwell on. And it's *definitely* not a possibility I want anyone else to dwell on.

"The Reduciata," I continue, "lost access to whoever created it. Whether the creator died, or was silenced, or what, I don't know."

"That long ago, virology would have been…well, nonexistent," Dr. Martin muses. "There were a few vaccines, but poorly understood. The loss of an advanced researcher in those days, particularly one capable of actually engineering biological weapons, would have been a setback indeed."

I remember—recently, though now it seems a lifetime ago—the young Curatoria doctor, Audra, speaking of finding ways to introduce advanced technology into civilization at large. The dark side of that undertaking hadn't occurred to me at the time. Even with all the details I've kept from her, Dr. Martin is assembling a pretty clear picture of things for herself.

"It's possible they thought they'd gotten everything they could from their…researcher," Thomas adds helpfully, "and didn't want anyone around who might be able to stop them. Regardless, the end result is that now they have to grow the virus, and that takes time and resources."

"I still don't like the idea of letting you go," Dr. Martin says with a sigh. "Most of them don't know it, of course, but we've got a whole planet clamoring for access to, well, *you*."

"And they should have it," I say, my voice sounding choked. "It's not fair to withhold something that can save literally billions, just because I happen to be American." *I certainly haven't always been*, I add to myself.

"Then you plan to leave the country?" Dr. Martin asks, her voice brittle.

"I thought to fly somewhere new every day," I say, shaking my melancholy away and resuming the business-like tone I started this meeting with. "Every other day at the slowest. New identity, new country every flight. Not in any kind of linear path; chaos is going to be our friend. I'll sleep on the plane, arrive, and do just what we've done before. Create as much vaccine as I can, eat, sleep, eat. Create more. Then we're out of there. Before the serum even ships to clinics. Gone before the Reduciata knows we've landed."

"You make it sound easy," Dr. Martin says. "And truth is you'd be making it easier for me—I can maintain our subterfuge longer by pinning some blame on the inefficiency of international bureaucracy. But I hate to expose you like that—if these Reduciates are as well-connected as you say, every flight you take is one more chance for their people to recognize you."

"I can't imagine that'll be a problem," I say, transforming myself into a perfect mirror image of Dr. Martin.

Her face flushes and then turns white so quickly I almost laugh. Even the others draw in a quick breath of surprise. As either a creator or a destroyer you can alter elements of your appearance, but it's permanent. I imagine that, as a mixed pair, Alanna and Thomas could manage something like this, but not in the blink of an eye.

"Oh. I—I see that you're on top of that," Dr. Martin says, her voice strangled. She looks away and I take the opportunity to return to my usual appearance.

I glance at Thomas and Alanna and get to the part I know they're not going to like. "I want to take Benson with me. And Thomas—I might need to consult with a doctor at a moment's notice."

I feel Benson's hand tighten around mine under the table, but he doesn't speak. I know that he'll go where I ask him—whether that means staying with me, or leaving me alone. Alanna's mouth tightens but she doesn't say anything. She's waiting to hear my reasons.

"And Alanna?" Thomas is clearly trying to hide the tightness in his voice, but he's not doing a great job. It occurs to me that with the way the two of them have tried to always keep a low profile from both brotherhoods throughout the last many lifetimes, they likely have had very, very little separation after connecting.

"Someone needs to stay behind, with Dr. Mar—with Kat. Someone who has experience with the Reduciata."

If Dr. Martin is uncomfortable with being assigned a bodyguard, she doesn't let it show.

"Then why not leave Benson?" Thomas snaps, then seems to recover himself and nods toward his son. "No offense."

Benson's wordless grunt evokes an impressive blend of *none taken* and *get bent*.

"For the obvious reasons," I say simply, not attempting to recast my motivations as noble. "And because I need to sleep. Let's not forget that it's been less than a year since I was the sole survivor in one of the worst plane wrecks in history." I swallow hard. "I've managed to stay fairly calm as I've presented all of this to you, but don't kid yourself that my throat doesn't feel like it's going to close up and choke me every time I think of getting on a plane."

The room is silent all around me and I struggle to keep my breathing shallow and inaudible.

I turn and look in Thomas' direction and continue, without waiting for the cascade of murmured sympathy I'm so sick of hearing. "I suspect I'll need to be sedated for at least the first few plane rides, and maybe the longer ones after that. I need Benson to sit by me, fend off flight attendants and chatty seatmates, and be a soft shoulder to sleep on."

"Thomas could do all of that," Alanna says. And it's not so much an argument, as an acknowledgement that I haven't given her the real answer yet.

"This entire venture is very stressful and I think we're all aware that stress is the antithesis of sleep. The biggest stress in my world right now is Benson's safety. I'll sleep better, eat better, just plain function better if I can look up and know in an instant, that he's safe. Maybe that's selfish of me, but I'm saving the world—I think I'm allowed this one indulgence."

"But that indulgence separates me from Alanna *and* puts my son in danger," Thomas says in even tones. "I can't agree."

"I'm afraid that at the moment my selfishness trumps yours, Thomas."

"No, she's right." Alanna's voice is quiet, but it draws

everyone's attention. "Any world traveler knows the key to fast travel is to pack lightly. Bring only what's absolutely necessary." She raises her eyes, peering at Thomas with an expression that begs him to understand. "Your ability, knowledge, and skills are crucial to Tavia's success, and Benson is crucial to her sanity. By default, that leaves me to hold down the fort."

"Thank you," I whisper, not brave enough to look at Thomas. I glance instead at the window where orange light from the desert sunset is slanting through the blinds. "Now, Dr. Martin, is there any chance of getting our hands on a few of your employees' passports?"

Her eyes widen momentarily, then she shakes her head. "In for a penny—"

CHAPTER NINE

It's not a lie that Monday morning is a fabulous time to fly if you're trying to blend into a crowd, but my reasons for waiting until morning to leave were far more personal than that.

One more load of vaccine on the planes.

I'm leaving the United States. Even if every dose I've created over the last ten days has found an innocent person's arm, I'd be shocked if that amounted to one American in five. Dr. Martin assures me that laboratories around the world are studying samples she sent them to try and synthesize their own vaccine, but for the foreseeable future, I'm the only supplier. I had to make a final effort before abandoning my homeland.

Plus, it gave Thomas and Alanna one more night before I forced them to abandon each other. Lovers should always get one more night after finding out they're going to be separated. Most of the time they don't.

I wiggle under the warm covers and snug closer to Benson at that thought. After creating cases of the vaccine until I was so exhausted I almost puked, our last night before leaving was far from romantic. Honestly, at this point our relationship might very well qualify as the least-romantic in history—hanging out and watching me sleep must be about the most boring thing Benson has done in his life. But the feel of him beside me, spooning my back, with one arm flopped over me—that's what lets me *rest*. Which is a different thing than merely sleeping.

And it's why I need him to come with me.

I've tried to hide just how much this whole thing is wearing me out. I spout platitudes about getting used to it, and I do have good days—days when I feel stronger, better. But I have just as many bad days, where even after twelve hours of sleep I can barely drag myself out of bed, and it takes every ounce of determination to fill those trucks. If I have to do my resting on planes *and* without Benson…it's never going to happen. And I don't have time for recovery days. Speed is our only advantage.

The alarm rings—it's strange to be waking up in the actual morning—and I turn to face Benson, wrapping my arms around his waist and kissing his chin. "Sleeping Beauty time."

"I know," he says. His eyes are still closed, but he doesn't sound like he's been sleeping.

"You okay?"

The smile he gives me looks forced. "Worried about the same things you are, I imagine. No need to rehash and make it all seem worse."

"No, tell me," I say, rolling onto my stomach and scooting

close enough that I can feel his breath on my cheeks.

The muscles in his jaw flex and I know he's deciding. But he's never been a great liar and he gives up pretty quickly. "It feels like filling a bathtub with a tablespoon. I mean, we have the vaccine, and that's amazing, but, it's taking so long. There are just so many people in the world."

"I know," I say softly. "People are dying every day from the virus. By the thousands. And we're too late for all of them."

Everyone's been trying to shield me from the news, but I'd rather hear bad news than know nothing at all. Maybe that's not the best outlook, but I've never seen ignorance pay off in the long run.

I smile, not because I'm thinking happy thoughts, but because at least he said it. At least he's sharing with me. "You know what they say about eating a whale."

"One bite at a time?"

"Exactly."

I make everything that was ours disappear, leaving no trace, and I know Alanna will have done the same in her and Thomas' room. It was her idea. The four of us meet at the side of the hotel, just out of sight of the main road, and both Thomas and Alanna look grim. Their hands are clasped together and Alanna's knuckles are white.

The air shimmers with heat even this early and I feel sweat break out on my back within minutes of leaving the air-conditioned room. I won't be sorry to leave the desert heat behind, that's for sure. Two black sedans pull up and Benson and I duck into the back seat of one, giving Alanna and Thomas some privacy to say their goodbyes.

Well, *I* do it out of courtesy; I imagine there's a pretty heavy squick factor for Benson, since Thomas is his dad and, from Benson's perspective, Alanna is basically the *other woman*. One thing Benson and I haven't talked about is how comfortable he is or isn't traveling with his—until very recently—estranged father. Maybe I don't want to know.

No, scratch that, I'm quite certain I don't want to know. I just need him to be with me and I'd rather think that's exactly where he wants to be, too.

Thomas slides into the front seat quicker than I expected, staring straight ahead instead of watching Alanna get into the other town car. Like ripping off a Band-Aid, the very first turn out of the hotel parking lot sends us in different directions and I can only keep sight of Alanna's car for about thirty seconds before it rounds a corner, off to the Mayo Clinic to manage with Dr. Martin.

"Which terminal?" the driver asks.

Covert looks shoot all around the car. "We're not sure," Thomas finally says. "International," he adds after a pause.

"Which airline?" the driver presses.

Thomas looks over and gives him a cocky smile. "We'll

decide when we get there," he says, as though such a thing were the most normal behavior in the world. "We're off on an adventure."

"Oh," says the driver. "In that case, terminal four." He makes a series of recommendations concerning airlines and connecting flights, but I tune them out. This part was Thomas' brainchild. Whenever possible, we'll decide where we're going next at the airport counter. Money's not an issue—thank you pre-paid Visa cards—but schedule is. Not to mention secrecy. The current plan is to check out the screens, find the timeliest non-stop flight to a major city, and get on it.

It's like a double-blind experiment; none of us, not me or Alanna or Dr. Martin, or anyone, knows where we're going until just before we board the plane. And during our flight, it'll be Dr. Martin's job to inform a clinic or hospital of our imminent arrival and to somehow arrange for them to receive the vaccine and get it immediately shipped out. I don't envy her the task, but she assured us she could make it happen.

It's only about a ten-minute drive to the airport from the hotel and already I'm getting nervous. Everything *should* work, but this isn't exactly a plan we've had weeks to perfect. I stare out the back window as we approach and Thomas points at a brightly lit sign displaying a bunch of airline logos and asks, "Any preferences back there?"

But I only give the sign a moment's notice before peering

around again. "Thomas, there's a car behind us."

"We're at the airport, hundreds of people going to the same place, of course there's a car behind us," he whispers.

"But it's coming up awfully fast," I say softly, squinting at a nondescript brown Ford Focus. Hardly the kind of vehicle you'd expect to be following anyone.

And yet ...

I see the gun a second before the back windshield shatters. The squeal of tires fills my ears a second before my body slams into Benson as the car pivots, careens off the road, and slams into a cement pillar. My head is ringing and the scent of matchsticks and burnt oil fills the air.

"We have to go." I know my voice is slurred, but the Focus wasn't very far behind us and I can imagine them screeching to a stop right this moment, well-prepared to capture us. "Thomas, this way!" I shout as the doors on the driver's side vanish. Thomas fumbles with his seatbelt and crawls over the driver's dead body as Benson and I exit the vehicle.

The fresh air helps a little, but we still need to run. "We have to get to people!" I say, probably too loud, but a fierce ringing fills my ears.

Luckily, the pillar we hit is part of a multi-story parking lot.

"This way," I say, then shriek when a bullet zips past my head, shattering a divot into the cement wall in front of us. Another wall, one of the same gray cinderblock that lines half the streets in Phoenix, springs up behind us, shielding us from further gunfire.

Not my creation. "Thomas!"

"They'll assume you did it," he breathes as I open a hole in the wall of the garage. He's been hiding his creation powers from the Reduciata and the Curatoria for so long sometimes I nearly forget about them myself.

Despite the sparkles still flashing in front of my eyes, I turn and focus on the opening in the wall that we just tumbled through and force myself to fill it in again. A solid, cement wall again.

"We can't stop," I say to them as we stand panting. "We have to get up, change, and get to a crowd."

"I—I'm not sure…" Benson's face is sweating from something more than the oppressive heat and I look down and see a large spot of blood blossoming on his thigh.

Weakness floods through me as I realize he's been shot. "Benson. Oh no. Ben—" I press my hand against my mouth to stifle a sob. I can't lose him.

"I'm okay. It's just my leg. But I…I can't…run." He sucks in a breath that tells me he's hurting a lot more than he's willing to admit.

I have to pull myself together and do my part or none of us is going to live. I force myself to reign in my tumbling emotions. "Okay. Thomas, patch him up. I'll change our appearances. We have like ten seconds. Ben," I look up into his panicked eyes, "you're going to have to bear it until we can do a better job. Can you make it?"

He gives me a grunt of determination and I nod at Thomas. He stares at Benson's leg for hardly a moment, and Benson lets out another groan as Thomas says, "It's bandaged, and the brace will redistribute your weight higher up your leg. Let's get you on your feet."

As I shift our appearances I consider trying to transform away Benson's wound, too, but even with my formidable Transformist powers, internal organs are a trick. Best let him heal mostly on his own. I scramble to my own jelly-ish legs as Thomas pulls Benson up, and a quick look around shows a small crowd heading toward the sound of the car crash.

Benson's eyes are wide as he takes me in from head to toe. "Who have you made us into?"

"Sixty-year-old tourists," I say apologetically, smoothing my hands down the blue floral shirt I'm sporting. With a rather large bosom.

Thomas is a perfect match in Bermuda shorts and a pastel pink polo. I tilt my head and then add a heavy gold necklace and several rings and bracelets to myself and a Rolex and winking diamond pinky ring to Thomas. "Rich, *impulsive* sixty-year-old tourists." Less likely to question why we're buying tickets at the counter. I hope.

"You actually look okay," I tell Benson. "You're red-haired and sunburned. Our slacking college drop-out son in his late twenties. Act entitled."

We're about to step out from behind the car when I grab Thomas' arm. "Wait. Here." I create an enormous jangly purse over my arm and a couple of sleek roller-boards in each of our hands. "Louis Vuitton," I mutter wryly.

"Nice touch," Thomas replies. We all clatter out from between the wall and the vehicles and fall into step with the crowd, still pressing toward the opening where our driver crashed.

Where he died.

A spasm rises in my throat, but I swallow it down and try to look like I haven't a care in the world. A soft grunt sounds from Benson and I turn to him, probably looking way more motherly than I'd like. "Are you okay?"

"As okay as I'm going to be, considering I was shot in the leg," he says in a pained tone.

"If you can avoid limping until we get inside, I can take you to a bathroom and fix you better," Thomas says.

"I'll try. Hurts like hell."

"You can do it." I reach for his hand, but stop just in time.

As we round the corner my head turns and Thomas hisses, "Don't look!"

"No, we *should* look," I retort under my breath. "Everyone

is looking. We want to be sheep today and do what all the other sheep are doing." I even go so far as to veer in the direction of the accident scene—where cop lights are already flashing—and crane my neck to have a look.

"I don't see the Ford," I whisper.

"No way he would have stayed." Benson's low voice vibrates beside my ear. My transformation doesn't seem to have changed his voice and I confess I'm relieved. "Not at the scene anyway. I bet he parked and is booking it to the terminal right now to look for us."

"Maybe we should stay and rubberneck a little longer."

"Maybe we shouldn't," Benson says tightly. "I don't know how much longer I can last."

He looks a little pasty even considering the pale complexion I've given him. At least the sweat popping up on his brow *could* be from the heat, but I know better. "Let's go," I say.

CHAPTER TEN

The airport is blessedly cool, but I guess an airport in the desert would specialize in that. I spot a men's restroom with a row of chairs along the wall beside it. "Should I wait here for you two?" I ask cheerily.

"I guess so." But before they turn Thomas lets out a sigh of exasperation. "Damn it. I'm so used to working with Alanna. I need your help. Let's all sit for a second—no, you on the other side," he says, pointing so he and Benson sit on either side of me. "It's not a through-and through, so I need you to get the bullet out," he says quietly, close to my ear. "I could go and pry it out in the bathroom, but that'll only make things worse. Not to mention bloodier. If *you* make it disappear it'll be the least amount of trauma possible."

Oh geeze. "Okay—what's the best way to do this?"

"Put your hand on his thigh, feel for the bandage. And at the same time wave your finger like you're lecturing him."

"I feel so stupid," I say as I swing a finger back and forth in front of Benson's face.

"Okay, got the bandage? I'm hoping that you can do this

without seeing it. You're powerful enough that you should be able to. Focus on the metal inside his leg and just—however you make stuff disappear."

I want to close my eyes to focus, but instead, I let my eyes glaze a bit and try to focus on what a spent bullet inside Benson's leg might look like. I blink and will it away and almost at the same time, Benson lets out a whoosh of breath.

"Wow, that feels better already," Benson says, pleasant surprise in his voice.

"Wait," I say, "I think I can—" I try to remember the way I closed up my stomach when Daniel shot me. In my head I knit his skin together just like I did then. The injury is still there, beneath the skin, since I'm not about to try knitting his muscles together. But without proper supplies—not to mention time—I'm not convinced even Thomas could do any better. At the last second I transform the bandage into a new one and carefully lift my hand, looking for blood. There's a dime-sized spot, but I erase it quickly.

"We're good," I say.

"One more thing," Thomas says. "I'm going to reach for you and create a syringe between our hands. Put your purse or something up to block the sight and then plunge the needle into Benson's thigh. Poke it right through his pants. Benson?" Thomas says, leaning around me to address his son. His actual son. "There'll be a burning coldness and it's going to sting like hell; be ready."

"My favorite," Benson mutters.

"Here," Thomas says. "Be careful. There's no lid." He smiles down at me lovingly and reaches for my hand.

I do my best to smile back the way a wife might and I feel a cool, plastic cylinder fill my palm. I peek down to double check which is the pointy end and then turn to Benson and flop my purse onto his lap, flinching when he grimaces.

"It's in here somewhere," I say loudly, rummaging through it with one hand while the other shoves down into his leg. *Way* too hard. The needle plunges through like a hot knife through butter and I whack his thigh hard with my fist. "Sorry!" I whisper, then quickly depress the plunger and hear Benson suck in a hiss of air.

He lets loose a string of cursing under his breath and I can't help but feel a bubble of laughter rise in my chest. I choke it down and then feel bad about it. But that blue streak was pretty impressive.

"The hell was *that?*" Benson hisses to Thomas, leaning forward to look around me.

"Lidocaine," he says blandly. "You're going to be very happy with me in about thirty seconds. Though you'll want some more in two hours or so. Tavia, we'll figure out the best way to do that later."

"No, no, no!" Benson interrupts. "I am *so* not doing that

again. That was seriously worse than actually getting shot..."
Benson's voice trails off and I look at Thomas, but he just
grins. I swing back to Benson and he's staring down at his leg
in wonder. "Wow. Okay, that's pretty awesome."

"Numb," Thomas says in my ear. "You'll still have to
consciously think about your gait," he says, addressing Benson
again. "You're leg's going to feel pretty dead, but it shouldn't
hurt."

"Thank you whoever's God, gods, or goddesses." His face
is relaxing and I feel a flutter of optimism in my chest. We've
managed to get through our first assassination attempt with
hardly a hiccup.

"Well," I say, pulling my stupid handbag off Benson's thigh
and pointing at the bank of screens on the opposite wall, "shall
we decide where we're going to go today?"

Thomas rises and offers me a hand, then smiles
apologetically at Benson. "Afraid you're on your own, young
strapping lad like you."

Benson rolls his eyes and I can't tell if that's his real
reaction or if he's doing his best to play his part of spoiled son.
But I can't bring myself to care too much when I see that he's
walking okay. That's the important part right now.

"I've got to get ahold of Alanna and Dr. Martin," Thomas
says as we stand in front of the shifting blue screens. "They
need to know about our tail. If they knew to find us at the

hotel, they know the Phoenix Mayo is involved. Everyone at the clinic could be in danger."

Frustration wells up within me. The last ten minutes have been one urgent problem after the other, without so much as a moment to think past our immediate survival. But he's right. The car tailing us knew where to find us. "Use the phone; we'll wait here."

"The phone is no longer in my pocket."

I squelch the urge to let out my own stream of curse words. When I transformed us I was in such a rush that I transformed everything. Including the contents of our pockets.

Which wasn't much, as we don't want to carry even the slightest proof of our actual identities. But Thomas had a disposable phone.

And now he doesn't.

And as powerful as I am, not only have I not learned how to make one, but the trick in this case isn't creating the hardware; it's hooking it up to functioning cell service. "Is there somewhere here to buy another one?" Panic flutters in my belly as I try to decide how long it's been since we all left the hotel. Twenty minutes? Thirty? It takes just over thirty to get from the airport to the clinic.

Assuming Alanna made it that far.

"I think we're going to have to get past security before we can do that," Thomas says.

"They still have payphones, don't they? Can you call collect?"

Thomas nods. "That should work; or I can make quarters or dollar bills."

"Go, go!" I whisper. "We'll stand here and look useless, just go."

He hurries off and, I have to admit, he looks very much like a legitimate sixty-year old standing at a payphone in slightly too-short Bermuda shorts.

"What happened?" Benson whispered.

"I screwed up." And at those words I realize what else I did. I had a pre-paid credit card in my pocket that was supposed to pay for today's tickets. While a payphone is easy to find at an airport, and a disposable phone is available in the shops once we pass security, nowhere around here is going to let me buy a pre-paid Visa with ten grand on it. In cash. "Damn it," I curse quietly. I'd been patting myself on the back for doing such a good job on Benson's leg, but the loss of the credit card could be devastating.

I stare uncomprehendingly at the departure listings for a couple of minutes before I feel a presence settle in at my right and give a quick glance to confirm that it's Thomas.

"I called Alanna, told her to watch out. She's going to contact Dr. Martin and arrange to rendezvous elsewhere." His voice is tense, but I can tell he's relieved that she's alive, at least. "I'll call her back once we get a better phone and we'll see what the damage is."

Tears prickle at my eyes as I realize it's time to confess that there's even more damage than he knows. "The credit card's gone."

"Smile, Tavia. We're on vacation."

I force my lips into a curve and try to blink back the sheen of tears. "What are we going to do?"

"I don't understand what the problem is; make another one."

"I can't. That magnetic strip. I don't know how to do that. It's the same issue as with the phone."

But Thomas is already shaking his head. "The magnetic strip is optional. We're clueless tourists—your took your purse too close to an MRI machine when I…had something done. Magnetic strip is screwed. She can type in the numbers and it'll be fine."

"I don't remember the numbers."

"Have you tried?"

"What do you mean?"

Thomas pulls me aside and smiles at me from his old man's face and says, "Remember what you told me that Daniel said, about how you can create perfectly any book you've ever read? How much you can create without giving yourself an aneurism is probably the simplest measure of an Earthbound's power, but another is the conscious effort you have to put into making something. And you're as powerful an Earthbound as anyone has seen in…millennia, probably. As long as those numbers are rattling around somewhere in your subconscious, we should be fine. Now think of the card, reach into your purse, and grab it."

This moment reminds me of nothing so much as the time I desperately needed a bus ticket in Portsmouth to save my own life. I was completely sure I wasn't going to be able to do it, and it wasn't until the moment I felt the ticket in my hand that I believed.

I grip the plastic card, pull it out, and hand it to Thomas. It *looks* like the one Dr. Martin got for us, but until someone actually runs those numbers, I can't know for sure. Turning back to the screen I try to force my worry down. "Where should we go?"

"The chances of getting anything directly international from here are slim unless we fly to Central America and, to be honest, that seems like something they'd expect us to do," Benson says under his breath, pointing randomly at the screen as he does. Sometimes I have to remind myself that he's spent most of the last ten years pretending to be someone he's not; of course he's good at it. "I suggest we head to LA or New York. We can get anywhere from either of those places."

"What do you think?" Thomas asks. "Better to have a short

plane-ride for your first time or a long one?"

I pause and look up at the screen where three flights for New York are posted. "As much as I'd like to say LA, I think I'd better jump right in with as long a flight as possible. How far to Europe from New York?"

"Ten hours, give or take."

"Then starting with four or five is probably a good jumping off point. That US Airways flight, maybe?" I point at a flight that's scheduled to leave in just under two hours.

"Let's go see if they have room in first class."

"First class?" I ask, trailing after Thomas.

"Absolutely," Thomas replies with almost no inflection. "You need to sleep, you need to eat, you're nervous anyway, money's not an issue, and on top of that they never fill up first class with frequent flyer people until the last minute. That's actually where you're most likely to get a seat."

"Sweet," Benson says from just over my shoulder.

As usual, Thomas is right, and although the woman at the counter looks skeptical when we tell her which flight we want to get onto, as soon as we mention first class, she changes her tune.

Believe me, though, it's a good thing money isn't an issue. first class tickets less than two hours before a flight are downright highway robbery. But we don't balk and she hardly glances at the IDs that I create as we all reach into our pockets.

It's more than a little scary just how much easier everything is with plenty of money. For us it's a good thing, but I consider all the scum in the world who have stacks of cash to throw around and it's downright shiver-inducing.

"Hmm," she says as she runs the card. "I'm not getting …"

"I told you not to take it so close to the MRI room," Thomas says gruffly, and I hope my face isn't white. I hurriedly create a touch more blush just in case.

"Oh, no problem," the woman says, not even looking up. "It'll just take another minute. Don't worry, you have plenty of time to get through security," she adds helpfully as her long fingernails click lightning fast over the keys. "Oh! You didn't have bags to check, did you?"

"No," I manage to croak after my heart jumped to about six hundred beats a minute when she squeaked.

"Good, I'd have to enter those numbers all over again." Her printer whirrs and she's lost in a flurry of ripping perforated cardboard and slamming her fist on the stapler. "Now this is your receipt," she says, handing one slip of cardboard to Thomas, "and these are your tickets. Don't mix them up—the receipt won't get you past TSA." She continues pointing up the hallway, telling Thomas where to go, but I may as well be deaf. My heart is pounding in my ears at the realization that it's over. The credit card went through.

I did it.

My first thought is to reach for Benson's hand and squeeze, but I stop just in time. Age thing aside, next time I give us new identities I'm not going to be my boyfriend's mother. It's too weird.

"Let's go," Thomas says, practically sweeping us along in front of him. I'm about to protest at his herding, but I realize he's worried about Alanna. Urgent problems solved; important problems loom large once more.

Security with first class tickets is a breeze. It does take some time to get all my jewelry off, but at least I didn't make us belts. As soon as we're through, Thomas focuses on a store ahead of us and says, "I'll meet you at the gate," leaving Benson and me without a backward glance.

"Alone at last," Benson says, raising an eyebrow at me.

"I want to kiss you so much right now," I say, just loud enough for him to hear. We so rarely get time alone these days—with both of us awake, anyway—and it feels like a colossal waste to not be able to even hold hands. "How's your leg?"

"Very numb." His smile is amused and there's a light in his eyes I don't know that I quite understand. "Wasn't this trip supposed to be boring?"

"That was the hope. Let's go find our gate so you can sit down."

We stop for food along the way and there's something fun

about going to whatever restaurant I want, and ordering anything I desire. The disruption we're having on the world's economy by inserting completely non-backed currency into the cash-stream is surely so negligible as to be entirely insignificant, right? Besides, we're supposed to look like rich, impulsive tourists. Nothing says rich and impulsive like a filled bakery box, a full-sized pizza, three drinks, and six churros.

Churros are delicious. Just saying.

"My life is sleeping and eating," I say, putting my Birkenstocked feet up on my Louis Vuitton suitcase. "It's rather a glorious life."

"Except that part where you drain yourself so much you faint or puke," Benson says, a strip of cheese hanging forgotten on the side of his mouth.

"You have a—a cheese," I say, pointing. Oh, so many ways this situation could have been romantic if we weren't currently playing mother and son. I'm seriously taking the time to think our disguises through next time. Maybe we can change in New York.

I barely notice Thomas before he smacks down on the seat beside Benson, eyes darting around wildly. "We called Alanna just in time. About ten minutes after she had Dr. Martin leave the Phoenix Mayo Clinic, it blew up. Should be hitting the news any moment."

Churros aren't quite so delicious the second time.

CHAPTER ELEVEN

"You have to trust Alanna," Benson says softly to Thomas as I try to get control of my stomach. I'm still fighting heaves, but I'm trying to disguise them, to avoid drawing attention. Luckily, I have a pizza box to shield my face, and this end of the terminal isn't especially crowded.

"Funny, coming from you," Thomas says, a mixture of parental patronizing and black humor that clearly rankles Benson.

"I don't *like* her—for reasons that are actually your fault—but I trust her to be able to take care of herself, and you should, too."

Thomas' lips—lips that aren't really his—are set in a tight line and I'm sure anyone walking by must think he's simply trying to talk some sense into his stubborn, spoiled son.

Not the other way around.

"I have to go to her," he finally says. "You two can make it to New York on your own; you've got the tickets."

"No," I say firmly. "You can't. And she wouldn't want you to. Benson's right. *Trust her.*"

"You don't understand. I have complete confidence in her capabilities, but she's a Destroyer. What she needs right now is to go on the run. She needs money and transportation and supplies. She needs *me*."

I roll my eyes. "You think the only way she can get what she needs is for you to create it for her? She's not helpless, Thomas."

"Easy for you to say—Benson is sitting here beside you, not out risking his life."

"How many times has Alanna been shot today?" I demand. My voice stuns him into silence and I wrangle a primal urge to lash out with my power, to put Thomas' little insurrection down hard.

I could kill him. And he knows it. There's not an Earthbound alive who could take me in a fair fight—not alone. And the way he's trivialized his own son's suffering in an effort to excuse himself—to rush to his *diligo,* the fate of the world be damned—has me very nearly boiling over with fury.

It must show in my eyes because Thomas visibly pales and begin nodding. "You're right. I spoke in anger—I'm sorry."

I force myself to unclench my jaw and try to remember how hard this must be for Thomas. I take a few calming breaths and speak gently. "She'll be okay. She's not just powerful; she's smart. In a few days you guys'll talk and you'll laugh that you ever doubted her." I trust Alanna. Benson's misgivings notwithstanding, I even like her.

Thomas stares into my eyes and seems to be pulling strength from me, buoying up his own resolve. "I hope so," he whispers. He doesn't sound confident, but at least he sits back and slumps into his chair. Not happy, not assured, but not taking off and running to her either.

"How long have we got before we board?" Thomas asks with his eyes closed.

"Twenty minutes," Benson says quietly.

At those words, the lingering heat of my anger is doused by ice-cold fear. The string of crises leading to this point has kept my mind on immediate concerns, but barring an attack on the airport itself, we seem to have weathered the storm. Time at last to consider what I've committed myself to do.

In twenty minutes, I'll be boarding a plane.

The last plane I was on fell out of the sky and killed my parents. Almost killed me. It set the entire disaster that has become my life into motion. Somehow I've *got* to get used to it—I'm going to spend the next several months flying crazy distances nearly every single day. But at the moment, I can hardly even breathe at the thought.

"We interrupt this program to bring you breaking news from Arizona."

The sound of the reporter's voice breaks the tense silence that had enveloped the three of us. Our attention goes to the nearest TV screen as the news program switches to on-site teams covering the now-familiar grounds of the Mayo Clinic. The ringing in my head blocks out the reporter's words as I stare in horror at the scene. The cameras mostly just show smoke and emergency vehicles. I'm reminded sickly of the way Logan's house was similarly decimated less than two months ago. Dimly, I wonder if any of the news people will make the connection in the weeks to come. Black smoke, a stark smudge against the sky, rises in an eerie column that I can only imagine must be visible for miles. Where once there was a cutting-edge medical research facility, now only fire and rubble.

"I wish they'd show the people," Benson says softly at my side.

"What people?" My words echo in my head and I'm not entirely sure I said them out loud until Benson replies.

"The survivors. Surely there must be some."

But I think of Logan's family—all dead—and I can't share his confidence.

"I thought you lived among them," Thomas says, and the edge in his voice cuts like a blade. "You should know better than anyone that the Reduciata don't leave survivors."

"Apparently I've gone soft," Benson shoots back. Tension crackles in the air between them, made somehow worse by the disaster unfolding before our eyes.

"That was meant for us." I give voice to the obvious, if for no other reason than to keep it from hanging over us like a dark storm cloud. I want to reach for Benson's hand—to thread my finger through his and hold on as though he were my lifeline. I've done it so many times. Back in Portsmouth, which feels more like years ago than just a few months. But I can't. Seriously, I am *never* disguising us as mother and son again. Ever.

"Was it?" Thomas asks, his voice strangely calm. "They knew we were at the hotel. Wouldn't it have been more effective to bomb the airport? Get the planes grounded until they could find us?"

I shake my head, staring at the TV screen. "Something like this would have taken hours to set up. We left the hotel—" I check my watch. "Ninety one minutes ago. I think it was too late by then and they must have decided that doing *something* was better than doing nothing."

"Hoping to catch Alanna at the very least, I'm sure," Benson adds, his eyes darting nervously to Thomas.

"But they didn't," Thomas whispers fiercely, not looking at either of us.

"Hang on, I don't understand," says Benson. "If they know we're here, and they don't want us to leave, they've still had plenty of time to get these planes grounded. It really would just take one phone call."

But Thomas is shaking his head. "It just means they haven't

guessed our plan. We've made several trips to the airport without ever boarding a plane, and if they think their attacks have put us on the run, closing down one airport puts us on high alert and only delays us by a few hours at the most. Plus, it's possible they need the airport open for their own purposes."

I barely register the words blaring over the speakers as an airline employee calls for first class passengers to board.

"That's us," I say. My throat feels like sandpaper and if there was anything left in my stomach, I probably would have puked again.

"Everyone have their boarding passes?" Thomas' voice sounds odd, like it's much farther away than where he's actually standing. I find myself gasping for breath and a wave of black passes over my vision; I start to choke and grasp at my throat, the pounding of my own heart like a drum in my ears, drowning everything else out. I look up with dry, scratchy eyes at the two men looking down on me, seeing them as if from underwater.

"I was afraid of this."

Thomas? I think so.

"What's wrong with her?"

"Panic attack. Stand in front of me."

A sharp sensation stabs at my leg and I want to cry out, but no sound escapes my throat. No air in or out. My lungs ache and the pain makes it somehow even harder to draw breath. I'm sure I'm going to suffocate when feeling suddenly returns to my fingers with pins and needles. I'm able to breathe again and I suck in oxygen so quickly my head begins to spin. Or maybe the whole airport is spinning; I'm oddly unsure and the sensation makes me giggle.

"I've got to help her walk. You grab the bags. They're not heavy; there's not actually much in them." Thomas' arm drapes around me and I try to turn to see Benson, but the world tilts crazily when I move my head and I jerk straight again. Thomas is half carrying me and I'm pretty sure they aren't going to let me onto the plane in this state.

Sure enough, the man at the gate stops us and I can feel all three of him looking at me. Why are there three of him? He's staring at my face and I try to focus, but distantly, I hear Thomas say something about being a doctor and anxiety, and he pulls something out of his pocket. A hastily created prescription, I imagine—or false credentials maybe.

It doesn't matter. They let us through and I feel the panic start to rise again as we make our way down the bridge toward the door of the airplane. Why do all airport bridges, all airplane doors, look exactly the same? I can practically feel my parents behind me as the three of us board the plane almost a year ago in Michigan.

I want to turn and tell them to stop. To not get on the

plane. I don't make it within even ten feet of the door before my eyes close and blackness takes over.

***

Consciousness returns slowly, which is probably for the best given that I'm on a plane.

A plane in the air, though even as I regain awareness the captain announces our final descent. The effect of whatever Thomas used to drug me retains some of its calming effect as I fight to fully return to myself and simultaneously stave off panicked paralysis.

I'm only half successful.

Something is binding me. I can't move my arms! I begin to twitch and fidget in my seat and quickly draw Benson's attention.

"You're awake," he says as I lift my head from his shoulder. "Thomas said to keep you wrapped up, even if you feel warm."

I nod spasmodically, only partially comprehending his words. It's just a blanket. It's not ropes. It's not a freaking straightjacket. I'm okay. I try to focus on other things. Like the two empty trays in front of us.

"I ate your dinner," Benson confesses, seeing where my gaze is going. "Better than regular airplane food, but trust me, you didn't miss much."

I nod again, feeling silly but knowing it's probably not a good idea to open my mouth at the moment. "Hold my hand?" I manage to force out through clenched teeth.

He reaches under the blanket and links his fingers with mine. Instantly everything seems just a little bit easier. It's not much, but it's something.

"Maybe close your eyes?" Benson suggests.

I nod woodenly and clamp my eyes shut, focusing on the warmth of Benson's hand holding tight to mine. I don't know where Thomas is. I don't think I could bear looking around to find out. My stomach is roiling and before I can consider too hard, I make a York peppermint patty inside my mouth and let the chocolate and mint cream melt slowly on my tongue—a trick I learned after the first couple of times I pushed myself too hard to fill an extra truck or plane with vaccine. The mint settles my stomach and the chocolate raises my blood sugar.

When the sweet mint is gone I make another and press my face into Benson's shoulder, my eyes still scrunched shut, not caring in the least what we might look like to other passengers.

Six candies and an eternity later, the plane lands fairly smoothly, and at last rolls to a stop. My legs are shaky when I stand, and as soon as Thomas hands me my carry-on I make all of its inner contents disappear, lest my shaky arms refuse to bear even its tiny weight. My knees feel like Jell-O and I barely make it up the walkway and into the terminal before collapsing in an empty seat.

"I admit, Tavia," Thomas says as he settles beside me. "I'm not sure this is going to work."

"What do you mean?" I ask, my hackles instantly rising.

"I don't think you're going to be able to handle these flights." His tone is grim. "If you're going to keep up a decent schedule—especially with the Reduciata sending out fake vaccines—you're going to have to be eating and resting *peacefully* on your flights. On much, much longer flights than this." He looks down at me skeptically and I fight the urge to touch my forehead to see if I'm sweating. "At this rate you're going to need two days to fly and another to *get over* flying."

"I can do this," I insist. "We all knew the first flight was going to be the hardest. I've done it now."

"Yes," Thomas says skeptically. "You've made it to New York City. A four-hour-flight, and you were unconscious for most of it. You want to get to Europe today? It's another nine to twelve. You really think you're ready to do that? Now? To walk onto another plane in the next hour or two?"

I narrow my eyes and just glare at him.

"I'm not trying to discourage you. Honest to God I'm not. I know what's at stake. But lying to yourself isn't going to help anyone, and repeatedly drugging you carries its own risks."

"I can do this," I repeat, willing it to be true. "Honestly, I think I'd feel better right now if I weren't fighting the effects of whatever it is you stuck me with."

His jaw tightens. "If I *hadn't* stuck you, you'd have never made it on the plane to begin with."

"I agree," I say, and almost laugh at the surprise on Thomas' face. "So it's a good thing you came along. But *now* it's just making me queasy."

"That's because your stomach is empty," he replies, brusque and clinical.

"Fine," I hide my hand in my empty bag and create a huge pack of trail mix, which I start shoving into my mouth.

Actually, it tastes really good and the dots of sweet and salty on my tongue work to clear my head. Another fake grab into my huge purse gives me a bottle of eggnog—one of the most calorie-dense liquids on the face of the earth—and within about five minutes, I'm feeling markedly better.

Without a word to Thomas or Benson I rise, shoulder my bag, and drag my empty rollerboard toward a bank of blue screens at the edge of the gate. I peer at the ever-changing lines of flight numbers and destinations, shoving more trail mix into my mouth as I consider them.

"So," I say when my travel companions sidle up on either side of me, "who wants to go to Spain?"

CHAPTER TWELVE

Thomas turns out to be both right and wrong. The flights are awful—every single damn one of them. With a little experimentation, we find a dosage of Valium that I swallow *after* I've boarded the plane of my own volition. Once I've filled my stomach with some warm, calorie-heavy food, I sleep. And if I nearly always lose my stomach as I get off the plane, well, nobody ever said saving the world would be easy.

But even with Thomas reluctantly administering benzodiazepines, I need a day to recover from each flight, as he predicted. Worse, I'm not able to create quite as much vaccine before hitting my limit. I'm sure that a couple days of quality rest would be marvelously restorative, but I have to weigh that against the possibility of being caught by Reduciates. The original plan was to spend twenty-four hours in each location, but a fast stop takes us thirty-six, and in most cities we push forty-eight.

Still, by picking our locations nearly at random we've managed to deliver millions and millions of doses to South Africa, Pakistan, Argentina, China, Australia, the Philippines,

Hong Kong, and—our first stop—Spain. We keep in contact with Alanna and Dr. Martin through disposable phones as they city hop through the United States nearly as quickly as we do abroad.

We have a system: as soon as our seats are called for boarding, Thomas calls Alanna and tells her where we're going. By the time we land—generally six to twelve hours later—she has instructions and contact information for us.

Dr. Martin sounds a little more shaky, a little less confident, every time I hear her voice, but so far the subterfuge has held, and everywhere we go, we find an empty cargo plane or warehouse ready to be loaded. Just trying to imagine how she's managing it all is enough to make my head spin.

We've worn a dozen false faces, though I've kept my personal commitment to never make Benson and myself look like relatives again. I need him too much. Not just his presence—I need his skin against mine, as though I can draw courage and strength by osmosis. There hasn't been time for more than stolen kisses here and there, even though we're physically together nearly every moment of the day. On the plane I lean against his shoulder and sleep as soon as possible, to block out my phobia. But even when we're on the ground— when I have time to sleep, and a bed to lie on—there's no time for making out. I curl up to him, press my face against his chest, and drift into the slumber of the utterly exhausted.

I suspect he's been watching a *lot* of foreign television.

He never complains.

Thomas complains. Some days Thomas seems to be a professional complainer. But I try to remember that while I have Benson, he hasn't seen Alanna in weeks. And there's absolutely no guarantee that he'll ever see her again.

I've asked both of them to risk the greatest sacrifice an Earthbound can be asked to make. And I haven't asked myself to do the same thing. Not really. I'm separated from Logan, and I ache for him the way I can only imagine one might feel a phantom limb. A throbbing awareness that there was once something there—something that maybe I ought to miss more than I do.

But we don't have the connection Thomas and Alanna do. Or, at least, I don't have it with Logan. I try not to think about that too much, either. Still, it would be nice to know if he's still alive. Should I be mourning? Or merely missing?

We're in Indonesia today. Bandung. Thomas suggested we avoid capital cities when possible because they seem like the most predictable places to go. At least half of the vaccine I make will be transported immediately to Jakarta, but *we* are not going to Jakarta. At the moment we're waiting for confirmation from the administration of a hospital thirty miles away, that they've made a warehouse available for us. Unfortunately, after the town-wide epidemic in Wilton, the

Reduciata has hit six more towns, two outside the United States. The fact that there's a "bioterrorist group" bombing hospitals and sabotaging vaccine shipments has finally been openly acknowledged by several world governments, which keeps people vigilant—and that's good. But it also tends to complicate our deliveries.

"Took them long enough," I grumble after Alanna tells us the news.

"It did," Alanna says, her voice tinny through the earpiece of the cheap cell phone, "but at least they eventually made an official statement."

"Three guesses why it's taken so long," Thomas says grumpily.

"What do you mean?" I ask.

"I mean that I guarantee there are Reduciates in the government doing everything they can to complicate matters for us."

"You think so?"

"Yes," Alanna, Thomas, and Benson all say at one.

They share a tense laugh, and Thomas runs his fingers through his hair in the nervous gesture I'm used to seeing in Benson. "You can't rule the world from the shadows without a few spies in the government. Don't you ever read tabloids?"

I think he's joking about the tabloids, so I give him a pity laugh, but I'm a little horrified to realize that he's not joking about ruling the world—I just never thought about it before. Of course the Reduciata have people in the government. And not just the U.S. government; the brotherhoods have always been international organizations. I've done fairly well so far at keeping the idea of danger a nebulous, faceless force. Danger is out there—fearful and fatal and comfortingly non-specific. The thought of very real, very specific people—people like Benson's brother, or maybe actual Earthbound—occupying positions of significant power in governments around the world makes the danger feel uncomfortably well-defined.

Thomas' second phone chirps to life and he looks at the screen, then stands. "That's them. Let's go."

***

Even with the warmth of Benson's skin curled against my back and the low hum of voices from the television serving as a white noise machine, sleep is elusive. I hate to admit it, but after the exhausting task of filling yet another warehouse in yet another city, the enormity of my endeavor is starting to sink feelers into my soul.

Benson did the math for me one day when my head hurt too bad to add two plus two, much less the many-digit multiplication required for this particular problem. I can make between five and ten million doses of the vaccine per session—assuming I'm in top form, which I certainly haven't been lately. With travel, I average less than one session a day. At five to ten million doses per day, with a human population of just over seven billion, it'll take up to *four years* to supply the world. Even if I were safe in one place, getting plenty of rest and producing at maximum capacity, I'd still have two years of work ahead of me, seven days a week, every day of the year.

Minimum.

How many will die while I'm getting around to them? Assuming the Reduciata don't find me during that time. It's all so incredibly demoralizing. I felt like a veritable Superwoman when I started out. Millions of doses! *Millions!*

But a million isn't that much against the population of the entire world, and the strain is already taking its toll on my body. I've been tolerating the flights better lately—less Valium needed—but after three weeks I'm already worried about developing dependence. Hopefully I can stop taking it soon, but I *have* to sleep, and if that's the only way, what choice do I have? I'm losing weight, too, and not in a good way. My ribs stand out under a thin layer of skin and my hipbones are getting disturbingly well-defined. Almost reflexively, I create a large peanut butter and hot fudge milkshake and take a long pull on the straw. If I'm not sleeping, I might as well be eating. Can't afford to waste time doing nothing.

"Can't sleep?" The gravel in Benson's voice tells me that if *he* wasn't, he was pretty close.

"Having trouble shutting my brain down."

He runs his fingers through my hair, brushing it back and away from my face. It's short again—like it was in Portsmouth. Takes less time. No long tangles to brush or push out of my face while I'm working—funny how I used to hate my short hair because it represented my parents' deaths and my jacked-up brain.

Those things seem so small, now.

Benson's fingers are soft and warm as he massages my scalp. Sometimes I swear he knows my body better than I do, knows what I need before it even occurs to me to ask. So many nights—and mornings, and afternoons, depending on what times zone we've flown into—he lies beside me, stroking my arms, my legs, my head, rubbing whatever he somehow senses is tense, helping me to relax and fall asleep.

I never understood the concept of being too tired to sleep until we started traveling.

A loud slurp sound tells me I've finished the milkshake and I toss the cup across the room, making it disappear mid-arc. I turn to face Benson, running my fingers up and down his bare chest. That was my request. Around week two I'd lost enough weight and was exerting myself to exhaustion frequently enough that I had trouble staying warm. Blankets only help so much, but Benson's skin warms me from both the inside and outside. It's the only thing that does.

So when we're alone, he goes shirtless.

I press my forehead to the base of his throat and inhale, loving the scent of Benson's skin that has become my definition of home. He hasn't shaved in a few days and a rough patch of stubble on his chin chafes my forehead. Rather than pull away, I rub a little harder. My body is so wrung out these days that subtle physical sensation is nearly indistinguishable. Everything inside me craves strong feelings—pleasure or pain.

A spark of wanting flutters to life in my belly. I push my mouth up to his, pulling his lip between my teeth and fighting the urge to bite down—to convince myself that he really is here. Benson responds with tentative touches, his fingers wandering a few inches up my back, under my shirt. But I don't want subtle.

I find a way to let him know.

***

I'm feeling surprisingly rejuvenated when a pounding on my door wakes me and I wonder if we've overslept. But a quick glance at the glowing red numbers beside the bed tells me that not only have we not overslept, we've only been asleep for four hours.

I slip out from beneath Benson's arm, making myself

presentable with a thought. It's probably a misguided housekeeper. But the moment I turn the handle Thomas bursts in.

"We have to go. Now! Make all this go away," he says, waving vaguely at a few necessities scattered about the room. "Car's waiting."

"The hell?" Benson is blinking blearily and I turn and hand him his glasses. Like that'll help him hear Thomas better.

Thomas shifts from one foot to the other, peers out the door, and then grimaces and swings it shut. "There's been another Earthbound death."

"From the virus?" I ask, my heart pounding.

"It's mostly a collection of rumors at this point, but while everyone else is baffled, *I* know exactly what they mean. If we're lucky, it'll work in our favor."

"What's happening?" Benson asks, pulling on a shirt and trying to step into shoes as he speaks.

Thomas seems to have only now registered Benson's presence at all, and at the sight of his son tumbling out of bed and yanking on clothes he's momentarily paralyzed by what I can only imagine is parental horror. Luckily, he recovers quickly, looks away from Benson, and says to the wall, "Madagascar, South Africa, Botswana, and some of Nambia disappeared from the Internet. People are going to figure out pretty quickly that it's not just a broken cable somewhere."

We were in South Africa last week. Despair washes over me at the news of millions of lives lost because I wasn't fast enough. Benson curses viciously under his breath and I swallow hard, fighting back tears.

"We don't have time to discuss," Thomas says, pulling the door open again. "I want us in the air as soon as possible."

"We can't leave," I say, swinging my hand around the room and making everything I can see that doesn't belong to the hotel disappear. "I've got to get another two batches made."

"No time. Maybe if we were in Samurinda, or better yet, Jayapura, but no, we're in Bandung." He technically answered my question, but his rant seems more directed at himself than me.

"You're not making any sense. Why are we leaving? This is awful but it doesn't have anything to do with what we're doing now. We can't lose focus!"

Thomas shakes his head and turns to face me. "There's going to be a tidal wave. It might not reach us here, but that's not a theory I want to stay and test. If the disasters in the Pacific and South America are any guide, it'll take some time for the satellites and seismologists to figure out what's going on. But when they do, news will travel fast. We've got to get on a plane before there aren't any *left* to get on."

My knees feel weak and I half-wish I hadn't asked.

"Ten minutes," I say, before I can lose my nerve.

"What the hell are you talking about?"

"Give me ten minutes. I feel good. Rested," I clarify quickly. "Run me by the warehouse, let me fill it one more time. Whatever I can do. We owe them that much, don't we?"

Thomas hesitates, standing in the doorway with panic still flaring in his eyes. "Fine," he says. "But you both have to come now. Make whatever else you need in the car."

"Deal," I say, ducking under his arm and running out to the waiting vehicle.

Thomas drives like a madman. The streets are dark but there's a blood-red line of brightness beginning to emerge in the east. Dawn, then.

There are a few people out and about—those who rise before everyone else and clean the streets, bake the bread, cater to the wealthy who can sleep in until noon—but not many. Another hour and we'd be trapped in a mess of vehicles, but for the moment, it's manageable. It's the first time I truly ask myself if ten minutes is too high a price to pay. But I can't abandon this city, especially when their country is about to face an entirely different kind of tragedy. Bandung is about as inland as it's possible to get on the island of Java—but that just means, in the event of a serious tidal wave, they're likely to have an influx of refugees. Crowds are a great way to spread contagious disease; they'll need as much vaccine as they I can give them.

Thomas squeals the brakes outside of a warehouse that doesn't look familiar to me, even though I was here less than five hours ago. At first I figure it's just the difference made by the waxing morning light, but it could just as easily be that, after all the warehouse visits I've made in the past few weeks, my brain knows better than to bother making memories of them.

"I'll be quick," I promise, slipping out of the car.

"I'm coming too," Benson says, at the same time as Thomas warns, "It'll be locked."

"Like that could stop me," I say, though my voice is quiet enough I'm not sure he hears. I'm not entirely sure I was talking to him.

"Are you sure you're okay?" Benson asks as I make the locked handle vanish and push the door open.

"I feel good," I say, a little surprised at the truth of the claim. "Rested," I add. "I think I'll be fine."

I turn to the empty space and take a deep breath. I've learned that it's easier to fill up large spaces in a few parts rather than all at once, so I focus on each of the four corners individually, and watch boxes with the Mayo Clinic emblem emblazoned on them appear in neat stacks. By the time I'm finished my legs are weak and I wait for my gut to roll, but though nausea arrives as anticipated, it's not unmanageable.

"I'm done," I say unnecessarily, but it spurs Benson into

action anyway.

Precisely eighty-nine minutes, three ridiculously expensive first class tickets, and one sprint through the terminal later, we lift off from the Husein Sastranegara International Airport. Even before the flight attendant announces that we've reached cruising altitude, I'm fast asleep with my head resting on Benson's shoulder.

No Valium required.

CHAPTER THIRTEEN

Brisbane feels surprisingly familiar when we deplane. Perhaps simply because the signs and annoying airport announcements are all in English.

"I can't believe I slept so well," I say, stretching my arms as we walk through the terminal.

"I can't believe you *ate* so much," Benson ribs, bumping his shoulder into mine. I have to smile at that. I'm sure it must have been quite a spectacle, watching me wolf down nine or ten thousand calories on the way to the airport.

"The news must have come through." I glance around at what should be a bustling airport but, instead, is almost entirely empty except where travelers have crowded around ceiling-mounted televisions. It occurs to me that I don't see very many people crying. As a population we've become sadly inured to tragedy over the last few months. Grief gives way all-too-quickly to numb, hopeless acceptance.

"Let's just get to a hotel," Thomas says grimly. "We'll have a few hours of downtime at least, we should probably make the most of it. Maybe even get some beach time so we don't forget what the sun looks like."

For a second I think he's kidding, but there's no accompanying grin—and he really doesn't seem to be in a joking mood. I guess I'd be a little disturbed if he was. And I can't remember the last time I was in the sunlight for more than a brief walk between a parking lot and an airport, or a hotel and car. But surely, given our present circumstances, he can't be serious—a walk on the beach would be the height of frivolity.

Then I realize what Thomas is really telling me: we don't have anywhere to go. We finally moved too fast for Dr. Martin's logistical genius.

So I walk silently beside Benson, holding his hand, aimless and frustrated—when a jewelry advertisement stops me in my tracks. Benson doesn't notice until his fingers slide out of mine and he turns with a flash of panic in his eyes. "What?"

My fingers rise to my throat, even though there's nothing there. "It's my necklace," I whisper. There, in a framed poster on the wall of the terminal, is a lovely antique silver necklace with curving tendrils embracing a large, sparkling ruby. Below it, elegantly scripted, is a phone number and an invitation.

For inquiries or to schedule a showing, contact Audra Taylor.

I barely manage to keep my wits about me enough to reach my hand into my purse, hiding my creation of a notebook and pen. The necklace, coupled with Audra's name is too big a coincidence.

He's alive. Logan is *alive.*

He must be. I lost the necklace in that first transformation at the airport in Phoenix. We all lost everything. Logan is the only person who could have recreated it in such perfect detail.

"Come on," I say, shoving the notebook into my bag. "We have to catch up with Thomas."

"That means what I think it means, doesn't it?" Benson whispers.

"Maybe. Probably. Or it's a trap." But no. It could only be a trap if they had Logan's cooperation. And the one thing I know about Logan is that he would never, ever betray me.

Not even after you left him behind? a tiny voice taunts.

"Don't tell Thomas," I whisper to Benson when we spot him, turned around and regarding us with mild impatience, a cell phone pressed to his right ear. I have enough doubts of my own without Thomas encouraging them, and whatever I decide to do with the phone number, I don't want it to be because Thomas is still cross about being separated from Alanna.

We get directions to a touristy part of Brisbane from the rental car attendant and leave the airport in stony silence. Alone and on the road, Thomas hits the speakerphone button and Alanna's voice fills the cab. Tears prickle at the corners of my eyes at the familiar sound. When Kat chimes in a few seconds later I start to smile. The world is in a hell of a state right now, and I'm an emotional wreck besides, but the sound of friendly voices helps to ground me a bit.

All the way from the airport I catch snatches of ocean on my right but it's not until we actually pull up to the hotel on Sunshine Coast that it feels real. I can't remember the last time I was at the ocean. And never at an ocean like this.

"Are you sure we're safe here?" Benson whispers to his father after the call ends.

"Safe as anywhere. A tidal wave from Madagascar isn't going to reach the east end of Australia. Not unless the whole continent goes under," he adds in a hollow voice. He stares through the windshield for a moment then seems to recollect himself. "I actually do need some sleep, but you guys go…be regular teenagers for a couple of hours, okay?" He gestures at the two of us vaguely and says, "Transform your clothes into, um, whatever. And sunscreen. We do *not* need you to burn and your skin has been quite under-exposed lately."

"Yes, Father," Benson says with a snort, but I recognize the wisdom in it. Hard to sleep with a bad burn. And sleep is the second-most important thing in my pathetic life right now.

"And keep these faces," he adds. "I'll leave your keys with the concierge, so you'll need your IDs."

"Easy," I say with a nod.

"I'll try to get you some new phones. In the meantime, I'll call your room if Dr. Martin finds us a drop."

I nod, then glance at Benson. I'm tempted to make him some kind of pink floral swim trunks, but somehow now doesn't seem the time for levity. I replace his cargoes with plain black board shorts instead, and an emerald green tankini and sarong morph into place on me. As he climbs out of his side of the vehicle Thomas creates some fake bags to lug in. I turn my face to the tangy breeze rolling in off the ocean and give myself permission to simply not think about death for a couple of hours.

"I admit, as nice as this is, I like it better in the hotel room when you look like yourself," Benson says as we walk along the sand, hands clasped, the waves lapping at our ankles. Despite being mid-summer in the states, it's winter here. Temperate enough—upper sixties, I'm guessing—and while a swim would be bracing at best, I enjoy the feel of the sand and surf on my toes.

"Better? I don't know—this is pretty amazing." I give a wave that encompasses the sapphire blue ocean and sparkling white sand, the line of greenery that somehow extends almost all the way to the shoreline, and the calm beachgoers. The last several weeks have been so isolated that seeing people enjoying themselves—not the hustle and bustle of busy travelers at the airport—is almost as refreshing as the breathtaking scenery. "But yes, I do wish I could look up and see the real Benson."

Benson draws me close to his chest and leans down to kiss

the tip of my nose.

"Your eyes are the same."

His bark of laughter surprises me. "What are you talking about? My eyes are *brown* at the moment."

"But I can still see you looking out through them."

"That's because no matter what kind of shell you put me into, the person inside loves you more than anything else in the entire world. No disguise can hide that."

"I love you too," I whisper. "And I'm so glad you're with me, even if it has been awful for you."

"Being with you could never be awful."

"Oh please," I argue. "It's been pretty bad."

He shrugs, almost casually. "Nothing could be worse than being away from you. And those aren't just pretty words. I lived them, Tave. Those weeks when we weren't together, and I was sure you hated me, it—" He takes a shuddering breath and his eyes cloud over. "Life without you is no life at all."

Then he leans down and wraps his arms around my thighs, picking me up as I shriek. He spins around and, though I get dizzy, his arms hold me firm and I'm not afraid.

"So give me international flights every other day, and bad airplane food, and running from tidal waves, and people shooting me." He lowers me again slowly, until our faces are level. "As long as I can stay with you."

I kiss him hard before he puts me down and we run in and

out of the chilly waves for a while. When my feet grow sufficiently numb we find a food stand and fill our bellies with warm Thai curry and rice, a bowl of freshly peeled lychee, and for dessert, eight flavors of gelato, because I couldn't decide on just one. "I've got to taste them all so I can make this stuff later," I say, spooning up bites and trying to memorize each flavor.

As the sun touches the horizon we head back up to the hotel. Back to real life. Back to midnight vaccine drops and unfamiliar beds and red-eye flights. Back to saving the world.

Logan's cryptic message—it *must* be from Logan—is the elephant lurking in our peripheral, but for a few more stolen minutes we don't discuss it. When we reach the courtyard of the high-rise hotel the immaculate building seems as imposing as a fortress. Sensing my hesitation, Benson pulls me down on a lounge chair and takes the sarong from my hands to wrap it around both of us, shielding us from the cool evening breeze. "Ten more minutes," he whispers in my ear. "Let's watch the sunset."

The sunset is beautiful, blazing the sky with the oranges and purples of radiant embers. But as the sun sinks over the western horizon, like sand through an inverted hourglass, it seems to set the city of Brisbane itself aflame, and I find myself increasingly disturbed by the illusion.

CHAPTER FOURTEEN

It takes two days to work up the courage to tell Thomas what I found at the Brisbane airport, and Benson doesn't push me. I think I would have, had our roles been reversed. I don't have his patience. I wonder if perhaps his best quality is simply that he's always been more willing to trust me than I have to trust him.

Not that I haven't had justifiable provocation to doubt in the past, of course. Still.

"Don't stop!" I whisper-hiss at Thomas as he totally pauses in front of the ad in the terminal. I try to yank on his arm subtly to pull him along and, luckily, he has the grace to only stagger for a step or two before melting back into the crowd with Benson and me. "If it is some kind of trap you *know* they're going to be watching for anyone giving it special attention."

"You're right," Thomas says ruefully. "I'm usually the one reminding *you* of this sort of thing." He glances over as we continue walking. "Actually, you've been remarkably clearheaded the last few days."

"I feel remarkably clearheaded," I confess. I haven't wanted to say anything about it, lest I have to confess that the change has coincided with getting some ... quality time with Benson. There are definitely some drawbacks to traveling with one's boyfriend's father.

Thomas purses his lips, looking rather stodgy with the salt-and pepper hair and prematurely lined skin of a Mayo security guard in Memphis—his face for today's travels.

"The question, of course," Benson says from behind the face of a cute, nerdy-looking doctor who vaguely resembles the real Benson, "is whether it's genuine, or a trap."

"Logan would never willingly betray me," I say, not looking at Benson. "But that doesn't mean he isn't being watched."

"Or manipulated, if that Audra person is with him," Thomas says darkly.

"Not her," I snap back so quickly I forget to lower my voice. A few heads pivot in our direction at my tone—drawn to the potential of public drama—but I give Thomas a playful grin and the eyes slide right by us, back to their own business. "I know you were only vaguely aware of her in the Curatoria Headquarters, but Audra's the one who gave me my first real proof that Daniel wasn't who he was pretending to be. I'd trust her almost readily as I trust Logan."

"Too many questions, not enough answers," Thomas says, scanning the departures board for our gate number.

"It's a risk I've got to take," I say, my voice cracking at the end. The whole point of keeping Thomas in the dark was to make up my mind in advance—to not let his doubts color my decision. But after I've spoken the words, I find it's Benson whose eyes I really want to avoid. Not because our relationship is in danger. Not because I've changed my mind. But the fact that Benson is the most important person in the world to me doesn't change the fact that Logan is number two. "I can't abandon him. Again," I add, guilt nearly buckling my knees.

A million times I've relived that moment in my mind: Thomas carrying me out of the Curatoria headquarters, the tiniest glimpse over his shoulder of Logan saving me by tackling Daniel, then all of it vanishing from sight as the door closed between us. Me leaving him, both because of and in spite of, my certainty that no one could escape such close proximity to Daniel.

Though I would never have admitted it out loud, I'd come to peace with the fact that Logan was gone. I wasn't even entirely sure that *gone* meant *dead*. Part of me hoped it did, because the other alternative was that he was a prisoner of the Reduciata—perhaps even infected with the virus to ensure that, even if I did thwart their plans in the present, my eternity would be spent in misery.

But now there's a tiny spark of hope and I know I can't turn my back on him again without knowing for sure.

"You have to consider everything you're risking," Thomas chides. "This isn't just your life anymore."

"Was it ever?"

Thomas has the grace to clear his throat and look away.

"I left him there, Thomas. If he's somehow under Reduciata influence, or even just being watched by them, it's my fault."

"Or possibly mine," Benson says. I look over at him and he flashes me a cocky grin that seems like it should feel all wrong, but somehow, it's exactly the tension-breaker I need.

I hide my smile while Benson continues. "Seriously though, we have the perfect opportunity here. We have a new untraceable phone and we're leaving the country in less than an hour. The damage from the South Africa wave was minimal, so there's almost nowhere in the world we couldn't be going…except South Africa itself, I guess. If we called, Tave would know instantly if it's Logan—right?" he says swinging his attention to me.

"Absolutely."

"So we make first contact, tell him we're leaving, that we'll call soon, and that he needs to be ready. Then, in the next couple days while we're in Brazil, we figure out a code or something to let him know where we can meet that only Logan would know. That way, if he's a hostage, he can just lead his captors to the wrong place and if he doesn't show, we get it."

"What if he's unknowingly being tailed?" Thomas demands.

"If they're following him and haven't killed him yet, it's because they want Tavia. As long as they aren't sure she's around, they're not going to do anything that might tip Logan off, or endanger him. So we tell him he's meeting me, and that I'll be taking him to Tavia—that way, the Reduciata won't have any reason to just set off a bomb or something the moment they think a meeting is happening. But really Tavia will be there to disguise Logan, and if there *are* Reduciate spies on him, we'll give them the slip."

Thomas and I both stare at him. Thomas breaks the awed silence first. "You watch too many spy movies."

"You're just mad because the plan I came up with in five minutes is going to work."

Thomas shakes his head and looks away from us. "You guys go find a quiet spot—not too far. As soon as they announce first class I'll text you. Make the call—two minutes absolute tops—then hurry back here and board the plane."

"Got it," I say, clutching the new phone in my hand.

As soon as we're out of earshot I turn to Benson. "You didn't really think of your plan in five minutes, did you?"

"Of course not. I've been trying to come up with something since we saw the ad two days ago." He flashes me a grin. "I wanted to look good." He puts an arm around me and says in a voice that's only half-joking, "I have to do *something* to convince him I'm pulling my weight. It's not as easy as you might think, being a mere mortal when your father and your girlfriend are both super-powered gods."

"I like your normal-powers," I say, lifting my face for a kiss.

"I know you do," he growls suggestively.

I tilt my head toward an empty gate where only a handful of travelers are lounging. My stomach is a twist of knots and butterflies and I wait to speak again until Benson is settled beside me. "You know this doesn't change anything, right?"

"I know," he says, but he doesn't meet my eyes.

"He's my partner," I say. "You're my love."

"You love him too. And that's not an argument," he says, cutting me off before I can deny it. "You picked me, and believe me, I thank God for it every day. A hundred times a day. But don't act like it wasn't a close call." His fingers twining through mine soften his words, but nothing can take the sting out of the fact that they're true.

"Okay," I say, trying not to sound hesitant and *so* not succeeding. "But I trust him. Saying I trust him with my life doesn't sound very convincing after the last few months, does it? But I would trust him with the lives of the people of the world, which is good because I guess that's what I'm doing. Ben, if there's one thing I could use in my life, it's more people I can trust that much. Because right now I have you, Thomas, Alanna, and you." I force a smile at my own lame joke.

"What about Dr. Martin?" He's never quite warmed to calling her Kat.

"I—I trust her as much as I can trust any clueless human, but—no Benson, don't," I say, seeing the expression on his face. "*You* are not a clueless human. Honestly, even though they were Reduciates, the fact that you grew up with Earthbound is one of the reasons I *do* feel like I can trust you. You understand in a way that almost no one else on Earth can. Kat is incredible—don't get me wrong. But we've kept her very much in the dark whenever possible. It's not that she's human, it's that she doesn't really *know*. You do."

I can tell from the furrow between Benson's eyebrows that he's not entirely mollified—but at least he understands.

"But Logan, I...I can trust him absolutely. And, well, another point of view on this would be helpful. Always is when trying to solve a complex problem, isn't it?"

"I don't know," Benson says with a sheepish smile. "Ever heard that saying, 'Too many cooks spoil the broth?'"

I smile back and lean to the side to thump him with my shoulder.

"What about this Audra person?"

"I guess I haven't really told you much about her. She..." It's a little hard to even talk to Benson about her because the story of how we met is so entwined with the time I was with Logan. Really *with* Logan. And while I wasn't with Benson at the time—*quite* the opposite—talking about it still makes me feel vaguely unfaithful. Which turns itself completely inside out and makes me feel like I'm betraying Logan.

I'm saved from my hesitation by a little chime from my phone—the text from Thomas. "Showtime," I say, my throat drying up.

"You know the number?" Benson says, digging into his pocket for the piece of paper I gave to him for safekeeping. There's no need.

"Memorized," I whisper. I take a deep breath and punch in the numbers. My finger hesitates over the Call button.

"Here goes nothing," Benson's voice says, close to my ear, his breath warming my skin.

I siphon some of his bravery and hit Call.

The phone rings once, twice, three times. "Hello?"

"Logan!" The name is out of my mouth before my brain could possibly have any hope of stopping it.

"Tavia? By the gods, I hoped…we hoped…but I don't think I ever actually believed. Where are you?"

The word *we* freezes my spine the instant I hear it. There's no way…He *can't* be with the Curatoriates still. The stab of ice helps my mind clarify and when I speak again, my voice is cool. "It doesn't actually matter because in a few minutes we'll be gone."

I purposely throw my own *we* in there, but Logan doesn't

seem to notice. I hear his voice muffled as he not-quite-yells, "Audra! Audra!"

Some of the ice melts. Is *we* just Audra? But maybe *we* means more Earthbound. Has he gathered allies? Is he being used—or held hostage? Hope and despair war in my chest and neither truly wins, leaving me feeling empty and blank. The idea of having more people to help—more *Earthbound* to help—is so tempting.

But the risks...

I could accept Audra. Anyone else and I'd have to cut off communication with Logan, pretend I'd never heard from him. Break both our hearts all over again. The thought makes a sour taste rise in my throat.

"Tavia, I can't believe that ad worked. It was Audra's idea and I was like, 'No way,' and she was sure it would—"

"Logan!" I snap, cutting off his raptures. "Who are you with?"

"With?"

"You mentioned Audra; is there anyone else?"

"Anyone...? No. No, we had Christina—the other doctor—at first, but she died two weeks ago. There was nothing we could do. Audra kept trying but, you know, her powers aren't permanent yet."

"Tave," Benson murmurs in my ear. "That's two minutes."

"Logan, are you certain, absolutely certain, that the...that *they* don't know where you are?"

"Please, if they did we'd all be dead." He says it with a tone of confidence I've been hearing for *thousands* of years, but behind it I sense something else: A yawning chasm of failure that his bravado can't cover. One thing I know for certain, whether he's being watched unawares or not, Logan feels utterly and completely *alone*.

"I have to go," I say.

"Tavia, no—"

"My plane is leaving. I'll call you again. Soon. Be ready."

"When? When? Tavia please don't—" I hang up without saying goodbye.

It hurts like sawing off a limb.

CHAPTER FIFTEEN

"Are you crazy?" Thomas asks as we sit in a sunlit hotel room in Rio de Janeiro.

"That's what makes it perfect—because that's what they'd think. That I'd be crazy to go back to Phoenix," I argue.

"And for once they'd be right," Thomas shoots back. "I listened to you last time—when you told us to go to Phoenix after the collapse of the Curatoria headquarters. We made it work, but let's count how many times they've attacked you there. *Killed* people there." He ticks off on his fingers. "Logan's family, the entire Mayo Clinic, our driver at the airport, and very nearly *us*. If experience has shown us anything at all, it's that the Reduciata have an extremely effective surveillance network in Phoenix!"

Thomas isn't shouting, exactly, but the emphasis behind his words speaks so loudly he may as well be.

"I think we can get away with it one more time," I say calmly.

"Maybe. But *I* think it would be safer to do it somewhere else. You want somewhere busy? Hard to track? Go to Paris."

"An unfamiliar place where we'll already stand out as tourists? I actually don't think that would be safer at all."

"Then go somewhere no one typically goes. I don't know—Nepal."

"Oh, yes," I say silkily. "We wouldn't stand out like sore thumbs there at all. Think about it, Thomas. Logan knows Phoenix; he'll blend in. I know it well enough, and seriously, it's the last thing they'd expect. Plus," I say, leaning back against the pillows stacked against my headboard, "I have the perfect clue for him to know where to go."

"Oh?"

"Before he got his memories back—I think even before the Reduciata found me there, we had one date. Crowded Mexican restaurant, half an hour north of the airport."

"And then what?"

I grin. "And then I change him into someone the Reduciata will never find, obviously."

"Plus," Benson says, backing me up, "I know we aren't supposed to plan locations ahead of time, but if we call on our way out of Brazil tomorrow and give them three days, we can spend an extra day in Mexico stocking vaccine. Any agents the Reduciata has in border states will have their attention drawn south. It's not totally ideal, but unless you can think of a discreet way to tell Logan to meet us in North Dakota ..."

"No," Thomas says as Benson trails off, but he doesn't

sound convinced.

"I admit, I'm not really asking permission," I say, trying not to sound threatening. "Besides, with five of us on the traveling team, maybe…maybe one of us could take an occasional break. Go see his wife." I look up at Thomas from under lowered lids. I always intended to make the offer once I felt things were running smoothly, but doing so before we actually have Logan and Audra in hand may be the best or worst move I could make at this moment.

Thomas' face drains of all color and I don't think he realizes how hard he's clutching a decorative pillow with whitened fingers.

"Audra's a doctor too, but her creations aren't permanent. And I know Logan is at a low point, power-wise, but I'm thinking that maybe Logan plus Audra just might add up to one of you." I say it with a smile—I'm not trying to get rid of him, and I certainly don't want to alienate him. I just need him focused on the advantages instead of the risks.

"Maybe," Thomas says, just over a whisper.

"Come on, Thomas. Everyone needs a break." I say cheerily, trying for that tension-breaking humor that Benson is so good at.

But I apparently am not, because Thomas simply glares.

Benson snorts. "A break from *us*."

There it is. Thomas looks over at Benson and, after a few

seconds, he releases his hold on the pillow and throws it at Benson's head.

***

I gave Logan three days. I'm not sure where he *was*, but surely that's enough time to get here, to this bustling suburban restaurant. The clue had been vague, but hopefully not too vague—"In three days, at the place and time where we had our first date. Benson will find you and bring you to me." If he's a prisoner, he'll lead his captors somewhere else to protect me. If he's working with them, well, if he's working with them, then I'm already in trouble.

I'm not in the lobby yet—I arrived about an hour early to watch the doors from my car, nicely air-conditioned against the blistering summer weather and darkly tinted to conceal my presence. Thomas wanted to come with me—almost as much as Benson wanted to come with me. I didn't give either of them a choice.

But now that I'm here, I wish I had someone's hand to hold.

I spot Logan just as he's pulling open the door to the restaurant. He's done a passable job disguising himself, considering he and Audra have only one power between them—his hair is long, like it used to be when he was Quinn, but it falls around his face in a shaggy cut instead of being pulled back at his nape with a ribbon. It's also brown, instead of that lovely, distinctive tawny color that he's carried through so many lives. If I hadn't known his face as well as I know my own—if I couldn't identify him by the angles of his shoulders or the cadence of his walk as surely as I could by the sound of his voice—I might not have recognized him from this distance. He's even added some kind of padding around his stomach, thighs, and upper arms, and he must be wearing some kind of shoe with a hidden heel, because he's a touch too tall.

But I know him at a glance.

The urge to rush to him, to embrace him immediately, is nearly overpowering. After he enters the restaurant, I force myself to count to thirty before climbing out of my car and taking slow, measured steps toward the heavy wooden doors that stand between us.

Logan's waiting in the lobby, idly scanning photos of local school groups sponsored by the restaurant's owners. The hostess hands a pair of menus to a young couple as I walk in. "I'll be right with you," she says, shooting me a hospitable smile.

"Go into the men's room," I whisper to Logan in a low voice.

I practiced it on Benson until he groaned and declared that it was creeping him out. Which was my sign that it was working. Because although I *look* like a guy, I'm still myself on the inside. And vocal chords are on the inside. Logan's eyes slide over to me very briefly, but other than that, he gives no sign that he's heard me at all. I wonder fleetingly if I need to say it again.

"Why should I?" he finally mutters, hiding his mouth with his hand as he puts a piece of gum in.

"Because it's the only way you're going to see Tavia."

His eyes widen and he starts to turn his face in my direction.

"Don't," I say quickly. "Follow me, but don't act like it." I turn toward the darkened hallway marked *Restrooms*.

I push the men's room door open and breathe a sigh of relief not to find a bunch of guys peeing at the urinals. That's an element of TMI I really don't need in my life right now. Actually, the restroom is empty for the moment, but I know that can't last long—not in a busy restaurant.

Logan walks in a few seconds later and I cock my head, gesturing for him to join me in the handicapped stall. I hurry and step up onto the toilet, crouching there so my feet can't be seen.

"Do you have anything on you that's irreplaceable?" I ask in a whisper. "Because in thirty seconds it'll be gone forever."

"Yes!" Logan blurts out. "In my backpack."

I glance at the pack on his shoulder. I don't like the idea of leaving something so large unaltered, but the most important thing right now is that we get out of here. "Put it down. If you want your wallet, add it. Everything else on you is about to go away."

He looks at me warily and reaches into his back pocket to extract his wallet, tossing it atop his backpack. I stare at him and then come up with an appearance entirely from my imagination. Seeing as how we're in the southwest, I picture sleek, short black hair and brown skin. His features take on a Latino cast and his eyes grow dark—nearly black.

Black, and swimming with shock and fear as Logan feels the change overtake him. "What did you do to me?" he hisses, his fear manifesting as anger.

"Something like this," I say, giving myself a similar look. If anyone noted me walking into the restaurant, I don't want them to catch me walking out two minutes later. "Get your bag and follow me." I hop down from the toilet seat and hustle out before anyone can walk in and find two people having shared a stall. That would be memorable.

Logan fumbles with his wallet, trying to shove it into unfamiliar pants, then follows. The two of us step out into the sunlight and I remember with chagrin the last time I fled from this restaurant with Logan behind me. It was after I made a fool of myself trying to restore his memories. Tried, and failed.

What a different world we live in now.

We walk silently for long minutes, me slowly remembering the area I spent about a week in a few months ago. If I recall...yes, there's a park down this street where two young men sitting on a bench won't attract undue attention.

I approach the bench and plop down onto it, looking meaningfully at the space beside me.

"Sit," I say when Logan doesn't take the hint.

"I don't think I will," he replies softly.

"Don't be an idiot. You standing and glaring down at me is only going to draw unwanted attention. Sit."

"You tell me who you are first. Not to mention what you've done to me."

My jaw drops, but I collect myself quickly. Of course he didn't realize who I am. He hasn't been traveling with me; he doesn't know I can do this. And even Benson was totally taken aback when I gave myself the outward appearance of a guy. I guess we'd never discussed it before—it just didn't seem worth it to jumble up our genders and take the chance that we'd start walking into the wrong bathrooms or some other seemingly trivial mistake that could get us caught.

But Logan hasn't seen me do anything but lengthen my hair. Technically, superficial things like that are all any Earthbound can do for disguise. Create, or destroy. Destroying someone's skin, even for the instant it would take another Earthbound to create new skin for them, could have a host of unpleasant consequences. My ability to do both things at once—to, in essence, Transform—is what sets me apart.

"Logan, it's me," I say, reverting to my normal voice.

All that does is make him scrunch down his eyebrows and glare.

"You were supposed to meet Benson, but we couldn't risk you being followed. I had to come and change your appearance."

He still doesn't look quite convinced, but I don't think it's so much that he doesn't believe it could be me, but that the enormity of my ability is stretching his credulity.

"Perks of being a Transformist." I look up at him and, to help him out, I let my eyes turn back into their normal shape and color.

That does it.

Logan collapses onto the bench beside me, a sappy grin covering his face. "Gods, Tavia! It really is." He reaches out to grab my arm, his fingers sliding down to my hand, like he can't believe I'm truly flesh. His fingers find my face and I clear my throat.

"We're in public," I say awkwardly.

"No one's around," he says, and his hands are cradling my cheeks now, staring into my eyes; the one part of me that looks like the person he's always knows. For thousands and thousands of years.

I can't help but smile back and tears start to build up in my eyes as an emotional dam, the one holding back my relief and exhilaration at finding Logan alive, bursts. "I wanted so badly to believe it was you on the phone," I confess. "But I don't think I completely did until I saw you. Your disguise was terrible, by the way."

"Well, I can't do this," he says, an eloquent hand movement taking in my entire body. "*This* is amazing. I mean, seriously. Damn, I want to kiss you so badly, to hell with you being a guy."

I clear my throat and look away and in that moment something shatters between us and a curtain of awkwardness descends. Somehow, without having said a word, I know he *knows*. He swallows hard and his hand drops from my arm and he leans forward with his elbows on his knees.

This is neither the time nor place and I thrash about for something—anything!—to change the subject. "What's so irreplaceable in the backpack?"

To my horror, Logan sniffs and turns his face away, subtly rubbing his sleeve against his cheek, camouflaged as digging into his pack. He removes a large Ziploc bag with a few bulking shapes inside that seem to be cushioned in bubble wrap. "It was the last thing you asked me to do."

Guilt is a razor slicing my chest from the inside out as I take the bag from him. I don't know exactly what's inside, but

I remember the last task I sent him to accomplish.

"My artifacts from the headquarters," I whisper. "Greta Heindlund and Elysa Meyer." The names Alanna gave me as a token of good faith when she revealed to us who she really was at the Curatoria headquarters.

"And another one," he says. His voice catches and I pretend not to notice as he takes the bag back and opens it, pulling out a golden circlet.

I gasp. I saw its silver twin a few weeks ago, in a dream—a dream of Logan as Lord Jovan Williams and I his Ladylove. A dream where I sat watching my handsome husband, next to my dearest friend, the two of us wearing matching circlets on our foreheads.

CHAPTER SIXTEEN

"Logan," I say hesitantly, "you have to know that I trust you completely. That I absolutely believe that if you are being watched by the Reduciata, then it's without your knowledge—"

"We've been *so* careful," he says, cutting me off. "We've been on the road, actually, traveling as much as possible. Cash for hotels, nothing we need ID for—you'll love this," he says, laughing and laying an arm across the bench behind me. "I bought a car for cash in Delaware when we got beyond sick of riding the bus. I pulled out ten grand and I thought the guy was going to faint. It was epic."

"Not the point, Logan. Although, good!" I add belatedly when his face falls. "I mean, a good plan with the resources you had." I groan. "I'm butchering this and I've only got fifteen minutes left before I have to rendezvous."

"What do you mean? I thought…We're going to be together now, right?"

I don't know exactly what he means by *together*. "I travel with Benson." I finally just blurt out. "And Thomas."

Logan's face is a blank slate, but I know what it means.

That he's trying as hard as he can to cover his emotions. And I have a pretty good idea what those emotions are.

"And they're worried," I rush on. "Honestly, they're mostly worried about Audra, seeing as how they don't know her."

"Are you?"

"No." I say it so quickly there's no way he can doubt my sincerity. "But they want proof you're not being followed."

"How am I supposed to prove that something *isn't* happening?"

"Part of it is me transforming everything you have on you—so let's start with your backpack. What's in it that's irreplaceable other than this?" I ask, holding up the bag. "I'm making a judgment call on this one and saying it's acceptable."

Logan grumbles something I don't hear and leans over to unzip his pack. "Hotel keycard," he says, handing it to me.

"You can get another one." I make it disappear.

Logan looks at me skeptically, then shrugs. "Phone. Disposable. It's the only number Audra has for me."

"We'll get you a new one." Gone.

Logan's eyes widen, but he looks back down at his backpack and says. "I guess nothing else in here is irreplaceable. But—"

"Done," I say, making his entire pack disappear. "Things just got easier. Your wallet? Anything you can't create again?"

He shakes his head silently and I see his jaw muscles

clenched hard. I hate that I'm treating him like a criminal, but the sooner he gets used to it, the better. It's what Benson, Thomas, and I do every single day. Leave absolutely *no* trace.

"If it makes you feel better, I lost my necklace with my first persona change," I say quietly.

"The one I made you?" he asks, and even though it's just a *thing*, I can see that he misses it as much as I do. "The one we used for the ad?"

I nod.

"I'll make you another one."

"I'd like that."

He glances at me, and though I suspect he intended it to be just a glance, he gets stuck. Now he's staring. He doesn't take in any part of me except my eyes—and his are sad, but perhaps angry, too. It occurs to me that as far as he's concerned, the Reduciata has taken my love away from him again. They just haven't killed me in the process. At least not yet.

I feel his loss, and ache that I created it.

"After the transformation in the bathroom, everything else should be brand-new," I whisper.

"Now what?" he asks, tearing his eyes away.

"Now we do the same for Audra and then we meet with Thomas and Benson, and we leave the country in two hours."

"Wow," he says, sitting straight. "You guys move fast."

"It's how we stay alive." I quirk an eyebrow. "It's worked

so far. Once we're in the air, we can talk a little more freely."

"You guys are *flying*? How are you even managing that?"

"You'll see."

"Where are we going?"

"I suggest you don't voice any interest in that fact whatsoever if you want to keep Thomas off your back. But the truth is," I add, looking him in the eye, "I don't know."

"Only Thomas?"

The snicker is genuine now. "Not even him."

"Then how—"

"Where's Audra?" I interrupt. "The sooner we get her and get out of here the sooner I can answer any of your questions."

"Hotel. Not far from here."

"Not far as in walk, or not far as in find a cab?" I'm kind of hoping for the cab option. July in Phoenix is not for the faint of heart and I'm sure I'm showing sweat marks. I stow the large plastic bag of artifacts in my backpack, wondering when I'll be able to justify the energy it'll take to get those memories back. I guess it depends on what I might learn from them.

"Walk."

I can't help but think it's amateurish to stay in a hotel within walking distance of a secret meet-up place, but I don't say anything. A week or two traveling with us and they'll learn the ropes. Hopefully, soon enough that Thomas will feel confident taking a break to visit Alanna. I've heard the strain in her voice the last few conversations we've had with her and Kat—I think they both need to be together for a few days.

"Let's go, then."

In his defense, the hotel is nearly a half-hour from the restaurant, we just happened to have halved the distance when we walked to the park. Still too close for my comfort. Logan peers around him as he climbs a rickety set of stairs to a room on the second floor of a seedy-looking motel. He knocks on the door and I hear movement behind it.

"Who is it?"

I almost tear up at the sound of Audra's voice—the one light of truth in the darkness that Daniel made of the Curatoria. Without her I still don't know if I'd have put all the pieces together in time to save anyone.

"Logan."

There's utter silence and in my mind's eye I can see her peering out the peephole—barely tall enough, as she really does have another year or two to grow. Then, unexpectedly, I hear a scuffle of movement, running feet, even—but the door doesn't open.

Logan seems to know what it means. "Aud, I look different! I know. I couldn't warn you because she took my phone. Not that *her*," he amends desperately. "It's Tavia. I've got Tavia with me."

"I haven't got time for this," I mutter. Nor can I afford the attention we're surely going to start attracting. I make the door disappear and shove Logan through before stepping in after him. I take one second to replace the door and add a *much* stronger bolt.

The room looks empty. Messy, but empty. I hear the unmistakable crash of shattering glass and glance toward what must be the bathroom doorway. Audra is already halfway out a window.

"For the love of—" I mutter. But the days of not thinking immediately of my powers are gone and in a second's thought Audra is bound with ropes and the sharp glass sticking out of the windowpane around her has turned into a soft wall of vinyl.

Even as she tumbles to the floor, the ropes fall away, steaming slightly from a multitude of severed ends—whatever chemical concoction she summoned to escape the ropes will vanish in five minutes, but of course plenty of objects need less than five minutes to work. I replace the ropes with chains; there are probably lots of ways to dissolve steel chains with creative powers too, but not quite so quickly.

"Audra, it's Tavia—"

My own arms are bound by thick chains and it takes me an instant to banish them; lacking my destroying capabilities, Logan finds himself bound hand and foot, and gagged with a clean white handkerchief, and no obvious way to escape.

"You told me about Daniel cutting the spy's throat from the inside—"

Logan throws himself against me, knocking me clear of an oversized anvil—like something straight out of a Bugs Bunny cartoon, and I wonder how much hotel television Audra's been watching. It drops through the space where I was just standing, grazing Logan's head instead of crushing mine. He clatters to the ground as I banish the anvil before it can put a hole in the floor, then erase Logan's chains. He doesn't move, and I stifle a cry of dismay.

"You wrote on a notebook and let me watch it disappear, so I would understand," I shout. But I'm getting the idea that, though my Transforming abilities are likely to freak her out; if I'm going to get through to her I'm going to have to use my own face. "You told me about my brain damage," I say, letting my disguise melt away and becoming myself again. "You had to tell me how little I would ever remember. You're one of the only people who ever saw my scar." On a whim, I change my hair into the tight French braids I was wearing the day I met her. "I changed Logan's when we met at the restaurant, but it's him. Look," I add, thrusting my hand into my backpack and pulling out the bag of artifacts. "He brought me this. You both brought me this. It's the only physical item I allowed him to keep."

Audra's chest is heaving but at least she's stopped attacking us.

"I took his phone and his room key, all in case the Reduciata was somehow keeping tabs on you."

"How...how are you doing that?" Audra's voice is small and scared and even though the soul inside her is millennia old, there's still a part of her physical reactions that are limited by her fifteen-year-old body, full of hormones and adrenaline.

"You knew Daniel wanted me—needed me—but I didn't tell you why. I'll tell you now if you'll chill out."

She clamps her mouth shut and I think that's as good as it's going to get.

"I can create and destroy simultaneously. Transform. It's especially useful for working on things like proteins that don't react well to incremental change. That's what Daniel needed in his lab."

"That's impossible."

"Clearly," I say.

She points at Logan, out cold on the floor. "Change him back."

I do. "Can you make sure he's not hurt too badly?" I ask.

"Hurt?" Audra says, staring in horror at what she's only just realizing she's done. She hurries over to him, her nimble fingers fairly flying over his neck and head as she checks him over. When he groans, a small flashlight appears in between her fingertips and she raises each of his eyelids and peers into them. When she's finished she tosses her light onto the floor where it clatters and rolls away, reminding me of the casual abandon with which I used to discard things, back when *my* creations weren't permanent.

When Audra finds a spot that's bleeding—something I couldn't see when Logan's hair was black, but is all-too-obvious now that he's back to his signature gold—she makes a mew of dismay and something else appears between her fingertips, something apparently made for cleaning cuts.

"It doesn't look too serious," she says with the clinical evenness to which I'm more accustomed from her. "But head wounds bleed like geysers and I need to get this one closed." She holds out her fingers, now grasping a needle bent in a half-circle and trailing a long strand of black thread. "Can you make one of these?" she asks, glaring hard at me. "My other instruments can disappear, but I need the thread to last."

"For stitches?"

"Obviously," she grumbles, and again, I'm struck by how much our immortal personalities are subject to the mannerisms of our present incarnations.

"How's that?" I ask, handing her a needle and thread that looks, to my eye, identical to the one in her hand. She takes it from me, pinches the wound shut and knits the skin back together with a few fast stitches.

"Can I move now?" Logan asks, and I find myself blinking

in surprise, wondering how long he's been conscious. And feeling the needle.

"I'm so sorry," Audra says, helping him roll over.

"Don't be," Logan insists, touching his head gingerly. "We've told each other over and over again how vigilant we have to be. That's all you were doing. I didn't even think how much our appearances would freak you out."

Audra lets out a long, noisy breath, insinuating that it should have been the most obvious thing in the world. "Be careful," she says as Logan sits up. "You might feel nauseous when you stand. And you'll need some Tylenol—you'll have a headache once the adrenaline wears off."

"Well," I say, pulling her attention away. "I think we can bypass any interrogation to prove your identity." My tone is dry, but the truth is, I'm glad to know so definitively that this girl is exactly who she says she is. "But we're incredibly short on time and if I don't call Benson in the next two minutes he might burst in and murder the both of you without asking questions."

Audra looks abashed, but she has no idea how close we all came to disaster.

I pull out my phone and call Benson. There were a million reasons—some rational, some not—why I couldn't bring him to my meeting with Logan. But that didn't mean he or Thomas was going to let me out of their sight. The final stage of

APRILYNNE PIKE

Benson's plan calls for him and Thomas to follow me back to the airport without revealing their presence. That way, if I get attacked en route, I'll have some surprise backup.

"We're good," I whisper. "I haven't stripped down Audra yet, but Logan's clean. See you there."

CHAPTER SEVENTEEN

Audra gives no indication whatsoever that losing her every worldly possession bothers her in the least. Nor does she mind being given a new face. Then, to break the tension as much as anything, I conjure up two syringes of the vaccine and turn to each of them. "First things first. Arms." I don't even have to explain—they understand immediately. I clean the skin on Logan's shoulder and uncap the syringe. "Every Earthbound we can get immune is a huge victory. And millions of lives no longer in jeopardy," I add, sticking a Band-Aid over the little red spot on Logan's arm, then turning to Audra. Once both of them are immunized I feel much better about pretty much everything in the world.

The drive back to the airport in Logan's car is uneventful—the motel is right on the freeway and traffic is light. I can practically feel Audra's questions being glared into the back of my head as we trudge through security, but it's not until the three of us are settled in the fancy lounge that they always let us use when we fly Business Class on international flights that I let her talk. Not that she wants to talk until we've all filled a plate from the buffet lunch they've laid out.

"How did you come up with this?" she whispers. "The identities with driver's licenses and everything? And a credit card? How the hell are you using a credit card?"

"Very carefully," I say around a mouthful of pizza, not really answering her questions. "Listen, I'm not going to get too specific until we're on the plane—"

"In *first class*!" she near-shrieks. "Seriously, I've only flown a handful of times in the last two—cycles…" she says, catching herself before she says *lives*. "And never, never first class."

"Well, business class, technically."

"Whatever. The good seats. With this awesome lounge. And free food. Seriously, to an Earthbound who can't make her own permanent food yet, this rocks."

I laugh, remembering how big a deal instant, permanent food was to me when I first resurged, oh, *weeks* ago, technically. It feels more like a lifetime—and I know something about how lifetimes feel. "Would you believe me if I say it actually is a necessity?" I ask, repeating the rationale regarding first class that Thomas rattled off to me before our original flight out of Phoenix.

"Although with five it's going to start getting significantly more difficult," Thomas says grumpily. I try not to startle too much at his sudden appearance behind me—the last thing I want from him is a lecture on vigilance—so I'm glad when he seems not to have noticed. He looks around at the quiet, sparsely occupied lounge where we'd agreed to meet up. "I'd rather be out there in the busy airport where we're less likely to be overheard. You can hear a pin drop in this place."

"Always the pessimist," Benson teases, but Thomas doesn't crack a smile.

"Here they are," I say, rising to make introductions. "Audra, Logan, this is Thomas and Benson. In their current guises."

"Thomas!" says Audra, smiling up at him.

He nods. "Good to see you again. Seriously, though, we've got to work out some kind of rotation, and soon. Even finding three open seats on a last-minute flight can be tough, depending." He glances between our two newcomers. "You're sure you got rid of *everything*?"

"Everything except this." I say, tilting the opening of my backpack toward Thomas and giving him a glimpse of the bag of artifacts. "And I'll get rid of them as soon as I can."

"Maybe don't make them go away completely," Thomas suggests. "You might need them in the future."

But I shake my head. "I can only use them once. One artifact gives me back one lifetime. It's better to get rid of them entirely after I've used them."

"I didn't mean in this life," Thomas says and there's an ice in his voice that I don't understand. "Don't let your current predicament let you forget that in seventy years—if you're lucky—you'll have an entirely new life to worry about."

My mouth snaps shut. Of course. I'm thinking small. Far too small for a completely restored Earthbound like Thomas.

Too *human*.

Stung by his completely justified criticism I sit down again, letting my shoulder brush Benson's, and I nod. "Good point," I say weakly, hating the reminder that—enhanced powers or not—I remain hobbled by my brain injury. I have a spark of an idea and I offer it up, almost in apology. "Maybe when you go back you can take it with you and give it to Alanna for safekeeping."

But even as I try to offer peace, he grimaces, and I realize my mistake. He hates that I've said her name in front of these two new recruits.

Audra catches on immediately. "Alanna? Seriously?" Her voice drips with disdain.

"She's not who she appeared to be at the headquarters," I hurry to assure Audra. "It was a disguise as surely as the one you're wearing now. She's actually really awesome."

Audra lifts an eyebrow skeptically and simply says, "If you say so," before turning to look out the window. I try to shoot Thomas an apologetic look, but he won't meet my eyes.

***

Despite being angry with me, Thomas runs interference once we board the plane, seating himself and Logan together—with Logan in a window seat, as far away from me as possible—and Benson and I across the aisle and one row up. This leaves Audra with her own pair of seats—the second of which ends up being filled by a thin, middle-aged man who unfolds his chair into a flat bed, raises the barrier between them, and falls asleep almost instantly.

"Can you imagine getting on a nine-hour first class flight and just going to sleep?" Audra hisses to me, leaning far out of her seat to see around the rounded plastic wall separating us.

Benson peers back at her. "Yes, yes I can, since that's exactly what Tavia needs to do now. Rule number one when traveling with us: Never, ever, bother Tave when she needs to sleep. Got it?"

"Be nice," I mumble. The rumble of plane engines has become an almost Pavlovian stimulus, and I'm already getting sleepy—which certainly mitigates the need for drugs. "She's new. She's young."

"I thought you said she has her memories back."

"She's still young."

Benson rolls his eyes, but glances back and smiles this time. "You should watch a movie. They're free. Food, too. Seriously, ask the flight attendants for anything you want, but you're going to have to leave Tavia and I alone completely." His voice drops to a whisper. "She's trying to rely less on the Valium."

Prescription medication. Now there's something Audra can understand. She nods and gives me a tight smile. I stretch tall in my seat to sneak a glance back at Logan and Thomas, their heads close together in consultation. By the time we land he'll know everything about how our operation works. I know how key that is, because I guarantee that after her insensitive remarks about Alanna, Thomas won't trust Audra to do his job. I guess when we land in London in nine hours I'll discover just how much he's decided to trust Logan.

I nestle into a warm cocoon of soft blankets and a few extra pillows I created while the flight attendant wasn't looking. The double sets of business class seats aren't really made for cuddling, but Benson and I have learned the best ways to make them function in our favor, and Benson makes sure to stay in some kind of physical contact with me the entire flight. The engines rumble quietly below us as the rest of the cabin boards and I settle in. Thanks to the business class lounge my stomach is full just shy of discomfort and I'm wearing earplugs. I close my eyes and let my breathing deepen.

Still, I spend half an hour past take-off slowing the thoughts racing through my head. I try to hide it—I don't really want to talk to Benson about it right now—but traveling with Logan, having him so physically near, is messing with my emotions more than I thought it would. It's one thing to say you've made your choice; it's a whole different thing to shut down the very large part of your brain that's still in love with someone else.

From that very first moment when I saw him in the restaurant, my body has been tingling with awareness, as though my very cells know that he's near. My body calls out for him in a way that reminds me that, despite my choice, I'm *supposed* to belong with Logan. That I was with him, body and soul, only a few months ago. That it has always, always been that way before.

A week. A brief week when we were truly together. It feels short even to me, but must seem like the blink of an eye to him. And the worst moment was when he first realized who I was on that park bench, and he didn't know. I'd been back with Benson for almost two months. And Logan had no idea.

I left him.

Left him in the Curatoria headquarters, where he not only completed the near-impossible task of finding my artifacts, but was actively attacking the murderous head of the Curatoria in order to allow me to escape. Even as he was doing that, *I left him*, in every possible sense of the word.

I stand by my decision—I love Benson more. But *more* is the key word. You can only love someone *more* when you still love someone else.

CHAPTER EIGHTEEN

"It's okay. I'm okay." I fling my arm out as Logan and Benson both step forward to help me back to my feet. "I'm okay," I repeat, trying not to move around too much and half-wanting to lie all the way down on the cold cement, to press my sweaty cheek to the cool surface.

The cool, *filthy* surface—so I resist. I should have known better than to create such a large batch of vaccine in one go, especially with Benson and Logan alert for any opportunity to out chivalry the other. But there are a lot of people in London, and even more traveling through it. Dr. Martin says that immunizing international travel hubs can really slow the spread of disease. While the Reduciata's bioterrorism complicates that tactic somewhat, I need to be sure London is well-stocked before we run again.

Audra gives an impressed whistle, surveying my work with eyebrows raised before turning to me. "You sure you're okay? You look a little...green."

"I'm not going to puke," I answer in at least a half-convincing tone, waving Benson and Logan back as I gulp for air, suppressing a wave of nausea. I don't need to give them any more excuses to try to outdo each other.

"Ginger ale," Benson says, holding a hand out to his father for him to create it. *Not Logan*, I note, though perhaps that's simply out of habit. Benson ignores my half-hearted protestations and places a hand at my elbow, pressing the open can of my post-creating drink of choice into my fingers. The chill of the soda is refreshing enough to restore some semblance of rational thought to my brain. The hell am I doing, trying to stave off boy-drama when I can barely stand?

I gulp the ginger ale, the burn in my throat pushing back the weariness that threatens to render me unconscious. Within seconds I feel the sugar begin to radiate through my bloodstream. It's a feeling that used to be subtle, but I've become hyper-attuned. I feel for it as a sort of marker— because that's when I can resume the usually-trivial task of making my own food. One more long swallow and I replace the empty can with a tart raspberry smoothie. The first half hour or so after creating a batch of serum is simply about trying not to lose my stomach. Or, sometimes, trying not to lose my stomach more than once. Tart is soothing.

Belatedly, I realize it's been nearly a week since I threw up. Despite what Thomas says about our powers being finite and not something that can expand in strength or stamina, I seem to be getting better at this.

I lean my head against Benson's shoulder, my forehead still damp, and just lose myself for a few minutes, letting him bear up my weight.

"Let's get out of here," Thomas says, and I feel his strong but gentle fingers on my arm, prodding us toward the double-door entrance of the huge warehouse. "You did great, Tavia."

"Thanks," I mumble automatically.

We never stay long at the warehouses, and not only because I have to go back and sleep and eat in preparation for round two. The people Dr. Martin has contracted to retrieve the vaccine will be arriving any moment. Benson leads me to the roomy sedan we rented at the airport and we follow a routine that has become automatic. The two of us curl into the back seat and I create a warm blanket. Then Benson holds me, arms wrapped tight, until I stop shaking.

Today I'm acutely aware of Logan's eyes on me—

I don't have the energy for this.

Turning away from him, I bury my face in Benson's chest, focusing on the heat seeping from his body, warming me when my own system can't quite do it. In a few minutes I'll make something else to eat, but for the first little while, I just need to *stop*.

"Sit up here," I hear Thomas say softly to Logan. "Help me navigate."

God bless Thomas. It's funny how much he's changed

since the three of us started traveling together. In so many ways, he acts more like my father than Benson's. The two of them have at least moved past their unspoken cease-fire; their animosity seems to be thawing like spring snow.

But that's not the same thing as resuming a father-son relationship. With me, it's different. Thomas is protective in a way that, somehow, doesn't make me feel like an object being guarded. Sometimes I even catch him saying or doing things that remind me of my own father. Today, he's running interference between Logan and Benson. Logan and me? I'm not even sure. But Thomas saw the potential for emotional distress that I didn't even consider when making the decision to bring Logan and Audra in with us. I wonder if I would have seen it too, if I could remember my past lives the way he does.

Regardless, he's prodding a reluctant Logan toward the front seat and nudging Audra in beside Benson and me. I don't really mean to peer out at Logan right then, but I shift in Benson's arms and his face appears in a crack between Benson's shoulder and the blanket.

He looks like I've stabbed him in the heart.

***

Everything is dark as I untangle myself from sleep's cottony embrace, but in the world of blackout curtains that doesn't actually tell me anything about the time of day. Or night. The rhythm of Benson's breathing against my cheek—slow, but not too slow—tells me he's relaxed but awake. Watching TV, in fact—muted and captioned. How bored he must be all the time; I marvel at the lengths to which he'll go to give me the simple security of having him with me. He's assured me that he doesn't mind, but I'm still grateful.

I push my arm under his back and around his waist, wanting him closer still. My lips find the soft patch of skin where his neck slopes into his shoulder, and my fingertips trace his collarbone.

"Hey," he says, his voice gravelly with disuse. His arms tighten around me, curving his body into mine and nesting us a little deeper under the blankets. "Sleep well?"

"I think so. How long has it been?"

He checks his watch. "Eleven hours."

"Damn."

"No, it's good. You can have up to twelve without disrupting our schedule. You know that."

"Yeah, but any time I sleep more than eight or nine hours I feel like a lazy slug."

His laughter rolls through his chest, rumbling against my ear. I smile at the sensation. "Think of what you're doing, Tave. You could sleep for fourteen hours and still not be lazy." The tip of his nose lowers to touch my cheek. "Of course,

Thomas would be grumpy about his *schedule*," he says, using the British pronunciation.

I laugh at that. Of course, someone has to be the organized authority figure, and heaven knows I've got plenty of other things to do. But Thomas does take his role very seriously.

"Speaking of Thomas," Benson says with a note of disappointment, "he texted me two hours ago. He wants us to have a short meeting as soon as you're—" Benson makes air-quotes with his fingers. "—'available.'"

"He doesn't know I'm awake yet," I murmur, finding the ticklish spot on his ribs with my lips and making him jump.

"It was two hours ago," Benson says, but there's a distinct breathlessness in his words as I explore his bare skin.

"Mmmph," I say, leaning my forehead against his sternum. "This is my punishment, isn't it? For sleeping in."

"Come on," he says, pulling a shirt on and sliding out of the bed. "Let's get this over with and maybe we'll have a bit of time afterward." He strides over to the curtains and pushes them back, letting in a few scattered rays of early dawn. "Need some breakfast?"

"Mmmm, eggs," I say, "Think Thomas'll make me some?"

We both snort with laughter, but after only a few minutes of putting ourselves together, we pad across the hallway in socks to Thomas' door and knock quietly. We're all so used to seeing each other in pajamas that we haven't bothered to stand on ceremony in weeks.

But when Thomas opens his door, I see Logan sitting on the bed.

"Oh," I say before I can stop myself. Then I clamp my mouth shut, lower my gaze, and refuse to make another sound.

"Come in, come in," Thomas says, and I reach up to smooth my hair as I edge past him.

As soon as I'm out of the way I hear a murmur of voices and a scuffle; by the time I turn back around, the door is clacking shut, separating us—Benson and Thomas on one side of the door, Logan and me on the other. Benson's muffled protests sound through the heavy wood, but even though I can't make out Thomas' actual words, I know essentially what his response must be—that this is necessary.

He's probably right, but I can't imagine a more effective way to re-open every old wound Benson has ever suffered, endangering the camaraderie Benson has managed to develop with his father. And it doesn't help that the air between Logan and me is so thick it's essentially gelatin. I stare at his feet, the bed—no, *not* the bed—the wall, the doorway to the bathroom, the clutter of Thomas' temporary belongings on the nightstand.

Logan stands, and the formality of the gesture only makes things worse. "Hey," he says. "Sorry for the...ambush. Thomas was pretty insistent. I've apparently missed a few things while we've been separated, and I can't…I…I need to know where I stand."

"You knew about Benson," I say belligerently.

"I did, yes, but I seem to remember you telling me he was your ex."

"Logan," I say testily, "we weren't exactly on great terms when I last saw you. We weren't even sleeping in the same room."

"If I recall correctly, and I very much think I do," Logan says softly, "the last night we spent in the Curatoria headquarters we spent together."

My cheeks flush, remembering the way I'd run to Logan— *escaped* to Logan—after that awful day in the lab: after that moment when I realized I was still in love with Benson, and then turned my back on him.

I'm so ashamed of myself for what I did to Logan that night. And he doesn't know. He thinks it was a sign I had forgiven him. The things I did…that *we* did…it should have meant something. How can I tell him that even that night—the last time we were together—was little more than an attempt to push Benson out of my head?

"It was a mistake," I mumble.

"It's never a mistake with us, Tavia," Logan protests, rushing forward. "It can't be. We're too right together. I mean, I don't blame you for needing someone while I wasn't here.

You probably thought I was dead. I thought *you* were dead, until I started seeing news about the vaccine. And what you're doing…it's obviously so difficult. But Tavia, I'm back. Doesn't that mean anything to you?"

"Of course it does!" The words come flying from my mouth.

"Then why…why are you still …" He puts his hands on his hips and looks down at the floor. "Tavia, we haven't been together in *lifetimes*. Obviously we have to deal with the crisis at hand, and he's a valuable ally, but…we finally found each other. He's going to have to face that fact."

I feel heat rising in my cheeks at Logan's casual dismissal of Benson—and his presumption in acting as if I have no choice in the matter. Logan isn't hurt because he thinks I've chosen Benson; Logan is *confused* because I'm treating someone else the way I'm supposed to treat *him*. It hasn't even entered his mind that—

My anger recedes as quickly as it arose, because that's just it—*it hasn't even entered his mind.* I'm *supposed* to choose him. I'm *supposed* to be with him. It's absolutely incomprehensible to him that I would choose someone else, for the simple reason that he would never choose anyone but me. And it's been that way for thousands and thousands of years.

I practically crumple onto the small sofa, lost for words. I've tried very hard not to think of it in such stark terms, but

Logan loves me more than I love him. He loves me more than Benson loves me. He loves me more than any human being on earth could ever love another person—with a love so strong it spans lifetimes.

That's the love I'm supposed to feel for him—

But I don't.

If my brain weren't broken—

But it is.

As I sit there, speechless, Logan watches the struggle play out on my face—or so I assume, because somehow he puts it all together without another word from me.

"You honestly think you're...choosing him?"

My eyes are swimming with tears.

He paces in front of me as I sit there feeling rather like a naughty child instead of the most powerful being walking the Earth.

At the moment all that seems very far away. Because for all my abilities, I can't fix Logan's heart, even though I'm the one who broke it—even though it's my heart, too, because he's an inextricable part of me, and he always will be.

Finally, Logan stills. "I wouldn't have come back if—no, that's a lie." He turns to me again, and rather than the sadness I was dreading, his eyes blaze with a fiery determination. "I'd have come back even if you told me you hated me and never wanted to see me again." He bends forward, his hands resting on either side of me, his face only a breath away from mine. "Because I can win you back. You can't fight what we have, Tavia. And I'll be here, ready, when you remember."

"I don't remember, Logan. I'm never going to remember!"

His expression doesn't alter in the slightest. "You'll remember." He strokes a finger down the side of my face, along my neck. "Remembering a lover is like remembering how to play the piano. It might come clumsily at first—" His fingers run past my shoulder, down to my waist, brushing along the side of my breast, making my breath come in short gasps. "—but if you lose yourself in the music, it'll all come rushing back." His hand travels to my back and before I can protest he pulls me forward, his mouth devouring mine with a ferocity I only recall from the night he finally surged.

He pulls away before I've managed to gather my wits—stands and walks out the door, closing it behind him. Leaving me so very alone.

CHAPTER NINETEEN

"China," I say. "It's the most populous country in the world and we've only been there once."

"Twice, technically," Benson offers.

"Yeah, but half the vaccine we left in Hong Kong was headed to Vietnam."

We're standing in Heathrow airport with new faces, staring up at the screens of departures and debating between the flight to China that leaves in an hour and a half, and the one to Egypt that doesn't leave for three hours.

"Yeah, but Egypt!" Audra says. "I lived there in the eighteenth century. It's *gorgeous*."

"Sure," Benson says, clinging to my hand a little more possessively than usual. "But we won't be sightseeing. So unless you think the *hotels* in Egypt are particularly nice ..."

I stop listening, letting the four of them decide amongst themselves where we're going to go next. To be honest, I don't care. Wherever we go, my job will be the same. I rub at the back of my neck, trying to stave off a headache. I didn't get very many hours to sleep after creating the last batch of

173

vaccines in here in London but I've become quite good at sleeping on planes, so I don't mind. Not too much, anyway.

It feels vaguely superstitious to think of Benson as my good luck charm, but spending meaningful time relaxing with him seems to genuinely improve my abilities. For over a week now I haven't thrown up, I haven't taken Valium to sleep on the plane, and I've been able to make slightly larger amounts of serum without depleting myself quite so thoroughly. I couldn't just ignore Logan's attempt to contact me, but now that I know he's safe, I'm questioning the wisdom of bringing him along.

And I have no one to blame but myself.

"China it is," Thomas says. "Let's go get tickets."

We purchase five ridiculously expensive tickets and make our way through security, then to the lounge where I eat without tasting my food. I need to finish the sleep I started a few hours ago—surely I'll feel less fog-headed once I'm not so tired. And less paranoid, too; I don't mind airports generally, but I don't like sitting around for hours in a place full of surveillance cameras and armed guards while engaged in supernatural identity theft. I find myself grateful to not be waiting on the flight to Egypt—less time to be paranoid, less time with Benson looming and Logan brooding. The sooner I can get to sleep, the sooner I can stop feeling guilty and stupid and helpless and afraid.

But as I settle into my seat, a distinct feeling of unease creeps over me.

In addition to needing more sleep than most people, one of the lasting scars of traumatic brain injury is forgetfulness. In my case, that forgetfulness seems to center mostly on my past lives. Still, when I'm stressed or distracted, the coping techniques I acquired from months of rehabilitation tend to fall to the wayside. Organization, planning, and multitasking are all challenging for me in ways that demand constant vigilance.

I have not been vigilant.

"My bag!"

Leaping to my feet, I bang my head against the overhead luggage compartment with a cry of pain. Then I'm crawling over Benson in a blind panic.

"What—" is all he manages before I'm edging past boarding coach passengers trying to stow their luggage.

"I left my bag in the lounge!" The bag with the artifacts from my past lives—the only irreplaceable possessions I have, and I left them sitting under the table where we ate.

"Make—uh—we can get you a new one—"

"I'll be right back!" I insist. Thomas and Logan are on their feet, concern lining their faces. "Just wait here," I say, pausing to apologize to a middle-aged woman as I slide past her in the narrow aisle. "I know right where it is." And the least I can do is fix my own stupid mistakes by myself.

But as I emerge onto the jet bridge leading back to the gate, I glance back and see Benson and Logan working their way through agitated passengers in line. A stewardess tries to say something to me but I brush past her with a mumbled apology. The lounge isn't far; if I'm fast, I should make it back to the gate before Thomas can decide to de-plane with Audra in tow.

The bag is right where I left it, artifacts and all. With a silent prayer of thanks to the gods of air travel that no one decided to report the unattended item to security, I head back toward the gate. Benson and Logan catch up to me as I'm leaving the lounge; the moment they see the bag, the concern lining their faces melts into understanding, then relief.

"Good catch," Logan says.

"I'm so sorry, I should have noticed," adds Benson.

Logan's praise and Benson's apology only make me feel worse. Of course they don't blame me; if I murdered a sack of kittens in front of them, they'd probably try to tell me the kittens deserved it.

No—that's not charitable. I'm tired and I'm letting silly things get the best of me.

Still…

I wasn't fast enough—Thomas and Audra emerge from the bridge as we arrive back at the boarding area.

"I didn't think we should risk getting separated," Thomas

says apologetically, "But now we've called a lot of attention to ourselves. It might—"

His words are cut off by the deafening crash of a dozen windows bursting into shards. Someone throws their body over mine, shielding me from the jagged rain; when the world finally stops shaking, I try to raise my head, but I'm so thoroughly covered I can scarcely move. Slowly, Benson and Logan climb off of me, then each extends a hand to help me to my feet. I take both.

Smoky wind blows into my face through the decimated windows where I see fierce orange flames and a plume of black smoke rising from a pile of scarred and twisted metal that was once a plane bound for Beijing.

The next sensation I'm aware of is someone shaking my shoulders—not enough to hurt, but I certainly wouldn't call it gentle. I'm turning, though not by choice, and then I'm looking up at Thomas, his face deadly serious just inches from mine. His lips are forming words but I can't hear them over the ringing in my ears.

And then, gradually, I can—at first as if from very far away, then with growing volume and urgency. "—need to leave. We need to get away from this gate and then we need new faces. Tavia, can you hear me? People are already looking at us, wondering why we got off the plane that just blew up."

My brain is having trouble keeping up, but I force

everything back and focus on Thomas' voice. I know we can have *minutes* at most before we're surrounded by authorities of some sort and taken into custody. They have our names, our descriptions, a million pictures of us on camera.

Cameras. "How are we going to do this with the surveillance?" I slur.

"Bathroom," Thomas says quietly. "Against the law to have cameras in there."

We're able to slip through the crowds of frantic people—most of them going the opposite direction, to help or to gawk, depending. It's difficult to force myself to walk when my body is screaming at me to run, but somehow I manage. Once I've given us all new faces in the family bathroom it's touch and go for a long hour as we try to get out of the airport without drawing undue attention. We all agree there's no sense lingering considering the infinitesimal chance of another flight getting off the tarmac any time today.

Everyone seems to be staring at us, though I'm sure that's mostly my imagination. Thomas was right—airport security was quick to identify the five passengers who got off the plane right before it blew up. Grainy images of our faces are up on all the announcement screens and our assumed names have been called by the loudspeaker more times than I care to count.

I pity the five actual Mayo Clinic employees working

somewhere in the United States who are about to spend the next several days—maybe weeks—being interrogated as to how their names, faces, and passports happened to be in another country, possibly blowing up a plane. I hope they all have excellent alibis.

With trains shut down we end up taking a crowded bus out of Heathrow, exiting at the first stop. We all wait outside the office while Thomas rents a car—luckily he's near the front of the line—and then we silently load up without the usual squabbles of where everyone's going to sit. I expect Thomas to head for the highway and figure out where exactly we're going at that point, but instead he weaves along nearly-deserted roads until he comes to a stop in front of a dusty fence.

"Where are we, Dad?" Benson asks. He must be afraid. He rarely reverts to calling Thomas *Dad* unless he's scared. I don't blame him.

"I saw this place on the way in," Thomas mutters, gesturing toward a construction site that appears, for the moment at least, to be empty of workers. "Come on, all of you. Tavia, we should probably drop these disguises once we're hidden from view."

I don't know what he has in mind, but I trust him enough to follow unquestioningly and everyone else does the same. I remove a padlock from a chain-link fence and we slip through the gate, and toward the half-built structure where we're mostly hidden from prying eyes by shade-screens and sound-walls.

The site itself consists mostly of scattered construction equipment and a building-sized hole in the ground, lined with concrete. At its edges, skeletal steel girders jut into the air; walls but no roof yet. After I give everyone back their faces, Thomas leads us toward an equipment shed, big enough for a few cars or perhaps a bulldozer, though far smaller than the warehouses we've been filling with vaccine. As we approach I start looking for a lock to destroy and notice that Thomas has created something large and black in his hand.

I gape when I realize it's a high caliber handgun with a screwed on silencer.

"Thomas?"

He ignores my question and pushes open the door to the empty, unlocked equipment shed, then beckons everyone inside. As he follows the last of us in, a bar appears across the door and Thomas points his gun at Audra.

He has a second gun, now, too. It's aimed at Logan.

"Time to find the traitor. Create anything and you die."

CHAPTER TWENTY

"Thomas stop!" I say. I try to rush forward, but Benson holds me so tightly I'm not convinced I won't have bruises on my upper arms tomorrow. I've seen Audra react to a threat; she might not be able to take Thomas in a fair fight, but she could certainly give him trouble. Whatever concerns Thomas has about Audra and Logan, the fact that they followed him into an isolated building and let him point guns at them without putting up a fight—without uttering so much as a word of protest—should tell him everything he needs to know about their loyalty.

"We had zero problems before the two of you came along," Thomas says, and I can sense the red-hot rage bubbling just beneath the surface. "And now this. We may be alive, but there are over two hundred people who were on that plane who are now dead. So I think it's time to figure out which one of you is our mole. And considering Logan is who he is to Tavia," Thomas adds, his glittering eyes fixed on Audra, "my money's on you."

"She can't be a spy," I blurt.

"You really think it's Logan?" Thomas asks, fury burning in his voice. He clearly doesn't—to his mind, the possibility of Logan betraying me is so ridiculous that Audra *must* be the one. And I can't fault his logic.

"I don't think either of them is a traitor." I can't—I *won't*—believe it.

"Don't you?"

Audra's hands are trembling. Logan looks angry, but also resigned—ready to act if necessary, but unwilling to do anything that might make him look guilty, or result in our separation.

"I don't," I say. "I don't know how the Reduciata found us. But there is no way either of them would betray us on purpose and nothing you do can convince me of that. Especially not shooting her."

"While I appreciate your loyalty to your friends, Tavia, we're talking about the fate of the world here. If you hadn't forgotten your bag we'd all be dead, with most of humanity soon to follow."

My bag.

"A spy wouldn't have gotten on that plane," Logan says evenly.

"Spies get sacrificed for the greater good all the time," Thomas counters.

"Maybe this is the spy." I step forward, putting myself

between Thomas and Audra, tossing my backpack to the ground. I make everything surrounding the large Ziploc bag simply melt away.

"That doesn't make sense," Audra says quietly.

"It's the *only* thing that makes sense," I counter.

"You really think that Daniel thought *so* far ahead that he put a tracker in your other-life belongings? On the off-chance that you'd find a way to steal them *and* escape headquarters *and* go on to thwart his evil plan?"

"Two days before I got away, I mentioned the artifacts to him." I bend and pick up the bag. "It's possible."

But Audra shakes her head. "He was too confident that he would be able to kill you. He would have had a plan B, sure. Maybe even C, but you're talking about, like, plan Q."

"Doesn't matter," I say, my voice quavering, my eyes stinging with tears. "I can't risk it. I've got to get rid of them."

"Wait!" Logan now. "Don't. Or, at least, don't get rid of them until you've used them. And even then." He looks desperately at Thomas, before homing in on me again. "Why do you think we work so hard to keep our belongings safe? Not only would getting rid of them destroy your change of remembering those lives now, but in your next life you're going to have three less things to help you awaken. Don't cripple yourself for thousands of years in the future because you're trying to escape in the moment."

"There won't be a future if we don't beat them, Logan!" I say, and tears are streaming down my face. "They might not even be real artifacts."

"Then touch them and find out!" Logan shouts back.

"Not sure we have time for that," Thomas says, and finally, he's back to being the one with a cool head. "We know whoever bombed the plane is here in London. If they could track us to the plane, they can track us here. Retrieving a life could knock Tavia out for hours."

"I have to destroy them, Logan."

"Tavia." He pauses and he clenches and unclenches his jaw—an expression of pain so acute on his face that it's hard to look at. "Listen, this is more than just your choice. My eternal existence depends on you remembering who you are and finding me within seven lifetimes. The necklace is gone; the braid from when you were Sonya is gone. If you're going to destroy another three artifacts that might mean the difference between life and eternal death for me, I think a deserve a say."

He's not wrong, and feeling the weight of that responsibility on my shoulders—along with the weight of the world already there—makes it almost impossible to breathe.

"It's not the artifacts," says Audra.

I'm so shocked by her voice that I can only blink numbly in reply.

"Tavia *forgot her backpack.* You said it yourself, Thomas.

That backpack was never on the plane. But we were—all of us. And every person who came to live at the Curatoria was required to submit to a medical evaluation. I hadn't been at the headquarters for very long, and because my powers weren't yet permanent I had a limited role, so I can't say for sure. But any one of us could be fitted with a tracking device. A pinch here, a poke there, a tiny bump—no one would notice. It would have been simple."

"You didn't do anything like that to me," I argue weakly.

"You weren't a sworn Curatoriate who trusted whatever Daniel told you. But Glenn and Christina were. I believe they would have been willing to put that kind of device in the Curatoriates even knowing what they were. Or—how hard would it be to convince someone that a tracking device was for all the Curatoriates' safety?" She shrugs helplessly. "I'd probably have agreed to it."

"But I've *changed* you!" I argue.

"You don't make any really deep changes—and you do it mostly on instinct. At the risk of asking the centipede how she dances, how much thought do you give to the exact process of keeping our nerves and muscles lined up so we don't lose the power of speech with every transformation of our faces?"

I shake my head. I don't even have to say it; she knows. I give it no thought at all.

"That's what I figured. Whether Daniel planned this out, or

just got lucky, the fact is that any one of us could be carrying around a tracking device."

Thomas' gaze swings between Logan and me. "Tavia, Benson, and I have been traveling for weeks without incident. It has to be one of you."

"Thomas is right," Audrey says, her voice choked. "I seem like the most likely culprit. Leave me."

"Not alive," Thomas says. "I don't like it, but you know too much."

Tears skim down Audra's cheeks when she closes her eyes, but she nods. "Death is just a reset button," she whispers.

"No!" I shout. "Audra, what about the special scanner you used on the helicopter? Could you make one of those and use it to look for…implants? We could find it—take it out."

Audra looks to Thomas for permission.

I see the question in his eyes, but I know he doesn't want to shoot her. "Fine."

"I might have to make a few—they won't last."

"No time," Thomas says flatly. "I can spare you five minutes—one temporary creation—but that's all."

"I'll need some help," she says, looking at me.

I'm already nodding. "What do I do?"

"Take away my hair," she says, pulling her shirt over her head. "I need a bare surface for the sono-gel." She drops her pants as I make her hair disappear. She's standing bald and nearly naked in front of us without so much as a blush of shame; Benson and Logan turn away politely, but Thomas maintains his vigil against any trick Audra might try to pull.

"Ready?" she says, meeting my eyes. "You'll have to get the parts I can't reach, and I'll watch the screen."

"I'm ready." *I'm so not ready.*

"Here we go." She screws up her face in concentration and instead of the small scanner suddenly appearing, the way I make crates of vaccine, I watch as a series of metal rails pop into existence, then layer upon layer of circuitry, until a probe appears next to a screen. In the solitude of my task these days, it's hard to remember that most Earthbound can't simply make complicated things appear all at once.

"Head to toe," Audra says, her voice shaking. "Like this," she says, her hand over mine on the probe, guiding me steadily but quickly across her scalp, slippery with the warm gel. "Okay, down this way," she says, leading my hand along her neck.

I guide the probe down her back, my fingers starting to tremble, and I can hear my heart pounding in my ears. "Steady," Audra murmurs. Her eyes are fixed on the screen. I see nothing but vague black and white shadows, but have to trust that Audra knows what she's doing.

"I'll get my front," she says, and her whisper is tense as warm gel appears across her torso. A trickle of sweat rolls down my back as I realize I've been counting in my head and

I've reached three hundred.

Her hands are shaking so badly she almost drops the probe as she steers it up her arms. I'm staring hard at the screen, willing it not to disappear, when Audra lets out a shriek.

"There! Look! It's there."

As Logan and Benson turn to see, Thomas runs to the screen and studies what Audra has found on her upper arm, near where I injected her with the vaccine serum. Then, even as he reaches to touch the screen, it blinks out of existence.

Audra turns wide eyes up to Thomas and for an instant, everything is utterly still, all of us staring at Thomas, waiting for the consequences to unroll. Then Thomas grabs Audra's arm and says simply, "Grit your teeth."

I scarcely see the flash of silver in Thomas' hand before Audra lets out a stifled growl, and a stripe of blood trails down her arm. "Here," Thomas says, turning to me with something held between bloody fingers. "Make it go away."

I glance up at Audra, who's pulling her clothes back on, her hand clasped to her arm, blood seeping through her fingers. "You don't want to look at it?"

"There's no time. Make it disappear, Tavia."

I shake my head. "No. Then they'll know we found it. Make them come all the way here before they realize."

"Good call, toss it in the hole out there. Logan," Thomas says sharply. "Ever driven on the left?"

Logan hesitates. "Long time ago." Another life then.

"Good enough." Thomas throws him the keys. "Tavia," he barks. "Front. Navigate. I'll patch Audra up in the back. Benson, with me. Go!"

We run out of the warehouse and to the car—pausing only an instant for me to fling the tracker in the half-built basement. Once we're all loaded Logan kicks up a bit of gravel as he pulls away, driving like there's a gunman in his rearview.

Which there might be.

The fate of the world shouldn't depend on chance—but today, it did. How much longer can our luck possibly hold?

CHAPTER TWENTY-ONE

"I don't think we should even listen—" Thomas begins as Logan fiddles with the radio in our rented car.

"Spare me, Thomas," I snap. "I'm not a wilting flower. I need to know." Need to know how many people died because I wasn't careful enough. I should have suspected that Daniel and Mariana would have some way to keep track of their followers—should have guessed they wouldn't leave everything to underlings and spies. To spend lifetime after lifetime finding a way to meet and resurge secretly so Earthbound on both sides would eventually forget what he looked like—that's the kind of logistical genius we have to overcome.

In the dream I had a few weeks ago, I realized that even I had forgotten what Daniel looked like. Still, as Lady Williams I knew Mariana—met her again and knew her for a friend. I was going to help her find Daniel. Did I go on to do that? And in my dream she spoke of how many lifetimes it had been since she saw him. But was that a lie?

Ignoring the newscast I'd been hoping to hear moments ago, I reach into my backpack and finger the gold circlet through the protective layer of plastic. Based on what I remember of the clothes and buildings, my guess has always been the thirteenth or fourteenth century. I know the brotherhoods are even older. Daniel and Mariana must have been at least loosely established as the leaders even at that point. Was she coming to test me? To see if her best friend still remembered her lover's face? That would have been the ultimate victory, wouldn't it?

Or had the resources of the Reduciata failed her, left her truly needing my help?

I glance out the window and then up at the clock on the dash. Despite how long this day has seemed, it's only mid-afternoon and we're about two hours from Liverpool. If we're lucky, we'll be able to catch a flight out of John Lennon tonight. But even so, there will be no serum creating for at least twenty-four hours. I have a full two hours before I have to alter identities, and what's likely ahead of me tonight is a long sleep, whether on a plane or in a hotel room.

While I certainly didn't ask for this awful upheaval to happen today, it feels foolish not to take advantage of it.

I've already discovered all I need to learn of Greta. The entirety of her association with either Mariana or Daniel happened in those last few minutes of her life. I've seen those. And Elysa? I don't even know who she is. Logan didn't know either, which says that the two of us never met. Another dead end.

But Leona Williams? Leona was with both Logan and Mariana, however briefly. Possibly Daniel, too. Perhaps other members of the brotherhoods.

I turn my face up to Benson, who's already studying me. Despite the gravity of the situation, I can't help but glow inside a little at the fact that no words are needed. He can tell what I have planned, and an entire conversation passes between us with no words.

I snuggle closer to him and he pulls the blanket around me so I'm blocked from general view. As I open the bag I cough to cover the clicks of the zip top, and then a surge of nerves overtakes me.

Until this moment I'd put out of my mind that this is going to hurt.

Benson presses a warm kiss to my forehead and tightens his arms a little.

Now or never.

My fingertips brush the circlet, then grasp it tightly in my fist as a whirlwind fills my skull and I tumble into the past.

***

When I open my eyes again everything is still. Too still.

Damn it. Thomas has pulled over onto the side of the road

and everyone is staring at me. I squeeze my eyelids shut again; even the dusky twilight is bright enough to send pain knifing through my skull.

"Sorry," mumbles a voice behind me, next to my ear. "I tried."

"Dare I ask what I did?" I say ruefully, pushing myself up into a sitting position and rubbing at my aching head. My whole body hurts like we got in a major car accident and I peer around subtly to make sure we didn't.

"Um, there was convulsing and screaming," Benson says hesitantly. His voice sounds funny and I look back at him and gasp. He's holding a handful of tissues to his nose, but I can see spots of blood. He shrugs with complete nonchalance, like it's all just part of the job as my boyfriend. He ought to draw hazard pay.

"Why did you stop?" I ask no one in particular, the heels of my hands still pressed to my eyes.

"Maybe to make sure you weren't going to die," Logan says dryly.

And somehow, hearing that from him just makes me mad. "I was never going to die," I snap back. "Benson could have told you that." I don't add that he's the one who witnessed the memory pull that almost *did* kill me back in Camden. But if that didn't kill me, nothing else is going to.

"It was ..." Thomas pauses to clear his throat, "rather

disconcerting, Tavia." Trust Thomas to be so understated.

My temples are throbbing and I want to push my face into Benson's shoulder and relax. "Can we just drive?" I ask, not trying to hide the desperation in my voice. "The whole point of me doing this now was that I have time to recover before we get to Liverpool. If we hurry, we can leave this godforsaken country tonight." I'm letting my irritation get to me—it seems to be a perfectly lovely country—but I want to get moving as soon as possible.

"Did you learn anything important?" Thomas asks.

"I'm still sorting," I say evasively. "It's harder for me than it is for you guys. I need …" A sob builds up in my throat and I'm not doing well at forcing it down. "I need to sleep," I whisper as one tear escapes.

I feel Audra pull my feet onto her lap as Thomas nods grimly. "Okay. Off we go."

Lying across both Benson and Audra's laps, I pull the blanket over my head to block out the light and create a soft pillow and earplugs. I need to shut off my senses for an hour and let my poor brain rest from the beating I've just subjected it to.

I don't sleep though. I can't. I'm still sorting through a lifetime of dim memories that seem to grow brighter as I individually examine them. But it's not a conscious process; I just…remember.

After the promise I made to Mariana during my dream—that I would help her find him—with the resources of the Williams' estate at our disposal we traveled for weeks. On an evening that would never have struck me as significant while I was Lady Williams, something happened that stands out to me now.

We were sitting at a table, sharing a communal supper with a handful of other travelers. Logan—Jovan, as he was back then—was near the fire, commanding our passel of servants, visiting with other gentlemen on the road. Mariana and I huddled together, my hand on her arm. She looked around the room, her eyes empty and haunted, and spoke to me of her desolation, the hopelessness of her task, her certainty that they would never find her absent lover.

But he was there—sitting across from us. I saw him that night, nearly a thousand years ago, though the woman I was noticed nothing out of the ordinary in the brooding, travel-worn stranger. Short beard, sandy-colored hair, one blue eye visible, the other covered with an eye patch, an ugly scar peeping from behind it and traveling up into his hairline. I remember a slightly different scar he wore in another memory—the memory of a cold child in London. I wonder how many injuries he's inflicted upon himself to hide his identity.

Lady Williams saw him. *I* saw him. I just didn't recognize

him.

Then I urged Mariana up from the wooden bench and led her upstairs to her room. At the time I didn't notice Mariana pause at the top of the stairs and glance back at the man across the table—didn't see anything significant in the small smile he cast her.

It was a test.

The entire thing was an elaborate set-up. Because if Mariana's dearest friend didn't recognize her partner—even as she was seeking him—who else would? I suspect that if I were privy to the record books of the Curatoria, I'd discover that soon after this meeting in the oh-so-normal inn, Daniel emerged with the claim of newly awakened memories, to take control of the Curatoria once more. And I'd be willing to bet that from then on, Daniel became synonymous with the Curatoria, and that's when his and Mariana's true joint-rule of both brotherhoods began.

Because I didn't see what was in front of my eyes.

The more I discover of my past the more I have to fight the feeling that all of this is my fault.

After an hour I ask Thomas for a strong pain reliever, and by the time we pull into the bustling Liverpool John Lennon airport I'm feeling well enough to carry out my usual role in our unending masquerade. Wearily I close my eyes and picture the datasheet from Kat in my head. By the time we exit the car, we all have a new face, new IDs and passports, and new sets of luggage—props in our deception. I'm so tired I start to stumble as we walk in, but Benson wraps a strong arm around me and helps me stay upright.

Turns out we get to go to Egypt after all. It's one of six international flights we're on time to catch, but two are repeat destinations and two are booked—no chance of getting five tickets on the day of departure. The last possibility is too close to the most recent catastrophe in Africa for Thomas' comfort.

"Egypt it is," Thomas says wryly, sliding a glance over at Audra, who he seems to still be unwilling to like. He rolls his eyes when she bounces on her toes and clasps her hands together.

Benson has to encourage me to eat. I don't tell him that it isn't the memory pull making me feel sick, but guilt and a deep sense of disappointment in myself for wrongs I can no longer right. Logan keeps looking over at me and I know he wants to talk—and I owe him that. It was a life I shared with him and, at the very least, we'll need to compare our memories. He must not have seen Daniel in the inn that night either, or he would have remembered immediately on resurging… I think. I guess I still don't really know what it's like for others to have multiple lifetimes crammed into their head. And I never will. Not in this life anyway.

I ask Thomas for half dose of Valium as we board, and

though he looks worried as he makes it for me, I remain silent and let him draw his own conclusions regarding the cause of the relapse. The plane takes off and I'm grateful when I feel the drug suck me into a deep sleep.

But still I dream of Mariana.

CHAPTER TWENTY-TWO

"The problem is that I have two contacts in the Egyptian government, and each of them is assuring me that the other one has been blackmailed into diverting the vaccine from distribution as soon as it arrives. Meanwhile I've got a colleague reporting that their understaffed quarantine hospital in Al Bawiti is beginning to pose a danger to the surrounding community." Even through the tinny speakers of Thomas' disposable phone, Kat's voice is heavy with frustration—and apology.

"Not to be insensitive," Logan says, frowning, "but does it really matter if the vaccine doesn't end up where you're trying to send it? I don't like the idea of criminals or rich people jumping to the front of the line, but everyone has to get the vaccine eventually."

I resist a petty urge to tell him that it matters to me.

"Well, one problem is that we don't know who's plotting these diversion. If it's the Reduciata, they'll make sure to destroy the vaccine—or taint it." As Alanna's voice comes through the phone, Thomas' hand tightens around it. Over a month of separation from his *diligo*, always moving, always in danger, is wearing on him. When we pulled Audra and Logan out of Phoenix, I really had intended to send Thomas back to wherever Alanna was hiding as soon as I could. I still hope to do so, once things settle down a bit, but with the way things are between Logan and me right now...

"The other is that we have no way of knowing where these bioterrorists will cause a new outbreak." Kat pauses, as if hoping someone will contradict her, but when we don't she continues. "Until then, the best we can do is slow the spread of the disease by prioritizing at-risk populations in Egypt. That includes medical professionals, people who live in crowded conditions, and those who lack convenient access to modern hygiene."

"Then we'll just have to take it to them directly." The words are out of my mouth before I've given them any serious thought, but saying them feels good. Feels *right*. "We'll go to that hospital you mentioned and Thomas can administer vaccine to the staff. While no one's looking, I'll fill their basement with vaccine crates. Or their hallways, or whatever. We don't have time to worry about politics or even Reduciata scheming. If people wonder how the vaccine got there, let them wonder. I doubt anyone's going to seriously guess the truth."

For a long moment, no one says anything, and I worry

they're going to object—to tell me it's not efficient, or it's not safe, or something. I'm not the person who plans these things, after all. Thomas is the organized one.

But no one argues.

"Well," Alanna says with a soft, cheerful laugh that makes Thomas wince with obvious longing, "I'm sure both Thomas and Audra will enjoy touring the hospital."

Kat arranges for us to show up at the Al Bawiti hospital under some false pretense or another, and we rent a car for the drive. Soon we're following the hospital administrator through the most crowded, poorly-lit hospital I've ever seen, Audra and Thomas talking shop with a doctor while Benson, Logan, and I trail silently behind. All of the staff is dressed in hazmat suits— our little entourage looks rather odd, actually, dressed in simple scrubs and sneakers.

But we're immune, and none of these people are.

It's not so crowded that patients are lining the halls, but the doors are nothing like the doors in Daniel's labs. Or the Mayo Clinic. They're just regular doors with a window in each one. Hazmat suits or no, I'm a little surprised the hospital has any non-infected staff left at all.

The horror I'm feeling must show on my face because Thomas pulls himself away from whatever conversation he and Audra—her disguise adding years to her appearance—are having with the doctors. Thomas addresses me in a low whisper. "Life in the trenches."

"It's like this...everywhere?"

"Probably not everywhere," he allows. "In poorer countries, definitely. I'm sorry you had to see this. But you were right—I doubt there was any other way we could help here; this place is obviously at the bottom of everyone's priority list. I'd just rather not make a habit of it; I'm already feeling pretty exposed."

"Thank you for indulging me. Just this once."

He shakes his head. "While I appreciate the sentiment, you shouldn't make promises you can't keep. We've got a long way to go." A sad smile softens his words and I remind myself that, as hard as he can be at times, Thomas is as committed to our quest as anyone. "I'm going to tell the doctor I've sent you to fetch vaccine. You take the elevator down and come back up with a full box. Watch for storage closets; I bet if you started by filling those while no one—"

"Sergei!"

Audra's delighted shriek startles both of us into silence. She's standing in front of a door on her tip-toes, her hands splayed on the window, her desperation palpable even from across the hall.

"Miss, miss!" The head doctor rushes by, knocking against my shoulder in his hurry to get to Audra, to place a restraining hand over hers as she turns the door handle. "You cannot enter that room. The confirmed sick are in there."

"Sergei!" Audra practically howls, and then Thomas is at her side, pulling her back, whispering rapidly in her ear. She stops struggling, but continues bouncing on the balls of her feet like an impatient child.

I've heard that name before and everything inside me first jumps with joy and then melts into a puddle of despair.

Oh gods, I'm going to have to tell her.

"A friend," Thomas explains to the doctor.

"Oh." I see sympathetic understanding cloud the doctor's expression.

"She can safely enter the room," Thomas says. "She's immune. Come speak with me about your staff for a moment." He puts a hand on the doctor's shoulder and steers him down the hallway, turning at the last second to give me a meaningful look. It's all in my hands now.

"Tavia, I need my face back," Audra says. "He might not know me—probably won't—but he certainly won't in someone else's face. Please," she begs. "Surely we can break a rule this once."

"Of course we can," I say, though it feels like my mouth is full of sawdust. I pull Benson close to block the both of us, and restore her appearance which, luckily, wasn't too far from her own since we're not in an airport with hundreds of cameras. "Go to him," I say softly. "We'll have to pull you out in a few minutes to make a plan, but go." I force a smile onto my face and hope she can't see the agony behind it.

She slips through the door into the sickroom and I can't bear to watch through the window. "Benson," I say, tugging on his arm. "I've got to do something for Thomas. Watch her. I don't think she'll try, but just in case, do *not* let her leave."

Benson nods soberly and I walk away, pulling Logan with me. I glance back several times as we approach the elevator. I don't like that this sudden shift leaves Benson standing there utterly unprotected, but I have to trust that he can take care of himself.

Sergei or no, we still have a job to do.

The elevator is mercifully empty and as soon as the doors close I collapse into tears. I hardly feel Logan's arms at all as he crouches beside me, hold me against him. I grasp at his forearms, clinging, my sobs growing loud and ugly as guilt and agony, mourning and regret rip through me. I'm not sure how I'm going to face her, but I know I've got to let out what I can before I have to re-erect that emotional dam.

"I don't think she realizes," I finally choke out. "Daniel didn't tell them. Now I have to."

"No, I'll tell her," Logan says. "It might be better, coming from me. Considering ..." He gestures helplessly between the two of us and I feel even worse.

"No, I have to do it." But I can't tell him why—why it's

affecting me like this. Can't tell him that there's still one very big secret I'm keeping from him. This is my consequence. So I say simply, "I owe her that."

The elevator reaches the basement and I take deep, fortifying gulps of air. I've got to keep it together.

"We're here for serum?" Logan says gently, his lips so close they brush my ear. I think how easy it would be to lose my grief in his arms, the way that—even though I can't quite remember it—I know I've done many, many times.

But that wouldn't change anything.

I nod and loosen myself from his embrace. "Will you hold it?" I ask.

He nods and extends his arms and I create a box full of serum right against his chest. Without a sound, he bears up its weight. As the elevator ascends, I create a small mirror and hold it up to my face, vanishing the redness in my eyes and creating a thin layer of makeup to cover my blotches. By the time the elevator dings on the fourth floor, I'm back to my usual self.

My usual, someone-else's-face self.

My eyes meet Benson's the moment the elevator doors open and it's all I can do not to race down the hall and throw myself into his arms. Then Thomas comes back around the corner, a small entourage of doctors trailing behind him. He raises his eyebrows when he sees me. The lines of weariness around his eyes seem to have deepened in just the last five minutes since Audra's pronouncement, and I marvel at how little his expressions really change from face to face. Or perhaps I've simply been traveling with him for so long, through so many disguises, that I no longer really see the face he wears—only the expressions upon it.

"Oh good," he says, eyeing me carefully. "Dr. Kamuzu is about to make a hospital-wide announcement gathering the staff. We have a room set aside for injections and you and William here can go supervise the delivery of the rest of the serum."

William? Was that Logan's fake name today? I guess I'm glad *someone* remembered. This secret identity stuff is way more complicated when you have to actually talk to people.

"I've arranged for Lisa to have an hour with her friend in room 414," Thomas continues evenly, meeting my gaze. "They'll want some privacy at this sensitive time, of course. But he'll have to return to the patients' ward when they're finished."

"I'll go speak with her, then," I say softly.

"We'll need to get back on the road as soon as the delivery is done."

I nod. We share a long look, then Thomas takes the box of vaccine from Logan and leads the doctors away.

I walk the hall on feet of lead, each step heavier than the

last. At the door, Benson says nothing, but gives my hand a fortifying squeeze. Forcing a smile I look into the window of the ward and beckon to Audra. Surprisingly, she's not the only one beaming and she whispers something to a very handsome young man sitting at the edge of his bed. He caresses her cheek and responds with something I can't hear before she slips off the bed.

They look amazing together. With their dark skin and glossy hair, I can't help but imagine them as a modern Cleopatra and Antony. Though I suppose it's possible that's exactly who they are—and I wonder, a bit idly, just how much of Mesopotamia owes its existence to them.

"Oh, Tavia!" Audra says, completely forgetting our false personas as she slips through the door. "I was so worried that we'd have to convince him of who he was and to come with us until we could find an artifact to restore his memories, but he's an archeology student! He awakened his own memories years ago. Almost the same time as me, actually. Can you believe it?" Her words gush out in a spill of joy and I cringe at the assumptions she's clearly accepted as fact, when nothing could be further from the truth.

"Audra," I say sharply, "you have to listen." I pull her a few feet down the hall, to an alcove that gives us a modicum of privacy. "He can't come with us."

Her exhilarated expression slips. "What?"

I lick my lips. "He's sick. He has the virus. He can't come with us."

"But—"

"The vaccine isn't a cure, Audra." I don't want to have to say it outright, but I don't have a choice. "He's not going anywhere."

Her jaw trembles. "Then I'm not either," she says softly. "I can't leave him." Her eyes flash. "*I'm* immune. I can stay. I'll…" Tears build in her eyes, but she blinks them back resolutely. "I'll stay with him until the end. I owe him that. We can…we can make the very most of the time we have."

"Oh, Audra," I breathe. "It's so much worse than that."

Her shining eyes stare up at me and now they're full of fear. She believes me, but doesn't yet understand how anything *could* be worse.

"The disasters—the ones in the Pacific, South America, the desert in Nevada, Africa—they were each caused by an Earthbound dying of the virus. The things they made on the Earth—it was all undone when the virus killed them."

"Oh, no," she says, closing her eyes. "I…we both created here in Egypt. That's why I was so happy to come back." After a pause, she gives a single nod—not to me, but to herself. "I'm staying anyway. If I die, I die. At least we'll be together."

I shake my head but she talks over me.

"You don't need me. I'm barely useful as it is. My powers

aren't permanent and Thomas is a doctor too. You won't miss me. My place is with—"

"Audra!" I snap, cutting her off. "You have to listen. They've arranged a private room for you. You can have an hour. Actually I'm relieved that his memories are already restored; hopefully you can resurge while I'm packing this place with vaccine. But that's all the time we can give you."

Audra doesn't speak, but her face is filled with stubborn fury and I can do nothing but let the final blow fall.

"If Sergei dies of the virus, he will not be reborn. He'll die *forever*. That's why the damage happens to the earth. An Earthbound life, ripped away forever."

"No, we don't—"

"In the Curatoria headquarters, we found the pair who created the desert, already with the virus. Mostly gone. We considered killing them right then to prevent disaster, but didn't know whether the infection had to be the cause of death, or if they just had to die while infected. When the headquarters collapsed there was no way for us to know if they died from injuries or from the virus, but either way, the dissolution of their creations was triggered." I gesture down the hall. "We know what happens if the virus kills him—we know he dies forever, and his work is undone. The only hope—"

My voice breaks and I swallow down a sob.

"—the only hope you have is—"

I can't say it. I can't tell her to kill her *diligo*. I don't know that it *will* save him in the long run, not for certain. And anyway I can't yet be sure there will even *be* a long run.

I see understanding dawn on Audra's face in a mask of horror. "No," she whispers.

"Thomas bought you an hour," I say, forcing myself not to break down and lose control. "All the privacy you want while we go down and fill every closet we can find. And when we come back up—" My throat closes off as though my physical body is fighting the words I'm about to say, but I choke them out at last. "You can kill him, or I'll do it for you, but in one hour, he has to die."

CHAPTER TWENTY-THREE

We drive to Cairo that night. By unspoken agreement, we simply cannot stay in Al Bawiti. The trip adds over two hours to a day that has already been hellishly long—even worse than two days ago in London—but we all seem to need distance.

I don't sleep in the car. I can't. When we finally arrive at the hotel in Cairo I slide out and stumble like I'm drunk, almost knocking Logan over. He rights himself and me, and attempts to gather me under his arm, but Benson wordlessly pulls me away and onto his other side, planting himself squarely between Logan and myself. He seems to understand I can't deal with any more drama tonight.

And that I need him.

I'm tearing at the buttons on his polo before the door to our room is fully closed. One pops off, but that hardly matters; I claw the fabric over his head and down his arms. I curse at the undershirt he always wears and, though it's kind of an unspoken rule that I don't bring my powers into our love life, I make the shirt disappear. He yelps, but I'm already pressing my head against his bare chest, listening to his heart, listening to

211

his breath—listening to his *life*.

He holds me tight, as tight as he can, so I can hardly breathe, but it satisfies my need for proof that he's there, that I won't have to let him go. Audra's ordeal has left me bereft. When I walked away from her at the hospital, I threw myself into creating as much vaccine as possible, filling closets and supply rooms and even empty offices when no one was looking. It was only when Logan yanked me, retching and heaving, from a cold cement floor and shouted at me that I had to stop, that I finally did.

After that, I couldn't go up to get Audra. There would be no way to explain my pitiful physical state to the doctors. Logan carried my limp form to the car instead, leaving Benson to watch over me.

Audra didn't look at me when she came down, flanked by Logan and Thomas. Her eyes were wide and sightless and, while I'm no doctor, I'm pretty sure she was slipping into shock. But when she eventually snaps out of it, in a few hours, or days, or weeks, she'll have a raging torrent of despair to face all alone.

I have Benson.

I find his mouth again. I've burned through my savage rage and moved on to intense longing. I *need* Benson—need him to show me that there's something good in the world, even if only between the two of us. And it's going to be up to him; I don't have much left to give. I'm already too tired to move. But I need Benson to help me get too tired to *think*.

***

Audra stays in her hotel room until we've finished in Cairo and are ready to leave Egypt. No one can blame her.

There were a few moments while I was so sick in the car back in Al Bawiti, when I wondered if Sergei having the virus at all—at any stage—would result in an Earthbound's permanent death. And I dreaded that I'd sentenced all of Egypt to death when I told Audra he had to be killed. We apparently found him early enough, so instead, only Audra suffers the consequences.

And millions of people will never know the sacrifice she made to save their lives. The exhaustion and fear of my own task feels miniscule by comparison.

I don't sleep well the night before we're supposed to leave for the airport, so in the early morning sunlight I slip out of my room and tip-toe to Audra's. I'm about to knock when a movement catches my eye and I see her sitting on a bench in a courtyard just down the hall, surrounded by palm trees and flowering bushes and lush grass. I'd always thought of Egypt as brown and sandy, but most of what I've seen has been verdant and fertile.

The glow of sunlight brightens Audra's wan features and a lit cigarette hangs from her fingertips. An ashtray at her side tells me it isn't the first.

"Hey," I say, dropping onto the spot beside her. My social impulse is to ask some version of *Are you okay*, but really, isn't that the stupidest question in the world? She just had to kill the man she's loved for longer than humans have had the power of speech, and she had to do it less than two hours after finding him for the first time in centuries. Of course she's not okay. To ask if she's okay is a selfish request: *tell me a pretty lie so I will feel better.*

"Hey," she replies, lifting the cigarette to her mouth. But instead of the long drag I'm expecting, she takes a tiny puff, shakes her head, and coughs. "My brain wants it," she says wryly as she stubs it out. "But these young lungs don't." She sits back in her chair, her eyes focused on the brightening skyline. "It's probably for the best."

"We're leaving soon," I say, leaning my elbows on my knees and resting my chin in my upturned palms. "I hope you'll come with us, but I understand if you can't."

She nods, and the movement sends a tear rolling down her cheek, but she's quick to raise a sleeved arm and wipe it away. "I want to. We're doing something good."

"Yes," I say tentatively, "but you've already done an incredible amount of good at a very high personal cost. No one would think any less of you if that's all you can give."

"What is there here for me?"

"Solitude," I answer quickly. "Sometimes that's the most helpful thing."

But she lets out a scoffing snort. "I've had a hell of a lot of solitude these last few years. I'm sick to death of solitude."

I feel like she's waiting for a response, but I don't want to speak. I want her to feel like she can talk.

"Have you talked to Logan about the weeks we traveled together?"

I shake my head. Of all the conversations we haven't had time for ...

"We had Christina with us at the beginning. But she died."

"Of the virus?" I wonder if that's what triggered the disaster in South Africa, but Audra shakes her head.

"She was injured in the collapse. Logan dug her out, like he dug me out. He saved us. I mean, I wasn't injured—not badly—but I couldn't get out until he came. He saved us both. But Christina..." Audra takes a deep breath. "She was injured internally. By the time we got her out the damage was done. In the beginning she made medicine for herself and we thought we'd gotten all of her internal bleeding stopped. But after a while she slept all the time. And then we couldn't wake her up at all and I couldn't help her because my powers weren't permanent, and the life support equipment we really needed was too complicated for Logan to duplicate. It got to the point where we were sleeping in shifts, keeping her alive by manually filling her lungs with oxygen. I fell asleep at the wrong time and she...she died."

I try to imagine the young girl—even if she is older on the inside—struggling to stay awake, to keep her mentor breathing. Acting as a living form of life support.

"And I felt like it was my fault because I couldn't give her what she needed."

"It wasn't your fault," I blurt, because I can't *not*.

"I know," she says, waving my words away like an irritating fly. "I failed her. But I didn't kill her." She takes a long shuddering breath. "I *killed* Sergei."

"I know," I whisper. "I made you do it."

"Do you know what I did?"

I force back a gag as I realize she's about to tell me precisely *how* she killed her love. But I make myself keep my mouth closed and listen.

"It was easy, really. I had to do something that was fast, and not obvious, because Sergei is a Destroyer and he can negate anything I do, if he's quick enough."

Another mixed pair, I think, shaking my head slightly at the awful waste, and cursing Daniel and Mariana for their terrible virus yet again. Then I remember Thomas telling me about him and Alanna—how they thought they were one of two mixed pairs. This was not only another mixed pair, it was *the* other mixed pair.

"I created a blood clot in the vessels in his brain." She doesn't look at me, instead staring into the rising sun intently enough that I'm a little worried about her eyes. "A catastrophic aneurism. Once he was dead I laid him back in the bed, tucked the blanket around him, and walked away."

"I'm sorry I wasn't there. I—I pushed myself too hard. I couldn't."

She shrugs. "It wasn't as hard as I expected to just pretend I hadn't done anything." She turns to me and her dark eyes are so wide. "How can you not be with Logan?"

The question and the accusation in her expression catches me so off-guard that I couldn't have said anything if I'd wanted to.

"He loves you so much and he's here and you've resurged and still?" She sits up straighter and turns her whole body to me. "You weren't there. He was so heart-broken when he was sure you were dead. But that was nothing compared to the way I see him look at you now. Being separated from our soul mate by death is part of our life. Part of our curse, really. But you have the chance and you're wasting it!"

I can't speak. Can't even conjure up appropriate words to say. This isn't the conversation I expected to be having with her this morning. And she's not wrong—I have everything she just had to give up.

And I don't want it.

No, even that isn't quite true. I don't want it *enough*. But I can't say that to her. I can't explain any of that.

Audra opens her hand to reveal a smooth blue stone. "Sergei gave this to me once. A thousand years ago. I'm going to keep it until I find him again."

"He had it with him?"

"No, it's not the real one. I created it. But now I can keep it."

It takes a few seconds to register what she's just told me. "You resurged?"

She nods.

"That's great! It means—" But I cut myself off. She doesn't need to be told what it means.

She says it anyway—the part that matters most. "It means that we have seven lifetimes again. Not that I think we'll need them. I have the advantage of my memories and my powers with permanence. I know exactly when he died, so I know when he'll be born again. My chances of finding him again in this life are quite high." She turns to me with a brittle smile that makes a twinge of discomfort curl in the bottom of my stomach. "Eighteen years isn't so long, really. I'll only be thirty-two by then. And who doesn't love a good May-December romance?" She stands and the wind blows her hair across her face. She brushes it to the side and says softly, "I'll get him back." She starts to walk away and then turns back to me and says, "But only if we save the world first. When should I be ready to go?"

"An hour," I say, my voice cracking.

Her calm façade worries me. For the moment she's holding it together, but I can't help but believe she's going to feel a lot worse before she begins to feel better.

CHAPTER TWENTY-FOUR

We're a silent group as we head to the airport in Cairo. I didn't realize how accustomed to Audra's excitement and happy chatter I'd grown—and I miss it. Everyone keeps giving her silent looks and, like me, they seem to realize how volatile she is. But no one makes her talk. I'm not certain whether it's the right or wrong thing to do. Certainly it seems like the only *possible* thing. I've even taken the front passenger seat for a change, leaving Audra to sit between my boys in the back.

But I'm completely unprepared for Thomas' announcement that he's going back to Alanna. I shouldn't be—I've been looking for an opportunity to send him back for days—but I am.

"Only for a while," he says, even though no one argues. "Things are getting increasingly complicated for Dr. Martin and the Reduciata are getting bolder with their bioterrorism. I think I'll be more helpful working closely with them to smooth the way for the rest of you." He looks back at Audra, even though she won't meet his eyes. "And with Audra's powers now permanent, you're in as good of medical hands as before.

Better, actually," he says with a self-deprecating laugh. "I was a physician in the sixties. Audra's been one almost constantly for the last hundred and twenty years."

He pauses for a response, but she doesn't give him one.

"I'll take the artifacts with me, just in case. I won't go right to Alanna," he adds when I start to sputter in protest. "I'll hit a few random cities first. Hide the artifacts away in safe places Alanna and I have set up over the years. By the time I go back to her, we should be certain that the Reduciata can't track us." He turns to glance at both Logan and me. "We'll make sure you know exactly how to find them when you need them. We're not exactly the Curatoria…but then, I suppose, even the Curatoria wasn't really the Curatoria, in the end."

Logan nods stoically and I look at my feet in guilt. I've been plagued by the things Audra said to me this morning. It's like I'm personally offending her by continuing to keep Logan at arm's length. Part of me feels like Audra should understand better than anyone; she was the one who saw my brain scans, who explained to me why I would never be like the other Earthbound. Why I would always be more human. But after being forced to give up her *diligo*? I can't blame her for being upset that I'm not sacrificing everything in the world for mine.

For a few moments I allow myself the idea that perhaps she was so protective of Logan because she was hiding her own romantic feelings for him. But even if that weren't a blatant insult to the sacrifice she just made, the truth is, it's nothing but a wish that everyone could be happy. That everyone could have someone. If there's one thing I've learned about the people I'm working with, it's that we're not all going to get our happily ever after and no matter what I do, people are going to suffer. Myself included.

"What face will you wear?" I ask.

"My own," Thomas says. "I'll have to manage my own disguises for a while, anyway."

I nod, then lean over the center console. "What will we do without you?" I whisper.

"Thrive, probably," Thomas says with a sad smile, pulling the car into a parking spot. His eyes dart to the back seat where the others are climbing out with only the most necessary of muted conversation. "Trust Logan," Thomas whispers to me. "I know you were the one who was saying that to me last week, but really. Every flight we've been on I've spent hours telling him how and why I do the things I do. He's...smart. Resourceful."

"I know."

"I'm not implying anything about that," Thomas says, one finger under my chin, lifting my face so I meet his eyes again. "I want you to let him do my job. *You* chose Benson to be your companion—*I* choose Logan to be my replacement. I'm not choosing you, Tavia. Not because you aren't capable. You have your job. Benson has his. Now Audra has hers. And you need to let Logan do his. Don't shut him out. There's too much riding on this."

He's right, of course. He so often is. And it's only in that moment that I realize how difficult it'll be to let Logan step in as the shot-caller. But Thomas' warning is completely true. I don't have the time or energy to be the leader. I have one job—and I'm the only one who can do it.

"Okay," I say. "I promise."

I give everyone their new identities—and give Thomas back his old one—leaving it to Logan and Audra to provide everyone with a couple of rollerboards. I also give Thomas a passport and he constructs his own temporary disguise, which I then alter the passport photo to better reflect. "Be careful," I blurt, somehow needing to say it.

He looks serious and for a second I don't think he's going to reply, then he leans closer and whispers, "If I screw this up, Alanna will die. No one on the face of the earth will be as careful as me."

The walk through the airport is somber; it's hard to let Thomas go, even though I'm happy for him. And he'll be back. If I know him, he'll be back sooner rather than later. This trip is for so much more than him. Although we're pretty sure we're safe from Reduciata tracking at this point, his plan for dropping the artifacts in different places before going back to

Alanna is brilliant. It hasn't escaped my notice that his great idea means that if anyone dies, it's him. But that's just such a Thomas thing to do.

To keep from drawing attention—as well as to send him off with zero information that anyone could potentially torture out of him—Thomas goes to the ticketing counter alone, nothing but a small shoulder bag as his luggage, and purchases his ticket to the United States. Other than the quick stop for Logan and Audra—and a couple of weird layovers—I haven't been in my home country for over a month. Nor do I expect to go back any time soon.

Thomas doesn't so much join our group as simply come and stand near us, while looking off in a different direction. "No scenes," he says softly. "I just wanted to suggest you guys fly east." Because, of course, he's flying west.

I start to nod, then remember that he's not looking at us.

"I should be able to talk to you in about a week. Be safe. Do good." He turns his head just a little and catches—though doesn't hold—my gaze. "Don't forget, T, let everyone do their jobs."

And then he's walking away.

The four of us are careful not to look very long in Thomas' direction as we subtly watch him go. Once I can no longer see him out the corner of my eye, a strange sort of slump settles over the group.

"What now?" Audra says quietly, voicing the sentiment I'm certain we're all feeling.

But I'm wrong.

Logan is paying no attention to Thomas as all. His eyes are fixed on the Departures screen above our heads and he says, almost breezily, "I think we should go to Tokyo."

I open my mouth to argue. *We went to Osaka three weeks ago! Thomas has been avoiding capital cities! That flight doesn't leave for two hours and the one to Incheon leaves in ninety minutes!*

But I remember what Thomas said, and I close my mouth. Thomas has been working with Logan since we picked him up, grooming him for this job. I'm certain Logan already knows all the arguments I could bring up. If he's making this decision anyway—if he's decided to change things up for reasons of his own—he needs my support. Because Thomas is right; I can spend my energy arguing with Logan, or I can spend it saving the world.

I look over at Logan, who has just made his first decision as our new leader, and I smile. "I think that's perfect," I say softly.

***

Worthy motivation seems oddly able to overcome nearly any obstacles. And as our plane rumbles to a stop in Lisbon,

Portugal, that thought really hits home. I stretch my arms and legs that are sore and awkward every day. I shuffle off the plane, Benson's arm around me, guiding me when I can't seem to shake off the last vestiges of sleep. In spite of our successes—and, I suppose, precisely because of them—I'm practically a sleepwalker lately. The last time I felt this way, timing meant that Thomas gave Benson and me a day in Brisbane.

Somehow, I don't think Logan is going to be quite so accommodating.

Not that I have room to complain; he's been a great leader. Once I gave in and made myself trust his judgment, things went quite well. He takes his decisions very seriously and I see so much of Quinn in him when he's studying departure lists and planning our next move. And I know he spends hours on the phone with Alanna and Dr. Martin while I'm sleeping, the same way Thomas used to.

There's been little to no rest between cities for two weeks, and once Thomas joined Alanna and Dr. Martin on logistics, the way forward got even smoother. We've given up on cover stories almost entirely and gone straight to bribing officials to just look the other way. Logan's discovered he's quite good at making obscene stacks of gold. I try not to think too hard about the ethics of his methods; I certainly can't argue with his results.

Even so, about half the cities we visit now are repeats—places where we know we'll be welcome. Thomas and Alanna are trying to fight bad press with good press. For every community that falls victim to a town-wide epidemic of the virus—thanks to the Reduciata—we counter the panic with a huge city of successful immunizations.

It's all we can do. The Reduciata are managing to hit a new town every two to three days, but with the incubation period of the virus, there's no way to detect it until it's too late and the entire town is exposed.

I can't read the news anymore. It's too demoralizing. The death count for South Africa finally came in and even the most modest experts are estimating over thirteen million. That lovely surprise came side by side with a report on two small towns in my home state of Michigan that were brought down by the Reduciata's virus. Benson would have shielded me from it as he so frequently tries to do, but we were in Canada that day, and the headlines screaming out their tragedies from the newspapers all around us were very much in English.

I needed Valium on the next flight.

It's a race against an opponent we can't see, who reaches out to trip us up at every opportunity. We've managed to avoid being found by Daniel and Mariana, but they won't stop looking. I recall the story of Damocles, who had a sword hanging over his head, held by a single hair from a horse's tail, and have to wonder how many swords are hanging over my head every instant. A whole armory full, at least.

The trip to Lisbon was a shorter flight—only six hours—but we've arrived in the middle of the night, so I'll be able to get more sleep once we get to the hotel. I'm having such trouble shaking off my exhaustion though, that as we emerge from the walkway and into the terminal, I stumble on my own feet and start to fall. Benson's not expecting it and I slip through his arms—but Logan catches me, and pulls me tight against his chest.

"You okay?"

"Yes. No. I'm—" What I am is exhausted. At our last stop we went right from the warehouse to the airport and I simply haven't had enough time to recover.

"I've got you," he says, tucking me against his side and abandoning his rollerboard. "Could you get that?" he asks Benson, without looking back.

I don't have the energy to argue, and really, Logan and I are still very close. We always will be. Benson's got to understand that. I feel guilty, but I can't muster up the will to protest.

"Let's get a cab," Logan says at the front of the airport. "There's a minivan there, it should be at least as roomy as a rental." He nods his head in the direction of a long line of cabs. "Plus, there's a ready queue."

I can feel Benson's frustration rolling off of him—

especially when Logan points him toward the front seat and hands him a small piece of paper. "This is where we're going; show the driver?" When he settles us into the back seat, me lying across his chest, I slip back to sleep within seconds.

I awake to hushed but angry voices and a soft blanket tucked warmly around me. I vaguely sense that I'm lying on a bed and realize someone carried me into the hotel. Logan? Benson? I'm stuck in the middle of something I don't have the energy to take part in.

"It's *my* room."

"That's bullshit and you know it. If she's here, it's my room. *Our* room."

"Don't trust her alone with me?"

"Screw you. I don't trust *you* alone with *her*."

"What? Think I'll ravish her in her sleep? What the hell kind of man do you take me for?"

"The kind she hasn't been choosing to share a room with."

"She needs to *sleep*. What does it matter whose room she sleeps in?"

"I agree. So go find your own room."

With a moan I roll over and smoosh my face into my pillow, refusing to let myself get sucked into their drama, and slip off to sleep before I find out who wins.

CHAPTER TWENTY-FIVE

When consciousness returns I'm cocooned in warmth and listening to the sound of slow, even breathing. I don't want to open my eyes—don't even want to *guess* whose breathing it is—so I focus on myself instead. I feel better. I really zonked last night and if I had to wager, I'd bet that it's been eight or ten hours since we got to the hotel, on top of the five to six hours of sleep I got on the plane. That's happened a couple times. I crash worse than usual and sleep for fourteen hours or more. I guess it's time, things have been going on unusually.

Still, we have a job to do and I think I'm ready to do it again.

I let my eyes flutter open and sunlight is streaming in through the window on the opposite wall.

Logan's breathing, then. Benson would have pulled the blackout curtains. He's nigh-neurotic about protecting my resting space, wherever it may be. I often have to sleep during the day, and he knows I hate it, so he always does his best not to let me know what time it is when I wake up. I haven't woken to a sunny morning in ages.

It's kind of nice.

I don't move, not wanting to let Logan know I'm awake. Not yet. His presence is familiar, not only from our time together at the Curatoria headquarters, but in a way that gathers itself weakly from my tattered memories. I breathe deep, savoring his scent. How odd to be drawing comfort from this sleeping person I've chosen not to be in a relationship with.

But I love him.

And I can't fall back on the *I love you like a brother* platitude because no one should love their brother this way. My body calls to him in a language I'm certain I don't speak anymore. Being with two people, loving and wanting them equally, seems like the most obvious solution in the world.

Except that it wouldn't be fair.

But for a minute, I let myself imagine.

There's nothing particularly intimate about how we're lying—we're scarcely even touching. I'm on my back and he's next to me on his side, with one hand encroaching on my space, sitting rather innocuously on my stomach, just above my hipbone. The sunlight illuminates his features and, even though he's sleeping, his face shows signs of weariness that have nothing to do with sleep. Tiny shadows smudge the skin beneath his closed eyes and I chuckle inwardly at the thought that I don't remember what my own eyes look like without those circles.

I blink at the realization that I don't remember changing Logan back into himself last night. But I evidently did. I know his body so well I can restore him to it in my sleep. I'm not sure if I should be disturbed by that fact or not.

Logan snuffles gently and rolls toward me, his arm pushing all the way across my torso and pulling me closer.

I don't resist, even though it sets our faces so near I can feel his breath and count the tiny freckles on his cheekbones, just barely visible against his tanned skin. Several minutes pass before I realize there's a slight shaking against my stomach.

"You're awake!" I scold, realizing it's Logan trying to hold back his laughter. "Open your eyes, you faker."

He does, and at the sight of those emerald green eyes my mirth melts and I know for certain I should have snuck away while he was still asleep.

I once described Logan's love for me like looking down off an endless cliff into the greatest expanse you could ever imagine, and this is the first time I've seen it so unmasked since the headquarters. It's seductive, his love for me. The knowledge that no matter what I do, what I say, what I look like, this person will love every cell of my body, every thought in my mind, with everything he is, until the day that he dies.

And then some.

It terrifies me. It exhilarates me. If I chose Logan, he would never leave me. Would never love me less than this endless expanse I can see right at this moment that takes my breath away. Benson might theoretically stop loving me one day, despite how he'd protest the very possibility if I voiced it. Logan never will.

As though he can read my mind, Logan moves his face closer still. He's smart, though. He doesn't go for my mouth. That smacks too much of cheating. Instead, he kisses my forehead. Something that *could* be considered friendly and chaste if not for the lightning bolt of desire it sends shooting down my legs.

"How did you sleep?" he whispers, and his lips find my cheek, dragging across the skin to the sensitive spot behind my ear.

I gasp, my arms shaking with the effort it takes to stop myself from pulling him in. Not to go from toeing the line to full-on betrayal. He kisses his way down my neck and my limbs turn to rubber beneath his touch. He reaches my collarbones and his fingers gently push the strap of my tank top off my shoulder, leaving it lying on my arm as I clench what I think are the sheets in my fists, only to discover it's the front of Logan's T-shirt. His lips move lower and my head is starting to swirl with wanting. Still lower those lips travel until they reach my rather low neckline and his finger hooks the edge of the maroon cotton and starts to pull it down.

"No," I say, shoving myself away from his warm body and rolling from the bed to my feet. I pull my strap back onto my shoulder and fold my arms across my middle like I'm cold.

I'm definitely not cold.

I must have changed myself last night, too; subconsciously got comfortable. I can tell I'm in my own body again, and I'm wearing a soft cotton strappy tank top and black pajama pants. My cheeks flush at the realization that they're so loose because they're Benson's—or rather, replicas of something I've seen Benson wear. They hang low, about halfway down my hipbones, prominent since I've gotten so thin.

As though reading my thoughts, Logan eyes those very bones. "You've lost a lot of weight," he says softly, voice laced with concern. "I didn't realize how much. You hide it well."

I resist the urge to transform the pants into sweats and add a floppy sweater. He's right, though. I do hide it. I don't want Logan to know how taxing this quest to save the world really is on me. Logan, or Benson, or anyone. But it is—the travel, creating vaccine, somehow always managing to trail death and destruction in my wake. Benson has learned that it stresses me out even worse to mention it, or to constantly tell me to eat, but Logan doesn't know that yet. I can hardly resent the impulse; I'd do the same thing for someone I loved. But I still grit my teeth when the next words out of his mouth are, "You need to eat. Let me get you some breakfast."

"Thanks, *Dad*," I say, succumbing to the temptation to don a sweater. After all, I could conceivably be cold. I'm no longer under the blankets.

With Logan.

I can't be here.

As soon as Logan's back is turned I flee. I flee from Logan, but I also flee from myself, from who I want to be when I'm with him. I lunge for the door before he can stop me and don't really succeed in not slamming it behind me. I lean my back against it as soon as the bolt clicks and, with a groan, I cover my face with my hands—only to be distracted by movement at my feet.

Benson.

He's sitting right beside the door, with his legs pulled up to his chest. Judging by his bleary eyes and the red marks on his forehead, he's been sleeping with his head propped on his knees.

I drop to a crouch beside him. "Have you been here all night?"

"That depends," Benson says, still blinking as though trying to make out the features of my face. "Is it morning?"

"Indeed, it is," I say dryly. "Come on." I reach out for his hands and pull him to his feet, though he groans in discomfort and his joints pop audibly as he straightens.

Of course Logan picks that moment to burst through the

door. "Tavia! Oh," he says, nearly running into Benson and me. "Well," he says with a smirk I don't appreciate at all. He raises one arm and leans against the doorframe, studying us. Mostly, studying Benson. It doesn't help that Logan isn't wearing a shirt. And it *really* doesn't help that I can't remember if he just took it off, or if he never had one on. I stare at the ground, hating the way they both make me feel like I've done something wrong.

"You don't look like you slept," Logan says, taking in Benson's rumply appearance.

"You look like all you did was sleep," Benson retorts calmly.

I scrunch my eyes shut with a moan. "Don't we have an appointment with a warehouse?"

"Two hours," Logan says smoothly. "Just got a text from Alanna."

Perfect. Two hours to make this all into a much bigger deal than it is.

"Well, I need breakfast," I grumble.

"Come right back in then, Tavia," Logan says, hiding all trace of challenge in his voice. "I don't think Ryder even knows where his room is."

Oh good, we've moved on to last names. "You guys seriously want to have this out in the hall?" The semi-truce between them has been threatening to explode for ages and I'm a little afraid of how loud it's going to get if I can't get it behind closed doors before it boils over.

"Did you expect me to give up and slink away?" Benson asks, ignoring me. "Taking care of Tavia is *my* job right now, and I don't care if you manage to worm your way into her bed, I'm still going to make sure she's taken care of."

Shit. All of Thomas' talk about letting people do their jobs. I thought it was only about putting Logan at the helm. Was he referring to Benson, too? A bit of father-son protectiveness? Or was he warning me not to let a scene like this happen?

"Did you expect *me* just give up and slink away because *you* wormed your way in when she thought I was dead?" Logan retorts. "You can't fight this, Ryder."

"I know."

I turn, open-mouthed to Benson. Logan's been shocked into silence as well and the moment hangs between us for several long seconds. "You can't fight with love at all. You start using it as a weapon and it dies. I'm not fighting. I'm just waiting. Because that's what I'll always do."

"Pretty words," Logan snaps back. "But still selfish at their core." He steps forward and says softly, "You will never love her as much as I do. Not a *fraction* as much. You can't. It's not even your fault. If you really wanted to give her the greatest love in the world you'd walk away and let her have it."

"You think I don't know how big what the two of you have

237

is? You think I don't wonder every day why the hell she stays with me?" He straightens and I remember for the first time in this conversation that Benson is taller than Logan. "But as long as she does, I'm here for her. And you can't stop me."

"I could."

"But you *won't*. Because then you really would lose her." They stand nearly chest-to-chest, but they've reached the end of the argument and they both seem to know it. "I love her," Benson whispers.

"I love her more."

"Then there's a good chance you're going to win in the end."

My heart splinters and I know I can't stand here a moment longer. I can't listen to them saying these things. I push past Logan, back into the room, but as soon as the door closes I transform the bolt into a new one and add another for good measure. I know Logan could use his powers to break in, but I have to trust that he won't. Pushing boundaries is his specialty—not breaking them.

Sure enough, one of them tries the knob, but when it doesn't open, nothing more happens. Once I'm certain that not only is no one going to burst in, but that they've both left the immediate vicinity, I pull my sweater off and head toward the bathroom. What I really need right now is an extremely hot shower and a very large omelet.

CHAPTER TWENTY-SIX

Four hours later I'm coughing behind a bush as I lose most of my breakfast. With the shaky stalemate somehow back in place, Benson is bending over me, making sure I don't fall over, while Logan sees to final preparations for whoever it is we have coming to pick things up.

Let everyone do their jobs, I remind myself, including Benson in that thought as my stomach lurches again.

"You've got to stop pushing yourself that last step when you're angry," Benson says softly, proffering a napkin. "You make yourself sick every time."

"That's rich, coming from you," I mutter, wiping my face.

"I deserved that," he says, not countering it, or trying to explain or justify. "Ginger ale?"

"Seltzer," I say, declining the bottle he's holding and making one for myself.

"You need sugar too," he says.

"I know. But I need this first."

Several minutes later Logan and Audra join us and I've managed to get a couple of saltines down and have moved on to light cookies and ginger ale. The nausea is beginning to abate.

"You okay?" Logan asks, with more concern than I think is really justified. The sad truth is, he's seen me in worse shape than this.

"I'll be fine. As always." I conjure up a cool cloth and pat my face and the back of my neck. "Can we get out of here now?"

"Did it feel any different?" Logan presses. "The batch today, I mean. The whole process."

I shake my head. "My concentration was a little off," I say, shooting him a significant look. "I was kinda going on auto-pilot if you know what I mean."

"Yes," he says, drawing out the 's' in a quiet hiss. "But you made almost a hundred more boxes than usual."

"I got a ton of sleep last night." I'm too tired and irritable to hide my bad mood. Puking will do that to you.

"No, like significantly more than you've *ever* made before. Even before I got here, based on Thomas' guesstimates. Even in Egypt, when you wrung yourself out so badly you couldn't lift your own head." He sends an apologetic look at Audra, but she's staring away from all of us as though the view of the gates surrounding the warehouse is the most fascinating sight in the world.

"That's good, right?" I say, making myself a lemon gelato

and digging in. I've entered the phase where—like the night I scarfed the huge hamburger in Camden—I just have to fill the black hole of my stomach. Sugar begins to hum blissfully through my body and it's a lovely feeling to have the energy to eat.

"I mean, it is, I'm just leery of any kind of change."

But I shake my head. "Same thing happened in Brisbane. Everything got a little easier. I think it's just from pushing myself to the limit often enough. Thomas said no, too," I add as Logan starts to shake his head, "but really, how often have Earthbound pushed themselves like this so frequently and for so long? Rarely if ever would be my guess." I offer a huge carton of sweet potato fries around the circle, but everyone declines.

We all jump when a loud beeping sounds from Logan's pocket—the phone that Alanna calls. Logan has adopted Thomas' approach to buying the same brand and setting the same ringtones whenever possible, so we'll know when a call is important.

"Hello?" Logan says after dropping his clipboard to dig the phone out of his pocket. "Yes, we're fine. No, why?"

We all stand around, but when the color drains from Logan's face, I know it's bad news. He lowers the phone and presses speaker and Alanna's voice blares out mid-sentence. "—New Orleans, Manhattan, all under water. News coming in from London, France, Spain, Japan, Australia. Everywhere with a coast. Flooded."

"Back up," Logan says weakly. "I just put you on speaker."

"A Destroyer somewhere his been killed by the virus," says Audra's voice, sounding all too innocent, even unreal, bursting out of that tiny phone with such dire news. "An island—practically an entire continent—has appeared in the ocean between North America and Europe. It's raised the levels of the ocean by an entire foot in...in moments, really. And the flooding is only the beginning. Every landmass with an Atlantic coastline is going to be hit by a massive tidal wave sometime in the next twenty-four hours and the word is only just starting to get out. We've got some government contacts feeding us the info, and they're saying that while the flooding will be catastrophic, the tidal wave is...it's cataclysmic."

"Can't we do anything?"

She hesitates and a shelf of books could be contained in the words Alanna *doesn't* say at that moment.

"There might be something I can do. And something Tavia can do. But we won't be able to hide it. The Reduciata will know."

Silence falls heavy around us. With a growl Logan kicks his clipboard and it flies at the wall of the warehouse and cracks into pieces. I vaguely realize there's a pain in my hand and I look down to see Benson gripping it so tightly the bones are grinding together.

"Ow, Benson, stop. Ben!" I have to say his name twice before he pulls his attention away from the broken clipboard. He loosens his grip, but his eyes are wide in horror when he pulls turns to look at me.

"Your power increases," he whispers, still staring at the clipboard. "Brisbane. And now. Tavia, I know why you're getting stronger."

And when he puts the two events together, it instantly comes clear to me, too. My mind travels back to so many months ago when the words came directly from Sammi: *That's what the Reduciata are trying to do. They believe that if they can permanently kill enough Earthbound, their power will revert to the remaining gods.*

I feel sick again.

"What am I missing?" Logan asks, reading part of my discovery in my eyes, but not yet seeing all the pieces.

"Sammi, she told me—" I suddenly remember that the entire reason Alanna and Thomas are on our side is because of Sammi and Mark. "Alanna! Did Sammi or Mark tell you why they thought the Reduciata were trying to kill the Earthbound?"

"To harvest their power, basically."

"The...the..." Bile rises in my throat and I have to swallow it down before continuing. "I had a sudden surge in my powers in Brisbane. The morning after the disaster in South Africa. Today it happened again." Alanna is quiet and even Thomas doesn't pipe up. Their stunned silence, more than anything else, convinces me that I'm right. "Before that, even," I say, shifting back and forth on my feet, letting my thoughts flow out in a jumble. "My best breakthroughs in the lab came right after the first death that erased the South Pacific. And the Andes Mountains, that was the day before I made my first batch of the vaccine. Oh gods, it's been happening from the beginning."

"But what you said earlier," Benson says, "about stretching yourself to the limit so often, that's why you're noticing. Small amps wouldn't normally even register, but when you're giving everything you have, you see the difference."

"Well, I don't feel any stronger," Audra says. "But I'm not nearly as powerful as you, Tavia. If we're all getting stronger in proportion to the strength we've already got, then Daniel and Mariana will be more dangerous than ever. Because I suspect they're the second and third most powerful Earthbound in the world."

"You're almost certain right," Alanna says and something about her voice gives me a few seconds of calm. Enough to grasp onto and cling. I take deep breaths, centering myself.

"What do we do?" Logan says. "This revelation is disturbing to say the least, but it's over; we can't change it.

What we need to face now is the flooding and the multiple tsunamis headed toward about a billion people right now."

"During a normal flood there's in influx of water and you have to either divert the water, or wait for it to recede, or to seep into the earth," Alanna says, and she sounds strangely nervous. "We can't do any of those things. What we need is for the water to simply *go away*."

Then I understand. This is something only she and I can do. But like trying to vaccinate the world, it feels like too big a job for one person—even two people—to accomplish. And the idea of going right back to work makes tears of exhaustion prickle in my eyes.

"Alanna, I…I can't. I just finished…I'm too—"

"I know," Alanna says gently. "I'll start. We're near the coast, though secrecy hardly seems necessary now considering…anyway, water is a *simple* substance. It's not like the vaccine. It'll take very little energy to make it disappear. It's doing so for hours at a time that will get wearying, but it might surprise you how much water you can destroy in one go. I want you to go back to your hotel and rest. Eat, sleep, have Audra give you something if necessary. But be ready."

"Ready for what?" I ask, my voice quavering.

"For the Reduciata to take me. That'll be your sign to start."

"What?"

"You're halfway around the world and far more powerful than me. While they're distracted with me, you can do some amazing work."

"Can't you work for a while and then hide? The same way we're doing it now?"

"No," Alanna says firmly. "I need to start, and not stop, for as long as I can. There's no time for travel." She chuckles. "I suppose if I collapse before the Reduciata finds me, I'll do two sessions. But I very much doubt I'll get that opportunity."

"Thomas! Are you even there? Are you hearing this?" I shout.

"I hear," Thomas says quietly, stunning me into silence. "She needs to do this. If I stop her she'll resent me forever. And with our kind, forever is a very long time. What else would you have me do?" When I say nothing he continues. "I told you, Tavia. We all have our jobs. And we need to let everyone do their job. Besides," he adds, a forced cheerfulness in his voice. "Remember what we had to do to Audra in London?"

The tracking device.

"I think turn-about is fair play, don't you?"

I gulp hard, a world of possibility opening up before me. A tracker in Alanna. Finding the Reduciata headquarters. Maybe even Daniel and Mariana.

"I—I don't want to lose her, Tavia. But what kind of future

can any of us have in a world where Daniel and Mariana live?" He pauses again. "I'd do it for her if I could."

"I know," I say, a sob in my voice.

"Now go," Alanna says, her crisp, business-like voice taking over. "I'm afraid vaccine-making will need to wait for a few days. But maybe...maybe by then we'll have a hell of a lot less resistance."

"Please gods," I whisper.

"Everyone does their job," Thomas says once more, and then we hear a click, and the call is over.

CHAPTER TWENTY-SEVEN

Despite the shorter-duration but very powerful sedative that Audra injects into me, my dreams are vivid. And they all feature Alanna.

In my mind I see her walk out into the ocean, far in, perhaps up to her neck. But she doesn't get wet; it's like the story of Moses and the Red Sea; the water effectively parts for her as she makes it disappear for ten feet in every direction. In my dream she's glorious and dressed in a stunning evening gown spangled with sequins that glimmer like the sun against her dark skin—though in reality bare feet and yoga pants are more likely involved.

I try to swim to her, to save her. I see Daniel and Mariana advancing on her from the other direction and I yell and scream and wave my arms. But though she can see me, she can't hear me, and she only smiles and waves as though she's having such fun. I point but she laughs, and when I try to swim to her, the water pushes me away. I try to make the water in my path disappear, but my powers are gone. I've used them all up.

Finite after all.

Salt water fills my mouth the next time I try to shout, and the water forces itself into my throat and nose, burning and choking me. Mariana sneaks up behind a smiling Alanna and the last thing I see as the waves close over my head is the flash of a knife and the unmistakable red of blood pouring into the water.

I sit up with a scream and my tank top is wet with a cold sweat.

"Shh, Tave, it's me."

My wild eyes turn in the direction of the voice and I wait for the dream to continue—for something awful to happen to Benson. But when I grip his arms he's solid and warm and real. I draw breath after breath, trying to push away the pain of drowning, begging for this quiet, dark space to truly be reality. My heart pounds in my chest it takes several minutes to calm down.

"Did you wake me up?" I ask when I finally start to believe that this darkened hotel is real. "Is it time?" I'm not sure what answer I want to hear.

I try to focus on the fact that she's attempting to save the lives and homes of billions of people. Almost a quarter of humanity, in all. Some morbid part of me suggests that it would sure move things along if I only had to immunize four billion people instead of seven. I recoil from the thought, and from the realization that most humans must see this as Kat did when she first came to understand my powers—as a sort of religious apocalypse being visited on them by an angry and incomprehensible deity. Governments are going to break down faster and faster, airports will close, and distributing the vaccine globally will become impossible. As if my quest weren't already absurd to the point of impossibility, now I've got to drain a continent's worth of water out of the ocean.

"No," Benson says, pointing the remote at the television and turning it off. "You woke yourself up screaming."

I look at the blank television screen and the hint of light coming through gaps in the blackout curtains. It's day. "What were you watching?"

He doesn't answer right away and I know he's considering if it would be kinder to lie. But he's always been shit at lying to me so he confesses, "The news."

"Turn it back on. There's no way I'm going to be able to go back to sleep."

"Do you want Audra to give you something to knock you out again?"

I shiver. "No. I'd rather be awake and tired then have that dream again. How long has it been?"

"Six hours."

"That's enough." I point at the TV. "Turn it back on."

"Are you sure?"

"When has hiding from the truth ever helped anyone?"

Benson says nothing, but clicks the TV back on. The volume is still muted, but the images need no accompanying explanation. New York City, flooded. A reporter is standing knee-deep in water in front of the Empire State Building. We watch in silence as the scene changes to a correspondent in London. More images, some stills, some videos, Europe, Africa, South America, cities all over the world, covered in seawater. Grainy videos from helicopters that remind me of the footage from the first incident in the South Pacific are on the screen now, and captions running along the bottom proclaim the new landmass that's about half the size of the continent of Australia. There have probably never been so many geologists on live television in history.

"Do you realize that even if we win, the entire face of the Earth has changed?" I ask Benson.

"Before he left, Thomas told me that he thinks that, best case scenario, the population of the Earth will have decreased by fifteen to twenty percent by this time next year." He rolls his head to the side from where he's lounging on a stack of pillows. "Doesn't sound like much when you say it that way, but we're talking about one to two *billion* people. Billion, Tavia."

"And the only thing either of us can do right now is wait."

Benson hesitates. "If you're not going to sleep anymore,

251

can't you eat and get started?"

I shake my head. "We need the Reduciata fully focused on Alanna before I make a single move." I cover my face with my hands. "I feel like the worst person in the world saying that."

"Maybe I just don't understand this. Why would they take her?"

"Two reasons—to stop her from ruining their destruction, and to dangle her as bait for me."

"And then you're going to walk into their trap?"

"Of course. But I'll know it's a trap."

"You don't think they'll know that you know?"

"Of course, they'll know, Ben," I explode. "Everyone knows everything here. It's a huge game of manipulation. Who can double-triple-quadruple-cross their opponent the best."

"Why then? Aren't we doing just what they want us to?"

I press the heels of my hands against my eyes. "Because it has to end, Benson. I can't ever really win while they're alive to fight me, and they can't win while I'm here to fight them." I drop my hands. "If they've felt the same increase in power that I have—and I suspect that's the case—they'll know their plan is working. And they'll up their game. But they've got to stop me from vaccinating Earthbound or they fail. They've spent almost three *hundred* years finding a way to kill Earthbound to steal their power. And there is one person standing in their way, and that's me."

"Then you shouldn't walk into their lair! You should hide."

"And how many people will die while I'm protecting myself?"

Benson chews on his lip for a while. "But in the long run—"

"*All* the people, Benson, that's the answer. *All* people everywhere will die. I can't live this way anymore." I scoot to the edge of the bed and stand, turning my warm pajama pants into small cotton shorts. "Look at me. Look at the circles under my eyes. My hair is falling out almost as fast as I can transform it into something healthy. Look, look at my fingernails. See how they're blue here at the base? Despite everything I eat, I'm suffering from malnutrition. I can't keep doing this. It's killing me in places I can't use my powers to fix. And if I burn myself out completely, they've still won." I straighten, suddenly embarrassed and cold, and I create an extra large hoodie and push my arms into it. "If I'm going to die anyway, I'd rather go out fighting."

"You won't die."

I smile tightly. "I hope not."

I eat until my stomach is uncomfortable and wait for Logan to knock on my door. After an hour I get impatient and go find him instead.

"Can we get ready?" I ask as Logan paces, looking almost as tired as I felt last night. "Alanna's been working for almost eight hours straight. How much longer can she last?"

Logan shakes his head. "I don't know. She's right that water is a simple substance, but she's got to be reaching her limit."

"And the news hasn't caught on yet?"

"Thomas said he took her to a pretty secluded area, and everyone's cameras are pointed at big cities right now."

"Why haven't they taken her, then?"

He shrugs. "But if they don't, you'll just be waiting longer while she sleeps and recovers and starts again. We can't reveal you until it's worth the risk."

"Worth the risk," I grumble mockingly, even though I know he's right.

"Tavia," Audra stands in the doorway, a huge book in her arms. "I hope no one minds, I stepped out to the bookstore for a second."

"No, no of course not," I assure her, rushing over to put a hand on her arm. Mostly I'm glad she hasn't been sitting her in her room staring at the ceiling. Or whatever it is she's been doing in her state of mourning. This is healthier, isn't it? "Reading's probably a good idea."

"Um, it's for you, actually." She pulls a thick, heavy book out of her shopping bag and I stare, devoid of understanding, at a copy of what looks like a college textbook on Anatomy and Physiology.

"For me?"

"Remember when you saved yourself in Daniel's lab because I taught you about the human throat?"

I nod, seeing where she's going, but the saying *Too little, too late*, is featuring very prominently in my thoughts at the moment.

"You also told me that Daniel once said you could recreate anything you had ever read in any of your lifetimes even if you didn't consciously remember reading it. And you're so powerful you really should only need the shallowest level of knowledge to be able to transform damaged organs into whole ones, even in yourself."

I stare at her. This might be the most brilliant thing any of us have ever come up with.

Audra must see a change in my eyes because she rushes forward and says, "I thought if we flipped through and did even a basic rundown of your entire anatomy, you could heal yourself if…if…"

"Just *if*," I say, letting her off the hook and reaching for the book. "Audra, you're a genius."

"Sergei would want me to be useful," she says, tears shining in her eyes.

"If he was anything like you, he certainly would," I whisper. "Come on, let's get started."

CHAPTER TWENTY-EIGHT

Heavy knocking sounds on the door less than an hour later, as Audra points out various blood vessels that would be most likely to cause fatal internal bleeding.

Logan rises to his feet as my heart races with fear. "Yes?"

"Let me in, damn it."

I'm on my feet and across the room before I've even thought about it; I swing the door open and throw myself into Thomas' arms. "I can't believe it," I babble into his shirt, overwhelmed by his presence. Somehow, having him back here and ready to fight with us—makes me think we might be able to win.

"Glad you made it," Logan says, reaching out to clasp his hand.

"You knew?" I gasp. "And you didn't say anything?"

"Just in case," he says grimly. And with those words the brief joy of our reunion snuffs out.

"Who's with Alanna?"

"Kat." I can tell it almost causes him physical pain to say that tiny syllable. "I left as soon as she was safely out in the ocean. The only way we have any chance against Mariana and Daniel is if we stay one step ahead of them. Part of me says don't put all your eggs in one basket, but a much louder part says stand together." Thomas' cell phone rings and he grabs it out of his pocket, bringing it swiftly up to his ear. "Yes?"

He listens for nearly a minute, then hangs up without saying goodbye.

"Showtime," he says weakly.

"She's gone?"

He nods, swallowing hard. "Just when they thought it wasn't going to happen. Kat said she almost made it to nine hours before she staggered back to shore. That's when the men in black came and took her—when she was at her weakest." He sets a heavy bag on the table. "Pathetic cowards." He pulls a computer out of the bag and several high-tech-looking cases, from which he begins pulling cords and stands and shiny metal bits. "Take her, Logan. Benson, I need you here."

"But—"

"Everyone does their job, Ben," I say quietly, cutting him off.

Thomas' gratitude shines in his eyes, and as he speaks, he focuses back on the pile of tech in front of him. "I need your help getting this all set up. Now don't wear yourself out too much," Thomas cautions me. "You're more powerful than Alanna, so you can get much more done in less time. As soon as we're sure we know where they've taken her, I'll call," he says, glancing back to Logan. "When that happens, you pull Tavia right out. Remember, we're just trying to do some good while they're looking the other way. I have a private jet waiting for us at Lisbon Portela Airport and Tavia can sleep and eat on the plane." He takes a long, shuddering breath. "One way or another, we're going to end this."

Logan threads his fingers through mine as he reaches for car keys with the other hand. I let him, needing something to hold onto right now. But even so, as I pass through the doorway I look back at Benson and mouth *I love you*. Logan pulls me forward before I can see if Benson says anything back.

"How far are we going?" I ask once we're in the car.

"Just a couple miles," Logan says, glancing both ways before pulling out onto the highway. "A swampy beach that no one visits because slimy seaweed somehow isn't glamorous. Who'd have thought?"

We're quiet for a few minutes. "I'm going to have to kill them, aren't I?"

"Someone has to. And I'm not sure anyone else is strong enough. Not to do them both in." He pauses. "You're sure Daniel's alive?"

"Sure? No. But he probably is. The jerks always manage to survive." I look out at the trees flashing by us. "I've never tried to kill someone."

"Not that you remember."

"I *am* my memories, Logan. If I don't remember it, it may as well have never happened."

"Funny, I have a very different point of view on that subject."

"I don't mean—gods, it doesn't matter, Logan. The point is I'm not sure I can kill someone on purpose. I—I offered to kill Sergei for Audra and regretted it later. Am I a bad person for being glad she did it herself?"

"Of course not. No one wants to kill someone."

"Well that clearly isn't true, or we wouldn't be in this situation at all."

"Granted," he mutters darkly.

"I've fought to survive, to protect someone else, and I've fought out of blind desperation. I know my actions have led to people dying, even. Lots of them. But I've never tried to make a specific person *stop living*. What if I can't do it?"

Logan pulls up between two trees on what looks like a dead-end dirt road. He turns in his seat to look at me. "When the moment comes, you'll do the right thing," he says solemnly. "As far as I can tell, the right thing is to kill those two bastards before they can ruin anything else. Then we spend the next few centuries seeing to it that they never, ever, ever get back together. But if there's a better way, you'll think of it."

"I don't think there's a loophole this time."

"Well, I guess I'm the bad person then, because I sure as hell hope you're right. I want them dead for everything they've done. I want them dead forever." He pushes his door open. "Let's go."

We tromp through a field of cattails for about thirty seconds before I grumble at my own stupidity and destroy all the plants in front of us in a small path to the open ocean. "I can't make silly oversights like that anymore," I say with a shaky voice. "From here on out, every moment counts."

"But don't overtax yourself in the process," Logan says, taking both my hands in his. "Like Thomas told us, we're just here to do some good before the real work begins."

I turn to the ocean, so eerily similar to my dream it this morning. After a deep breath I clear a path in front of me so I don't have to fight the surf. The waves disappear in a long line and gravity sends more green-blue water rushing into the void, but each new surge disappears as well. I walk forward until the rapidly disappearing wall of water around me is waist-deep, then I begin to expand my circle.

Alanna was right—it's not difficult work. *So* much easier than the intricate task of creating neatly packaged and labeled vials of a complicated vaccine. I take the opportunity to see how far I can stretch my powers.

I've always known in a vague sort of way that I have to be somewhat close to the matter I'm manipulating, but *how* close has never been an issue. In a few hours, it might be. I spread my arms wide and circle slowly, spreading the expanse of dry sand around me, making the water disappear in a circle of greater and greater circumference. When the span reaches about twenty feet radiating around me on all sides, I realize that while I'm not really pushing my personal boundaries on distance, I'm also not getting much more effective at eliminating the water.

I need to get *deeper*.

I walk forward, holding my circle—my *sphere* of destruction—and after a few minutes, the wall of ocean around me is gaining significant height, reaching my shoulder, then my head. I can feel the pressure of the water pressing in all around me as if testing the limits of my power—but I'm nowhere near that boundary, and I must be destroying millions of gallons every instant. Not much, in an ocean with millions of trillions of gallons in it—not yet. But the whole process is invigorating, like smashing bricks with a sledgehammer when I've spent the last two months painstakingly hand-assembling jewel-precision watches.

I'm hardly even aware of time passing as I watch the sun glint of the blues and greens of the ocean. My Transformist powers change everything that comes crashing toward me into harmless molecules of air—water, silt, seaweed, it's hypnotizing and freeing to simply let loose with such a large amount of power and so little specific focus.

Something tugs at the edge of my consciousness and I pull back very slightly, bringing my circle closer. From the corner of my eye I see a small, dark watercraft, and I gasp and drop my hands, barely resuming a much smaller circle before the thousands of pounds of water closing over my head can rush in and crush me.

"Tavia, come in!" Logan calls from a small boat listing perilously at the edge of my circle. I breathe a sigh of relief, having thought for a moment that I almost made an entire person disappear.

Pulling the circle of ocean close so Logan isn't caught in the eddy, I begin walking back to shore. I'm farther out than I thought, and when I reach the wet, sandy beach I release my powers and let the ocean fall back together. My legs tremble and I collapse onto the gritty sand, tired, for once, in my muscles instead of that deep, bone-wrenching weariness that comes from overextending my powers.

I look down at my arms and push up the sleeve of my T-shirt to reveal a light pink line.

I'm sunburned.

How long was I out there? Or have I just seen so little sun the last two months that my skin is this sensitive?

Logan rushes up to me, his shoes kicking up cascades of sand behind him. "Are you okay?"

I look up and nod. It's hard to put into words how I feel. Ever since the collapse of the Curatoria headquarters I've been pouring masses of power into one tiny, intricate thing, to the point that it's become easy to forget just how powerful I truly am.

But out there in the ocean—the endless, fathomless ocean—pouring everything within me into that basic, life-giving substance, I feel enormous. Like my power could fill the world. Instead of the nauseating emptiness when I'm done making vaccine, I instead feel the kind of revitalizing tiredness I might feel after an intense workout. Worn out, but stronger.

"Yes," I say, when I realize Logan's still waiting for an answer. "I'm okay."

"Look what you've done," Logan says.

I blink and have to force myself to focus after the dazzling reflections of the sea and sun. His arm is spread wide, indicating the entire beach, but I'm not sure precisely what I'm supposed to be seeing.

Oh.

Beach.

I look back at the car, checking before I let myself believe.

It's back where we started, right behind the bed of cattails. And between those and the ocean is a small expanse of beach.

Beach that was underwater when we got here.

"Is it enough?" I ask. Even my hearing seems different after standing in the rush and roar of the ocean. Now there's nothing but the gentle lapping of small waves on the sand and the call of gulls above us.

"I don't know. You were probably destroying water faster than it could arrive from elsewhere; lowering the waterline here doesn't lower it everywhere else, not all at once. But it's definitely something." He lays a gentle hand on my shoulder. "It's a start."

"How long was I out there?" I'm a little embarrassed to admit that I haven't the faintest idea.

"About five hours."

I let out a sharp laugh. "No wonder I'm tired. And thirsty." The buzz of a headache is beginning and I instinctively create a bottle of water to do what I can against the encroachment of dehydration.

Once I've finished drinking Logan stands and reaches out two hands to me. "Let's go."

And in one terrible moment, the bliss and magic of the last five hours—five!—vanishes. "Did Thomas figure out where she is?"

"Not yet, but he says they've stopped flying, so we should start."

"Where are they?"

"Canada."

"How far is that from here?"

"About seven or eight hours, according to Thomas."

"And we have no idea how long we're going to have to drive once we get there?"

Logan shakes his head. "He's got some high-tech stuff back at the hotel, but we may not know for sure until we're on the ground again."

He takes my hand, twines his fingers through mine, and I let him. It doesn't feel wrong; it doesn't even feel romantic. I know that in past lives, even when we were passionate lovers, we must have been friends too. And that's what I need from him at the moment.

"Logan?"

"Yes?" His voice is quiet, like he's afraid he's going to ruin something if he speaks too loudly, and I know he's feeling the moment of closeness too.

"They know we're coming, don't they?"

He's quiet for ten steps. Twenty. We're almost to the car and I'm not sure he's going to answer. "They must. They're not stupid."

"It's a trap."

"A trap we dared them to set."

"A trap within a trap."

"Possibly within another trap," he says wryly.

"But …" I pause, trying to put my feelings into the right words. "In the end, it's not even really about all these games. These puzzles and disguises and manipulations. It's about getting me in the same room as Daniel and Mariana and seeing which of us can kill the other."

He turns to look at me.

"Don't lie, Logan, please. At this of all moments, tell me the truth."

"Yes, Tavia. They want to kill you; you have to kill them. I guess in the end, you're right. It is as simple as that."

"Am I ready?"

"Ready?"

I turn to face him fully. "I'm broken, Logan. I can't remember fighting them before—I won't have the experience and memories you do. And I'm not strong. Not emotionally. Two weeks ago Audra killed the most important person in her universe less than an hour after she found him. I can't even give up Benson to save *you*. And—and—"

"Tavia." Logan's hands are on my shoulders, his thumbs massaging just beside my collarbones in small circles. "You just changed the depth of the *ocean*." He leans forward and brushes my lips with the softest of kisses then whispers, "They should be terrified."

CHAPTER TWENTY-NINE

It's strange to travel without covering our tracks when we've been so incredibly careful for so long. We don't even bother to change our appearances. There's no one to hide from anymore.

Thomas is waiting in a big van when Logan pulls up to the hotel in the little rental car. It feels wrong to ditch an entire vehicle, but the rental company will probably get it back eventually, and anyway we always spring for the best insurance—seems the least we can do given that we rent them with counterfeit credit cards funded with non-backed cash. With a little effort I could probably just create a car, and even Thomas might have that kind of power and understanding of machinery, but creating money has always been so much simpler.

"We've got a seven-hour flight," Thomas says while we all begin to settle ourselves into the small but comfortable private jet. "Tavia, have we worn you out too much?"

I shake my head. "I feel good, actually. I do need some rest, but it's not like with the vaccine. I just need a break."

He stares at me in a way I can't quite interpret until he

whistles between his teeth and crosses his arms over his chest. "Logan told me about the change in the shoreline. For that kind of thing to have simply made you *a bit tired*—you're incredible, Tavia." He laughs bitterly. "I'm glad you're on our side."

This is a Thomas I've never seen before: Bitter and brittle with a palpable air of fear. It's because of Alanna, of course, but it's hard to watch. Especially when I know how much he's depending on me to save her. Still, I try to take the compliment as it's meant and feed it to my dwindling confidence, knowing that even in this state of mind, Thomas wouldn't say it if he didn't believe it was true.

"We have a bed for you in the back," he says, not looking at me, instead pointing vaguely toward the rear of the plane. "Sleep while you can."

I nod, but when the pilot comes in to talk to him I turn to Audra, who's starting to buckle her seatbelt in one of the dozen seats lining the walls. "Did you bring the book?"

"Of course."

"Will you come back here? I have an idea." If she can be creative, so can I.

She joins me in the back where we find a small room with a double bed, adorned with pillows and a beige comforter, as well as a cushy armchair and a small desk off to one side. I don't even want to know what Thomas had to pay for this plane, and I try not to think about how much easier my flights might have been if we hadn't been so worried about traveling incognito.

I explain my idea to Audra and her eyes brighten.

"You're the brain specialist," I say. "Do you think it'll work?"

"I think it's worth a try."

I nod, not pressing her for a more solid answer. "Will this be comfy enough for you?" I ask, pointing at the armchair.

"Totally."

I turn to find both Logan and Benson in the doorway. "Everything okay?" Logan asks. But I know what he's really wondering. Even though it felt more supportive and friendly than romantic, his kiss still burns like fire on my lips.

"Perfect," I say, making myself smile. "This is great."

Then the awkward silence. Cheery.

"I need Benson." I speak more to my shoes than to either of them. I don't want to see if Benson is going to take the opportunity to flash a triumphant smile at Logan; I'd rather pretend he doesn't and believe it to be true.

I don't move my gaze upward until I see Benson's feet slide forward, but when my eyes meet Logan's they're burning with betrayal. "I'll sleep better this way," I say softly. "I need the routine. Now of all times," I add firmly.

The crestfallen look snaps into acceptance and he nods, not

liking it, but understanding.

I've given him far too much room to interpret what I actually said.

"Should I close the door?" he asks tightly.

"I think that's best," I reply, feeling ridiculously formal and stuffy.

He pauses, then seems to need to say something, anything, before retreating. "We'll be taking off soon. I'm pretty sure there's an intercom button back there somewhere. Let me know if you need anything."

"Just sleep," I blurt.

He doesn't reply before closing the door.

It's true, though. Beyond the fact that Audra's sitting right there, seeing everything, Benson has learned in the last two months just how important it is to let me sleep. Within minutes the cozy little jet is lifting of from the runway and we leave Portugal behind. Between the all-too-familiar rumbling of the plane, Benson's comforting presence, and the gentle cadence of Audra's voice, I'm asleep in minutes.

The bump of the plane touching down in Canada jolts me awake and I blink a few times at the room. Audra is still in her place, looking up from the book with questioning eyes, but the desk beside her is covered with the remains of a meal and several mugs and tissues. Benson is lying beside me, headphones in his ears, and until I sit up and stretch, he doesn't notice I've awakened.

"Are we there?" I ask blearily.

Audra reaches for a cup of tea and takes a sip before saying, "Should be."

"Audra!" I say at the sound of her raspy voice. "Did you read to me the whole seven hours?"

"I took a little break in the middle, to eat," she protests.

"Like ten minutes," Benson says, removing his headphones. "It was incredibly boring. I finally had to ask Thomas to make these for me." But I can tell he's impressed with Audra's stamina and determination.

"Do you think it worked?" Audra asks.

"I guess there's one way to find out," I say, as I begin to hear the people in the main part of the cabin moving around. I take a deep breath, and spread my hands. A weight fills them instantly and I send a little hope out to the universe before opening my eyes.

The cover of the book is there, but that's far and away the simplest part. I look up to meet Audra's eyes, but she's leaning forward expectantly and her fingers are clenched white-knuckled around her own copy. I open to about halfway through the book and start flipping through the pages and Audra gasps and then starts half-laughing, half-crying.

"I can't believe this! I was so sure it would work, but that doubt. And there was no way to check and—damn my throat hurts, but it was all worth it."

Her glee is contagious and I grin as I page through the textbook that's nearly complete on the inside. "What about places like this?" I ask, tipping the book to show her a blank section.

"Oh, I skipped things I thought wouldn't be helpful. Like reproduction and fetal development," she says, flushing.

"Um, I think that's okay," I say, avoiding Benson's eyes, though I can feel his stomach bouncing with suppressed laughter.

"I just wanted to make sure we got through all the most important stuff. I skipped a fair bit of the physiology too."

"I hope it's useful," I say quietly.

She smiles and says, "I hope it's not! I hope you never have a reason to use it."

"I appreciate the sentiment," I say wryly, "but we both know that's not likely." This sobers us all, but I reach out and lay a hand on Aura's knee. "Thank you," I say. "Honestly, after what I made you do, I wouldn't blame you if you never wanted to so much as see me again, much less lose your voice trying to help me."

"It wasn't you," she says softly, a shimmer of tears in her eyes. "You were just the messenger. And it's like I told you, I'll find him again. I have a lot more to go on than I ever have before. Plus we resurged. That alone was an incredible gift.

Started the clock again."

The bedroom door opens with no warning and Thomas is standing there, looking grim. "Don major coats guys. Forget summer; it's freezing out there. SUV's waiting—we'll be able to drive for about two hours before we have to go on foot. We'll talk in the car."

And then he's gone.

I start to rise, but Audra catches my arm. "There're a couple of sections I marked to give you later. Possibly..." She hesitates and I don't understand her discomfort. "Possibly the *most* important chapters. But I wanted you to read them awake, when we *knew* it would work. The car ride is probably a good time for that. Here." She hands me the book with three Post-It notes marking spots near the end of the text.

There's no time to ask questions now. A chilly gust of air reaches me from the open cockpit door and I'm yanked back to the task at hand. "Benson," I say, making him a thick, hooded and down-filled coat. A near-matching one appears for me and I slip into it, gathering the puffy front around the textbook still held tight to my chest.

Snow is being blown into our faces like a pelting rain. I don't see Thomas right away, so I turn to Logan. "Where the hell are we?"

"Somewhere on Baffin Island. It's up north, almost to the Arctic Circle. Well, parts of it are in the Arctic Circle."

I shake my head, thinking how appropriate it is that the Curatoria headquarters was in the desert, and the Reduciata headquarters is in the Arctic. It's good strategy, though: both areas are flat and easy to see intruders approaching, and somewhat less than hospitable in terms of climate.

I reach out for Benson's hand as we jog toward the large black SUV waiting with doors open. "You failed to mention that the Reduciata headquarters is in the freaking North Pole."

But he shakes his head. "I was never any place like this."

"Weren't you at headquarters?"

"I thought I was."

"Then what is this place?"

"Wish I could tell you."

We squeeze into the back seat and I see that the two benches are facing each other rather than both pointing toward the front. I settle myself between Logan and Benson—and try not to see the seating as a microcosm of my life—while Audra and Thomas click into seatbelts opposite us.

"Who's driving?" I lean forward and whisper to Thomas.

He holds up one finger, then pushes a button, and what looks like a glass partition rises between our seats. "It's just a guy," he says. "Rental place sent him with the car. Like the pilot. He has no idea what's actually happening."

"Who does he think we are, just driving out into the Arctic Tundra in August?" I ask.

"Rich people are crazy, Tavia. And that's exactly who he thinks we are. Arrive in a private jet on a whim and go snowshoeing, I guess."

"Thomas, you know Benson lived at Reduciata headquarters for several years."

Thomas nods and Benson squirms uncomfortably beside me.

"He says this isn't it."

"I was afraid of that."

"What does that *mean?*" I ask, thoroughly confused. "Are we in the wrong place?"

"No, I'm afraid we're exactly where they want us to be." He heaves a sigh. "Think about it this way—Daniel and Mariana have been jointly running the Reduciata and Curatoria for at least a thousand years. And while each of them have a home base that's full of Earthbound who would literally lay down their lives for them individually, neither of those places is safe for *both* of them." He looks around and meets each set of eyes. "Directly or indirectly, we all know how strong the bond between Earthbound soul mates is. They would have needed a base where they could be together. Where they could put into action their joint plans. Where they could hide their artifacts and the resources they've been using to find each other so consistently over the last many, many lifetimes. A safe place."

"You think we're going to their safe place?" I ask, fear

pooling at the bottom of my stomach. "But it's got to be their most vulnerable spot in the whole world. Why would they let us discover it?"

"Why would *you* let someone walk into your safe haven?" Thomas asks, his face a mask of neutrality.

Logan answers for me. "I'd have to be pretty damn confident they weren't walking out."

CHAPTER THIRTY

"Alanna—well, the tracking device *in* Alanna—stopped moving about four hours ago," Thomas says. "According to our driver, we can get within a mile of the coordinates I gave him. I told him we wanted to go polar bear spotting," he adds with a roll of his eyes.

"Do polar bears even live up here?" Logan asks skeptically.

"Does it matter?"

"Point taken."

"What do we do from there?" I ask.

"Ever gone snow-shoeing?" Thomas says, more an answer than question. "It's the only way."

"Are we absolutely sure we haven't been lured up here by the tracking device and we're going to go out there and find nothing at all?" Benson asks.

"While there is certainly the possibility that Alanna's not really out here," Thomas says, his voice strained and brittle, "and the additional possibility that there's no actual structure, there's no way we've been lured on a fool's errand. They want Tavia—we've given them a way to get her. They're not going to waste time sending us traipsing around in the snow."

"Why not? Us wasting time means we aren't saving people from the virus. Doesn't that fit into their plans too?"

"Except that they know that'll only work on us once. We find nothing out here; we won't go for their bait again. They have one opportunity and they're going to make the most of it." Thomas leans back and looks at me again. "My money's on this being their safe haven."

"So why can't they have sent one sharpshooter who'll put a bullet on all our heads and leave us for dead?" Benson presses, and I suspect he missed a lot of talk lying with me on the plane.

"That only *sounds* easy," Thomas answers in much the same tone one might try explaining algebra to a six-year-old. "But consider the fact that we already feel like sitting ducks out there in the endless expanse of white. This guy would have to hide too. Secondly, it's hard enough to kill a resurged, fully-aware Earthbound under the best of circumstances. But one super-powered Earthbound Transformist traveling with *two* doctors who have a portable EB Scanner—would you make us one of those, by the way, Audra?—is nigh impossible." He shakes his head. "No, I'd wager an armload of my own artifacts that Daniel and Mariana are waiting personally at wherever that little tracking device is leading us."

"Cheery," I say after a brief silence.

"Here's the EB Scanner," Audra says, handing Thomas a small gray box. "And on that note, Tavia has some studying to do."

I open the textbook and lean back against the seat with my knees pulled up to my chest, careful not to lean toward either Benson or Logan as I spread the book open and begin skimming through the chapters Audra marked for me. I shut out the sound of the guys all discussing which weapons will be the most effective, and how best to create them without letting the driver know what we're doing. Weapons mean killing and I'm afraid dwelling on that aspect of our mission before it even really starts will just make me nervous. I focus instead of whatever subjects Audra has deemed important enough to receive my full, conscious, attention. My eyes widen as I understand why she said they were so important.

"Audra?" I say, and she turns to look at me with somewhat guilty eyes. "Tell me the difference between CC's and milliliters."

***

"That's the end of the road," our driver says when he pulls to a stop and taps on the partition a little over an hour later.

"How can you tell?" Logan asks under his breath, peering through the windshield in front of us.

I turn around and look behind us, where our tracks are still visible—though I suspect they won't be in five minutes—and I can't even distinguish where the road begins and ends to the right and left, much less turns from pavement to dirt.

I'd just finished skimming the last chapter that Audra marked for me when the SUV stopped, and now I find myself in the awkward position of having to trust what Daniel told me about how I can be only vaguely familiar with concepts and matter in order to Transform them. I sure hope he's right.

"Okay," Thomas says, "Everyone needs full snow gear: hat, goggles, scarf, coat, gloves, snow pants, and snow boots. White for camouflage. Tavia, you take care of yourself, I'll get Benson."

I nod, my mouth dry, my heart beating wildly. All this time it's been easy to focus on where we were at the moment, not where we are going. But now it's a short walk away from whatever's waiting for us in Daniel and Mariana's trap.

And I feel woefully unprepared.

We do put some effort into not letting the driver see us actually using our abilities, but I can't help but wonder, as we all awkwardly tromp off into the snow, where he thinks all these big white bags hanging over our shoulders came from, when we didn't bring them into the SUV with us. And surely he'd be horrified to discover they're full of semi-automatic handguns and assault rifles.

"Okay, come here, everyone," Thomas says after we've hiked down into a shallow dip, taking the big SUV out of sight. "I promise I haven't been wasting the time I've had with Dr. Martin and Alanna." He goes to Benson first and puts his hand on either side of the hood Benson has over his head. Benson stands still for a few seconds and then jerks away, reaching his hands to where Thomas' were.

"Bullet-proof helmet," Thomas says softly. "Get back here, son."

I can't help but smile. It's the first time I've ever heard Thomas refer to Benson that way.

Thomas puts his hands on either side of Benson's ribs this time and, though Benson doesn't flinch away, I see the moment when whatever Thomas has done takes effect. "State of the art Kevlar vest. Not available to the general public." He looks at me and grins. "Like I said, gotta have those spies in the government."

"Yours just happens to be your wife," I say.

"Hey, I have good taste."

It's a joke, but no one seems to be up for a laugh.

"Okay, guys," Thomas says, "come get 'em."

Once we're all outfitted in the heavy duty armor we start walking again. I don't like the feel of the vest, and the helmet makes my head too heavy to move efficiently, but I figure if it's really in my way, I can take it off once we get wherever we're going. This is for those sharp-shooters Benson talked about.

"What's that?" Logan asks, after we've been trudging along for about fifteen minutes. I only hear him because he's so close behind me he's almost treading on me.

We've crested a hill and there are rows upon rows of black rectangles as far as I can see. Thomas hesitates, then says, "Solar panels. Of course. They would want their safe haven to be entirely self-sustaining should something like, oh, the destruction of the world due to the permanent deaths of a dozen Earthbound, occur. Adjust your expectations if necessary. We should expect this love-cottage to essentially be a survival bunker that could withstand a zombie apocalypse."

Logan pipes up. "From what little I can see, it looks like a huge, square field of panels."

"Then I suspect we'll find the actual residence at the very center. Be careful guys; this is a great place for assassins to jump out from behind panels. Guns to the ready?" he asks Benson.

"Yeah, I think it's time," Benson says grimly.

Thomas tosses his duffel down and unzips it. I feel a little sick at the array of firearms within. Guns have never been my thing; not even back in the day in Portsmouth when people were shooting at me. Nonetheless, my dad taught me how to use several different kinds and I don't argue when Benson puts a semi-automatic pistol in one of my hands and two loaded clips in the other.

"I don't think you should carry a rifle," he says. "You're more dangerous on your own anyway."

"Thank you," I reply, and I don't really care whether he thinks I'm thanking him for his pseudo-compliment or for letting me off the hook. Some of both, I suppose.

We travel two abreast down the shallow dip to the wide expanse of solar panels, all pointing straight up despite the fact that they'll catch no sun today. I creep forward slowly, right in the middle of the pack, startling at shadows and expecting a wild Earthbound, hungry for my death, to pop out from behind a panel at any moment. But all that actually happens is that the heavy structures block much of the wind and everything is quieter than it's been since we left the SUV.

Logan begins to whisper something to Thomas, but Thomas cuts him off with a sharp hand motion and Logan goes back to scanning the peripheral with his gun.

We move so slowly it takes nearly twenty minutes before we reach the center of the panels. In the heavy snowfall the clearing appears quite suddenly and we have to back up to crouch behind the final row of solar panels to stare at the unexpectedly small gray structure, flanked on all sides by the fields of shiny black rectangles. It's hardly more than a single-room shed one might expect near a weather station.

"That's it?" I ask skeptically. "Do you think they're all just standing inside that door?"

But Thomas is already shaking his head. "They're Destroyers. They make matter go away. It'll all be underground. Better insulation, fewer materials. Alanna could be directly beneath our feet."

We all stare, unmoving at the small building. At that solid steel door.

"Think we're supposed to ring the doorbell?"

CHAPTER THIRTY-ONE

"No really, though," I add, when all five sets of eyes turn to glare at me. "What do you think they're expecting us to do?"

Benson hesitates, then says, "Make the door disappear and creep in?"

"Exactly," I say. "Why don't we take out the entire upper floor and leave a huge hole, exposed to the elements, for them to deal with on top of us?"

"She has a point," Logan says. "They'll expect us to be sneaky."

I look down at the ground. "I might be able to take out all this dirt and just let the solar panels collapse on top of it. Might cave in the entire thing."

"Let's not forget that Alanna's in there," Thomas says. "If collapsing an enormous pyramid didn't kill Daniel last time, I suspect trying to do so with a completely unfamiliar structure of unknown size isn't our best way to go this time around."

I have to give him that. "Okay. But that," I say, pointing at the small station sticking up out of the snow. "It can just go."

"All right," Thomas says. "Here's what we do. Everyone

take out a gun—you're choice," he adds before anyone can ask, "and we start to run. Tavia, right before we hit the building, make it disappear, floor too, please, if you can manage, and guys, we're jumping into a black hole."

We all nod somberly.

"Lose the snowshoes," Thomas says, quickly unbuckling his. Benson's strap gets stuck and I make them disappear with a glance. "Run quietly," Thomas reminds us all, and then he's out from behind the solar panel and sprinting toward the shed and there's nothing to do but follow and try to keep up.

I focus on the small building and, just before Thomas crashes into the door, I scrunch my eyes closed and when I open them Thomas is disappearing into a dark space. Logan follows less than a step behind.

I can't look. I get close and jump, and only once both feet are in the air do I look down at a sea of faces. I'm moving too fast to count how many and I land hard on stinging feet and am immediately engulfed in arms.

"We've got you," Benson says, and pulls me to the side an instant before Audra hits the ground, her fall softened by Logan and Thomas.

I spin, trying to take in my surroundings. We're in an atrium of sorts that stretches a bit farther than the top structure that isn't there anymore. On all four sides of the rectangular room are wide hallways that lead into varying levels of darkness. I hear footsteps and turn to see two people in black clothing running toward us. Thomas lifts his rifle and fires a volley of shots too close together to distinguish individually, and the figures fall to the ground.

"Thomas!" I scold instinctively.

"Tavia, this is not the moment to be confused about precisely why we're here," Thomas says in a voice so harsh I flinch away. "And that is to kill everyone who isn't on our side, and leave with as many people who *are* as possible." When I say nothing he looks away and says softly, "We're past mercy, Tavia. It's time for vengeance."

"Split?" Audra says coolly, seeming entirely unnerved. I have to remember that she has killed someone. Someone she loved. I guess after you've done that, killing an enemy isn't so hard. It's not something I ever want to find out for sure.

"No way," Thomas replies. "We're stronger together." He pulls a small instrument out of his pocket that looks kind of like a cell phone. "Tracker's roughly this way," he says. "Let's go."

I keep my gun pointing toward the ceiling as we jog down the hall together. I try not to think too hard about the fact that we're a bunch of amateurs engaging a private security force of some kind. Powers or no, it's completely insane—but I'm trying to remember that we're simply not going to be able to save the world while Daniel and Mariana are around to slow us down.

Here and there I see cameras and, like when we broke into the Mayo clinic that first night in Phoenix, I make them disappear. Whatever I can do. Even so, I can't fathom a scenario in which Daniel and Mariana don't know we're here. They hold all the cards and I can picture them in a room far underground, watching us on a screen and sending out whatever obstacles they think most effective.

And in that instant I doubt everything we're doing. For all it seems absolutely necessary, it also feels utterly impossible.

My steps slow, but Audra presses gently on my back. "All we can do is try," she whispers in answer to my unspoken thoughts.

I turn away when I hear Thomas' gun let loose another round of shots, but it's hard to miss the bleeding, twitching bodies as we slip past them, hugging the wall. The hall turns and then there are doors lining both sides.

"Tavia," Logan says, "can you take the doors out along the entire hallway?"

I'm not sure there's anything he could have asked that would have restored my confidence so significantly. With a grin I pocket my gun and fling my arms out in front of me. All along the corridor, the doors vanish.

The halls come alive with people dressed in that uniform black, swarming like a hornet's nest just knocked from the eaves. Thomas and Logan open fire. At least ten people fall and the rest duck behind doorways. At the first crack of return fire, Logan throws up a metal shield on wheels that we all crouch behind.

"Audra, Tavia, go on either side and push the shield forward as we take people out," Logan orders.

I spare just a moment to shed my heavy coat and position myself on the left side of the shield in a long-sleeved black T-shirt and my Kevlar vest. An earsplitting crackle of bullets sounds against the barrier. "Push!" Thomas says, and Audra and I slide the shield forward.

The shield reverberates ominously as bullets ping off its surface.

"Push!" Logan gives the order this time.

Audra and I shove together, but within seconds, we run into something. "Keep going—push through it," Benson says, and what he *doesn't* say tells me everything. We're running into bodies. I choke down a gag and push again, harder this time. In a few seconds a smear of blood appears as I continue to shove the shield forward and all I can do is avert my eyes and press with my shoulder again. I reset my feet but stumble forward onto a warm, unmoving body when the entire shield disappears.

"Destroyer!" Thomas yells as I roll off the dead body and scramble to my feet trying to look every way at once and decipher some kind of order or pattern in the chaos surrounding me.

A hand wraps around my upper arm and yanks me to the side so hard my shoulder burns. My gun is up and pointed directly between his eyes before I realize it's Benson, standing a few feet from Thomas. I thrust the barrel of my gun upward, pointing it at the ceiling before I can accidentally shoot the guy I love in the face.

"Hurry," Thomas says. "There's a door back here and that's where the tracker should be."

"But—" Logan and Audra are on the other side of the hallway, and every time one of them pops their head out to take aim and shoot, they're answered with a deafening volley of gunfire. There's no way they can get to us, or us to them.

"Everyone has a job, Tavia. Trust them to do theirs. We have to be fast. This way!"

As I run away from them I feel like my heart splits in two and one piece stays with Logan and Audra.

We hustle through a door and Thomas slams it behind him almost without slowing. There are two more sets of doors before Thomas enters what looks like a surgery suite in a hospital, complete with a gurney and those greenish-blue drapes all over the place.

Thomas stomps over to the gurney and yanks the drape off, but it was evident from the moment we walked in that it was empty.

Beside the gurney is a cart full of gleaming metal instruments and what looks like a large bowl covered in a bloodstained blue cloth. Thomas sweeps aside the cloth and grips a stainless steel bowl with both hands so hard the bowl begins to shake and whatever's inside rattles against the sides.

"Thomas?" I ask tentatively.

He reaches into the bowl and removes a bloody square. His jaw is clenched so tightly it makes my own mouth hurt, and I let out a shriek when he turns and lobs the tracker chip at the wall, where is shatters with a soft crunch. His anger boils over and he shoves the cart into a shelf where the instruments rain onto the ground in a clatter before he overturns the gurney with a growl.

I start to reach out to him, to remind him that we don't have time for this. But even as I do, Benson's hand closes soft but firm around my forearm and I pause. I remember how many years Benson lived with Thomas, even if it was a decade ago—he knows Thomas' temper better than I do.

And he's right. A few seconds later Thomas runs his fingers through his hair and takes a few deep breaths. Having regained hold of his control, he reaches down and picks up his rifle and spins in a slow circle. "Okay, this way is north; that's the direction the hallway was going when we were attacked. If we travel directly through the walls going parallel, we should run into something."

I stare, not quite comprehending the logic of his plan.

He shrugs helplessly. "It's a start," he says. "We can't go backward. The only way we have any chance of success is to move forward."

I want to scream at him that going backward is the best way to rescue our friends, but he's right. Achieving the big goals means continuing onward.

I look toward the northern wall, which is the same one he threw the tracker chip at. "Thomas, we know she was here less than four hours ago, when the tracker stopped moving. The blood on that chip proves it. Chances are she's still here. And if they had killed her when they removed the chip, there would've been more blood." I lay a hand on his arm. "Don't give up hope."

"I never give up hope where Alanna is concerned," he says, sounding weary, but not beaten.

"Then let's go find her." I open up a hole in the wall, transforming the soil I find there into a long tunnel, reminding me of Quinn's and my house in Camden.

Hopefully this tunnel will have a happier ending.

On the off chance that Audra and Logan not only get away, but figure out where we've gone, I leave the hole open and ask Benson to keep a good eye on our back and yell if he sees anything. *Anything.*

We stumble out of the tunnel into random rooms twice, and change directions each time.

"Maybe we need to descend to a lower floor," I suggest.

"Maybe," Thomas echoes, but he doesn't seem entirely convinced.

But a few seconds later I run into a steel wall.

"Can't you get through it?" Thomas asks, confused.

"I *can*," I say, laying a hand on it. "But strong walls don't only keep things out. I'll take it layer by layer to make sure we're not bursting into something like a nuclear reactor, because that ends the story for everyone here."

"Maybe it would be worth it," Thomas mutters and I glare at him.

"Or," I say acerbically, "it could be a high tech vault full of poisonous acid and we all die of painful death and no one rescues anyone and Daniel and Mariana win."

"I'm sorry," Thomas says quickly. "By all means, be careful, but hurry."

Turns out it's a normal wall with a thick sheet of steel on both sides, but the fact that is was so reinforced makes me edgy. I transform a tiny peek hole in the final layer of steel just to be sure nothing fatal is going to come pouring out, but all I can see is an empty room. Empty in that there's no movement; there's something in there, I just can't tell what.

"I think we're clear," I say, widening the hole. We step out tentatively, leading with our guns, shoulder-to-shoulder in a tight triangle with all directions covered. It's only at Thomas' cry of dismay that I drop my stance and turn.

He's running forward to a contraption I don't comprehend and is only a few feet away when Benson barks, "Stop! Don't touch her."

Thomas halts, hands outstretched like he can't help himself, but at Benson's warning he doesn't move forward. I walk up beside him and feel an awful sickness when I realize what I'm looking at.

It's Alanna.

She's lying on her back and draped in such a way that her bare stomach is exposed with a conical apparatus just above it. Perched atop the cone thing is a tiny round sphere made of very thick, transparent material that I assume is glass. Her hands are spread wide to each side, her legs extended straight down in a T, and her hands and feet are encased in some kind of steel that holds her captive.

She's not awake, she but appears to be sleeping, not dead or in pain or anything. Just not…conscious. "What is that?" I whisper.

"A prison for an Earthbound," Benson says grimly. "It's brilliant, actually. Sadistic and twisted, but effective. Stop!" he says again when Thomas takes another step forward. "Look," Benson says, laying a hand on Thomas' shoulder and pointing.

"Those spring-triggers there, and there. And I assume there are more at her feet that we can't see. And that," he says, pointing at the small sphere of thick glass with a marble-sized core of what looks simply like water, with disgust, "is dimethylmercury. A blood poison that kills you very slowly with only a tiny amount of exposure."

The words sets off a spark of memory, but it's not what I need right now, so I push it away. "How can you tell? It doesn't look like anything."

His face flushes. "They used to use it to...to question people back at the Reduciata headquarters. It didn't ever seem important before or I'd have said something. I'd kinda pushed the memory away, really. It's—it's more than torture. Worse than torture. And they would—" He takes a shuddering breath. "Doesn't matter. Point is, I'd be willing to bet that's what that stuff is."

"Her chest is rising," I say, catching the small movement. "She's alive, at least." I'm grasping for hope now. Seeing Alanna in this awful device feels like something is ripping into my chest and I can't even imagine what it does to Thomas who's standing silent and white-faced.

"For the moment," Benson says tightly. "But if she wakes up and moves, or if *we* try to move her, we'll spring those triggers and the mercury will be released. Even if we could get her out of those things encasing her hands and feet, she'd be dead in a couple months tops. I don't know that even Tavia could save her—the poising spreads and contaminates the inner organs so quickly and in such infinitesimal amounts."

"What about those things on her hands and feet?" Thomas rasps, his voice tight as a bowstring.

Benson swallows hard. "Judging by what I know of how the Reduciata thinks, I suspect that beneath that flat layer of steel is some kind of complex material laced with either poison, or a corrosive acid, or something. Something that would prevent Tavia—or at the very least they *think* will prevent Tavia—from vanishing it in a single go." His head swings right to left as he studies the set-up, and then he shakes his head. "No, even then, you'd have to be able to do all four limbs at the same time *and* get her off the table, or you'd spring the weight triggers and it wouldn't matter that you'd freed her hands and feet—she'd still be exposed to the mercury."

"What about vanishing the mercury sphere first?" I say. The sphere seems to be fairly straight forward—I think I could do that.

"No good. Look at those lasers." Benson points at four scanners still part of the contraption, but well away from the central sphere. "Four scanners—the wiring leading downward. I bet they go to things on her hands and feet and trigger them to release whatever is inside is the sphere is disturbed."

"So hands, feet, *and* mercury sphere all at the same time?" I ask.

"And exactly right on the first try."

"Gods."

"And, of course, the *coup de grace*, she's unconscious and completely unable to use her own destructive powers. Or help us. And if she wakes up, or even tosses about in her sedated state, it springs the triggers." He takes off his glasses and rubs his eyes. "I always wondered how to capture a fully-awakened Earthbound. Now I wish I didn't know."

"It's sadistic."

"Of course, two Destroyers who knew exactly what they were doing, working in tandem, could release her."

"We don't have two Destroyers."

"Which they know. No one but Daniel and Mariana can get her out of this."

"And they never will," I whisper. *She's here to die.* But I don't say it out loud. I can't. Not with Thomas standing here.

"What do I do?"

I've never heard Thomas sound so helpless. The man who has led us all over the world with his cunning and clear-headed plans is at a total loss, his arms limp by his side, a state of the art automatic handgun dangling uselessly from his fingertips.

It takes me only a heartbeat to accept the inevitable. "You stay here," I say. "You study this thing and try to figure out a different way. Also, if she begins to wake up, you'll need to put her out again, without setting off the springs."

"Because it would be just like them to only give her enough sedative to last long enough to let her die before my eyes." His voice sounds dead.

"They underestimate us," I insist. "They underestimate *you*. And they'll be sorry."

He stands so still he scarcely seems to be moving. "I can't even touch her," he finally says, his voice quavering.

I step close to him. "I'm going to find a way out of this," I vow. "I promise. I will not let her die."

He turns those empty eyes to me.

"I've spent months trusting you, Thomas. It's your turn."

He stares, his eyes dissecting me, peeling back layers. But I stand and stare right back, daring him to question me. After a few seconds he must see something that changes his mind, because the tiniest spark of hope reappears in his eyes and he nods resolutely.

I take the gun from his fingers and pull mine out of my pocket so I have one in each hand. "Come on, Benson," I say, low and steady. "I'm going to kill them."

CHAPTER THIRTY-TWO

We use doors, at least for now. Skin-crawling as it is, I'm starting to think like Daniel and Mariana, and I know without the slightest doubt that they wanted us to end up in that room. To see what they'd done with the bait we sent them. That means that there must be multiple ways to end up there, leading in from everywhere.

And if the hallways from everywhere lead to that room, those hallways also lead back out to wherever we actually want to be.

Sure enough, right after the first hallway is a corridor that splits three ways. One of them leads to a door that overlooks a flight of utility stairs leading downward. I glance at it, and then back to Benson. "I bet we find them at the very bottom of this hellhole."

"Agreed," Benson says, holding his rifle in front of him.

"Down we go."

We descend the stairs as quickly and quietly as possible, ending up on a floor that looks identical to the one we were on before. We jog down hallways, and I make doors disappear like before, but this time we see no one. After a few minutes we find another set of stairs and head down another level.

Three empty floors go this way—a labyrinth of corridors to find the next set of stairs, but every room we pass eerily empty despite other signs of life. Beds, belongings, machinery, rooms full of files and banks of server equipment, a kitchen, a cozy study. But no people.

"Do you get the idea we're going the wrong way?" Benson asks.

"Actually, I get the idea that we're going exactly the right way. According to them. False sense of security—wanting us to relax at just the wrong time. So *don't*," I add, unnecessarily.

At the bottom of the next stairway I pull up short. "This floor is different," I say, peering out the window in the door at the bottom of the stairway. "It's smaller. I think we're getting there. Guns ready." We step slowly from the stairwell and I spread my arms out to both sides, trying to cover as many directions as possible with the guns in my hands.

But this room is empty too.

It's a larger room—nearly the size of that first atrium—and there's only one hallway leading off of it.

"Wait," I say when the tip of Benson's rifle drops a few inches. "Footsteps," I add in a whisper.

We can both hear them now. The squeak and patter of a good half-dozen sets of feet. "Be ready," Benson says, his gun trained on the hallway. A few seconds later a group of the black-clad people burst around the corner, but these ones are better-prepared than the ones we met five floors up. Three drop to one knee with shields held in front of them. Their guns poke out around the sides of their shields and they begin shooting. I barely see the other three line up semi-protected behind them, and lower their guns to shoot over the tops of their comrades' heads.

I throw up my own heavy shield and Benson and I duck behind it as bullets clang against the metal.

"Give me some slits to see through," Benson instructs. "And a hole for the barrel of my gun."

I obey and make a similar pattern for myself, then peer through my slits and position the barrels. A smattering of shot sounds from Benson beside me and the force of his bullets knock one of the guards out of his crouch, exposing him directly to me. I focus, take aim…

And freeze.

My shot is clear and I can't take it.

Benson's eyes dart over to me and my paralysis must show in my face because he sets his jaw with grim determination and next thing I know a line of blood blossoms across the guard's chest. If he's not dead now, he will be momentarily.

Two more guards fall while I remain paralyzed.

Benson curses and flings his rifle away, grabbing the one

strapped on his back. In thirty seconds, it's over. The heavy smell of burning gunpowder burns my throat. Benson rises slowly to his feet, rifle still pointed forward, but the people are dead.

"Ben, I'm sorry," I start, my voice cracking. "I froze. I don't know what—"

"It's okay," Benson says. But his voice is tight. He's never killed anyone before today, either. He creeps forward carefully, but no one on the other side of the room moves. "I managed and we're still walking. Save it for Daniel and Mariana."

"I don't think so."

A woman's voice sounds from behind me and a sharp grip pulls on the back of my T-shirt, yanking the collar against my throat, as something cold and hard pushes against the back of my neck.

"Tave!" Benson whirls and lifts his gun, looking, from my perspective, as though he's pointing it directly at my head.

Whoever has me is attempting to be clever, holding the gun where I can't see it. They're assuming that if I can't get some kind of sense of it, I can't make is disappear. But I've learned a lot in the last few months. If this person were an Earthbound they would have attacked me with their powers—this is just a human.

And no human on earth can stand against me.

Benson's eyes widen in horror. "Mom?"

Well, maybe one human.

Benson's arms begin to tremble, making the rifle shake visibly. I have to restore his confidence within the next few *seconds* or this woman will truly comprehend her power over him.

"Ben, think about this," I say, forcing my voice to be steady. "I'm in absolutely no danger."

"No danger?" the woman mutters, sounding surprisingly like Benson. "Please."

I'm glad I can't see her. I only vaguely remember one snapshot, framed back at Benson's house in Portsmouth, and noting that he looked like her. I don't want to know if she has his eyes, his crooked smile, that wry arch of his eyebrow.

"She's here to get to you, but you have to know I'm good. You know that, right?" I stare straight at him, and his gaze darts madly from my eyes, to over my shoulder.

Finally he blinks, and I see control start to seep back in.

"Your decision, Ben, and no pressure. I'll spare her if you want me to."

"Someone's waiting to see you," the woman says gleefully, as though I hadn't spoken. She's pushing me toward the single hallway and I'm pretending to stagger, slowing us.

"You decide, Ben. No guilt, either way." I refuse to break eye contact, even as she mutters crazily in my ear.

"I saw them bring in my husband's bitch," she whispers.

"They're going to kill her too, when this is all over. Mariana understands. She understands what he did to me. She's going to let me kill her." She giggles. "And then him."

"Mom, no—"

"I hope they make him watch. That would—" She takes a deep breath, like she smells something delicious in the air instead of the acrid stink of gunpowder. "I'll finally be free," she says softly.

We're almost to the hall and I can only pretend to stumble over my feet so many times. "I need a decision, Ben."

Our gaze never breaks, that gun still pointing almost directly into my face, his hopefully calm finger tense on the trigger.

"She said I could kill you too, if I had to," his mom says, leaning forward to whisper the words in my ear, even though her voice carries easily around the silent room.

A deafening crash fills my head and I gasp as something wet sprays my face.

"Oh gods," I say, my knees feeling wobbly as I realize it's blood.

Benson's mother's blood.

He shot her when she stuck her head out too far to whisper in my ear.

He killed his own mother.

Benson hasn't moved—not an inch. His gun still points just

over my shoulder and I can hear his breathing coming in loud, heaving gasps as a tiny stream of smoke seeps out of the barrel of the rifle. I turn slowly, not wanting to take any chance of startling him at this volatile moment.

She's lying on the floor, her eyes open but unseeing, a hole in the center of her forehead. The wall behind her is sprayed with blood and worse, with more already pooling beneath her.

So much blood.

Even if I were to do everything in my considerable power right at this moment, there would be no saving her. She's so very, very dead.

I walk slowly toward Benson, my hand outstretched, entreating. I sidestep the barrel of the rifle and admit to myself that I feel better once it's not pointed at me.

"It's okay—she can't hurt you anymore. Or me. Or Alanna," I add, reciting all the people she just threatened to harm. "Or Thomas," I add for good measure.

The gun finally starts to drop and tears are streaking down Benson's face. He turns away and swipes at them angrily with his sleeve, but I cover the last two steps and take his face in both my hands, the tears wet on my thumbs.

"It's okay. You don't have to hide this from me. Oh, Benson, you never have to hide from me." I wrap both arms around his chest, bulky from his vest and packs of extra ammunition, but underneath all that, he's still my Benson, and

I hold on tight like I could squeeze everything that hurts out of him.

And into me.

If only it worked that way.

Benson's arms envelop me and his chest shakes as he buries his wet face in my neck. I know we could stay there, locked in our embrace for hours, and miss saving anyone, so as soon as he draws a long, shuddering breath, I push him back so I can look him in the face. "We have to keep moving," I say, feeling like the biggest jerk in the world for not being able to give him more time. But Daniel and Mariana knew exactly what they were doing when they sent Benson's mom in, and I want to stay out of whatever trap they're hoping to spring next.

"There's only one place left to go," I say, grabbing my handgun from the floor and handing the other to Benson. I turn to the single hallway that Benson's mother was dragging me toward. "And who am I to argue with Fate?" I whisper.

"Fate," Benson scoffs. "More like maniacal, sociopathic manipulators."

"That too," I say dryly. "Let's watch our back this time."

"Good plan," he says in a mock-chipper tone.

Handgun stretched out in front of me, I walk slowly forward. Benson is at my back, his own gun scanning the room behind. We work our way around the corner, encountering no further resistance. "There's a doorway at the end of the hall," I whisper. "The door's open. I can actually see into the room beyond. It looks like one of those super fancy hotel rooms."

Benson chances a fast glance. "Like the one we stayed at in Madrid."

"Exactly. I think this is…their room."

"Why would it be standing open? We haven't exactly been quiet. If they're in there, they have to know *we're* out here."

"They're waiting for us."

"Then what was the point of…all that?" Benson whispers under his breath. "Alanna, the guards, if they expected us to make it this far, it seems like a waste."

"It's a vendetta," I growl. "They hate—" Something shoots up from the floor, wrenching my ankle and knocking me over. Reflexively, I flail, dropping my guns and nearly spraining my wrists and shoulder against the cold, hard floor. I scramble to my feet and turn to Benson—

Only to face a stainless steel wall.

I almost destroy it with a thought, but then I realize what's really happening. Daniel and Mariana have known me for longer than I can remember. Have been *close* to me. They know the way I think, the way I react, better than anyone but Logan himself. Maybe. They've put obstacles in my way crafted to separate me from everyone I have left in the world— deliberately, carefully.

And now every single one of them is being held hostage,

even though Alanna is the only one in obvious chains. We're *underground*. If Daniel and Mariana wanted to simply kill us, they could destroy a few supports and bury us alive. I might escape, but Benson wouldn't have any chance at all. And even if Logan, Audra, and Thomas created something in time to save their own lives, digging their way out would be exhausting—maybe verging on impossible.

If I destroy this wall, I feel certain it'll release something that will kill Benson.

Daniel and Mariana want me alone.

I put my back against the wall and give myself a few moments, covering my face with my hands and forcing back tears. I can imagine Benson pounding the other side with his fists and probably shouting too, though I don't hear anything. I suppose it's possible he's dead, but I don't think so. Daniel and Mariana learned from their past mistakes. They know *I'm* willing to die, if that's what it takes to ruin their plans. I've given life up before. But as long as I have people too protect, there are things I can't do.

Of course, I'm in no position to share these insights with Benson. He doesn't know I'm alive; might not figure out why I'm not simply making the partition disappear. Briefly I consider trying to make a tunnel through the walls and around the ominous steel, but considering this is Daniel and Marie's private quarters I suspect there are Earthbound-proof traps everywhere.

Killing myself at this point will help no one. Thomas was right. There's no going back; there's only pressing forward. I spread my hand wide on the chilly wall and imagine I can feel the reverberations of Benson's fists.

Then I walk away.

I pause only to pick up one of the guns I dropped—it seems silly to walk in there with *nothing*. But the truth is, a gun won't matter, and all three of us know it. Daniel and Mariana are waiting for me and this gun may as well be a decorative fake for all the good it's going to do.

But it's something.

The double doors beckon me, inviting me into a room of thick, soft carpet, a hint of elegant furniture, paintings done in bright, brilliant colors. It seems an odd place to die.

I pause, my toes right at the line where the cement floor meets lush carpet. It feels like the boundary into a magical world.

Over the threshold I go.

Pain hits me first, followed by the sharp, staccato drum roll of automatic weapon fire. My head snaps backward and Thomas' protective helmet rings like a church bell in my ears; it feels like someone hit me in the face with a sledgehammer. My body is falling, back and to the left, but the drum roll continues, bruising me where I'm armored, piercing me where

I'm not. I distinctly feel a rib shatter and the breath of surprise I'm drawing is one more instrument in a symphony of agony.

I exist only in a world of pain and noise.

As I hit the ground, I'm struck with the absurd thought that I'm glad the carpet is so soft.

CHAPTER THIRTY-THREE

Audra's voice is whispering in my ear.

Arterial walls, superior vena cava, main stem bronchus, meninges, sympathetic ganglion, femoral and saphenous veins.

My heart is battered, but not bullet-ridden, and it delivers the dwindling oxygen in my system to my scarred and probably now concussed brain—also whole, thanks to Thomas' foresight. I hold my breath as I transform my screaming lungs into new, whole ones, and take a tentative breath.

Bearable.

Now I won't lose consciousness—not from oxygen deprivation, anyway. My face is wet with blood and I'm sure the throbbing agony on my cheek is a shot that broke both facial bones and teeth. Maintaining consciousness against the pain isn't easy.

But if I faint, I will die.

I'm not totally sure I can save myself even now, but the long hours Audra spent reading the medical textbook aloud while I slept seems to have dramatically improved my ability to instinctively proceed with internal transformations.

So far.

Several of my vital organs are surely shredded. If I don't want to die of internal bleeding, I should do them next. I start from the top and work down, replacing all the organs in my digestive tract. It's extremely complex work, tiring me almost as much as creating a truckload of vaccine.

But I'm nearly there.

"You were right," Mariana says. "That was incredibly satisfying. I'm glad Melynda didn't kill her."

"Celebrate on your own," says a voice I could never forget—one that has haunted my dreams for months. "I know what it's like to think she's dead. You'll excuse me if I'm skeptical."

"Examine her, then. Just don't forget we need her blood."

"Your confidence in me is staggering," he says dryly.

"Gods, she's been a thorn in my side for almost two thousand years."

My head feels floaty. I need to focus, to work faster—and I need more blood. It's leaking out everywhere. I fill the blood vessels around my heart and then transform the breath sitting passively in my lungs to fresh, oxygenated air. This has the added benefit of saving me from the pain of inhalation; I haven't gotten around to fixing my ribs, which hurt like hell.

"We should take her body to the others," Mariana says. "Her partner and the young doctor have just about finished cleaning up the guards we gave them, and Thomas is still sitting in that room with Alanna, trying to think up a way to save his lady love. Hmmm," she says after a moment, "our former ingénue is pounding at the partition again. I think he may have heard us shoot her. He looks upset. At this rate, he'll break his hands."

Her calm voice describing Benson in agony makes me burn with fury.

"She's a real mess," Daniel says, very close to me. I continue to feed oxygen into my lungs, not drawing breath. I can't stop my heart from beating without losing consciousness, but if he touches me to check for a pulse, I'll know exactly where he is. If I have to, I can simply destroy him.

I hope. I hope I have it in me.

But Daniel doesn't check for a pulse—he cuts my throat instead. My eyes fly open at the fresh addition of pain, and I find myself staring up at him. His eyes are filled with disgust, not surprise, and he's pointing a snub-nosed revolver at the space between my brows. "Till next life, then."

Instinct kicks in as he pulls the trigger and time slows to a crawl. A burning cloud of gunpowder sears my already-ruined face, forcing my eyes closed and causing me to flinch away from the heat. It propels a tiny metal slug toward my brain at hypersonic speed and I feel it pierce the skin between my eyebrows, spinning, drilling into the bone beneath. And then, as it begins to notch my skull, I dissolve it, millimeter by millimeter, into nothing. A rivulet of blood runs down from the aching spot on my forehead. I'm not that fast.

For a split second I can't do anything but be surprised that I'm not dead. When I think to open my eyes again, I see Daniel and Mariana huddled close together just a few feet away, a tray of medical supplies between them. Daniel is holding a vial of blood.

My blood—he must have collected it when he cut my throat.

My throat! I close my carotid artery again, before I lose consciousness. I have to be fast. Already Mariana is drawing blood into two syringes and Daniel is rolling up his sleeve.

Now is the time to make the decision I could never quite bring myself to make in advance.

What to do with them.

They can't actually receive my blood. Not even a drop—it would be a death sentence to the world. The cells in my blood will surge through any person's bloodstream, implanting themselves into the bone marrow and slowly turning all of their cells into Earthbound Transformist cells. It would make Mariana and Daniel Transformists with the same degree of power as me. It would grant them true immortality. It would be the end of all mankind.

Worse than the end. The utter enslavement of all remaining

humans.

In the end, Audra is right, as she so often is.

I chance a blink, closing my eyelids over my burning eyes and seeing in that brief instant of darkness one of the pages she marked for me.

It has to be done.

They look like a normal couple as they assist each other, heads close together, smiling. "Ladies first," Daniel murmurs.

That spares me the agony of deciding.

Mariana twinges briefly at the stick of the needle, but her face turns almost rapturous as Daniel depresses the plunger.

"Now you," she says seductively. Daniel proffers his arm and she gently slips the needle in.

"Damn. Burns, doesn't it?" he says, rubbing his injection site.

"Burns? Mine didn't burn. Did I do it wrong?"

"No. Probably just haven't got your tolerance for pain." But he's still grasping at his arm.

Mariana turns from him and steps slowly toward a bank of computer monitors—surveillance screens. Taking out the cameras I could see was apparently a wasted effort; every single screen displays some part of the bunker. All I got were decoys, I guess. "Think we can keep them alive long enough to try our new powers on them? I'm feeling...creative."

A gasp from Daniel draws my attention—he's clawing the

skin on his arm bloody. But it's only when he falls to the ground, sending the medical tray clattering, that Mariana turns around.

"Daniel?" It's the first hint of weakness I've ever heard in her voice. "Daniel!" She screams and rushes over to him, pulling his head into her arms and cradling it against her chest. "I don't understand! What's happening?"

But he can't talk.

He opens his mouth but only pink froth emerges, mingling with the blood pouring out of his nose. A few more seconds and his whole body begins to convulse. "No, Love!" Mariana shrieks, as though she could will him to stop dying. At this point, even I couldn't help him. "Don't leave me. Not yet. Please!"

She rocks back and forth and tears are streaming down her face as sobs wrack her chest. I've stopped thinking of them as lovers for so long that I forgot about their bond. An Earthbound's motivation for living, Sammi once said.

I can't watch. Can't afford to think of them as human.

It's too late to change anything.

I close my eyes and block them out, focusing instead on fixing my limbs and rebuilding my face. I can't do everything, but I need to be able to walk out of here, and I have to do it without bleeding to death.

When I'm sufficiently whole to sit upright, Mariana is too

fixated on Daniel to notice my movement. I take advantage of her distraction to look myself over—patching the wounds I can see—then rise, struggling, to my feet. When she does notice me, I want to be standing, towering over her. She'll never know how much it cost me.

The sobs from the corner grow suddenly faint, then stop altogether. Confusion spreads on Mariana's face and her hand goes to her throat.

"It's too late."

My words are weak, but they carry to her ears and Mariana's head jerks up. "You!" But it's hardly a whisper and she gags on it, her hands clutching her neck again.

I raise my hand to my forehead and wipe away the trickle of blood from Daniel's shot, leaving the skin there whole and unbroken. "You're already dead, Mariana. You just don't know it."

I find still more aches as I step forward. Though I try not to show it, I'm sure I'm wincing. Mariana rises to her knees, but almost immediately starts to choke. The floor splits beneath my feet—a weak attempt at destruction. I step off the spider web of cracks anyway.

"While you were lamenting your loss, you probably missed the beginning of the sensation of the Sarin injection taking over your body. But if you pay attention, you'll recognize the signs now. I apologize; it's a terrible way to die." My voice is hollow and I feel oddly disconnected from the scene in front of me.

The one I caused.

Mariana scrapes at her throat, her fingernails tearing into the tender skin, and it's all I can do to keep speaking calmly as the horror of what I've done washes over me.

"It's too late to stop it," I say, and I'm not sure who I'm really addressing—her or me. "I've been assured that the poison scrambles your abilities even faster than it kills you. You've got about two minutes left to live. And you're going to listen to me during those two minutes."

My hands are clenched behind me and I stop a few feet short of where Mariana lies dying—not really wanting to tempt fate by putting myself within arm's reach. "We both know that as soon as you and Daniel can get your memories back and reunite—and I'm sure you have people I don't know about in place to help you—you'll start plotting something new and awful. But by the time that happens, I promise you, I will have eradicated your virus."

Her body is shaking with pain, her lips turning blue from lack of oxygen. "I know it's hard to believe right now, Mariana, considering you're probably experiencing the worst physical pain of all your many, many lives, but I'm granting you a great mercy right now. I'm giving you another chance. You're not dying of the virus—meaning you won't be dead forever. Don't think I didn't consider it. Very seriously. Even with your immunity, I could probably fill your body with enough raw viral solution to overwhelm it. But I won't trade the millions of human lives your eternal deaths would cause merely for the convenience of the two of you being gone forever."

I edge closer, my stomach churning at what I've done to this woman I once considered my greatest friend, only outside of my eternal lover. "Listen carefully, Mariana. This is the important part." I raise my voice and pierce her with my eyes. "If you return and try to hunt me again, or try to kill the humans, I will change my mind. And even if there isn't a single strand of the virus left in the entire world, it will always exist in my mind. I can create it at any moment, in any lifetime, and no defense you could possibly launch will keep me from finding a way to get it into your body. Someday—somehow. And thanks to you and Daniel, no matter what happens with Logan and me, I will always be strong enough to make it."

Mariana's muscles go into spasms, forcing her limbs into unnatural angles that make me ache to see them. My voice is shaking and I have to take a breath to stabilize it—disgusted at myself for what I'm doing and trying to remember all the people I'm making safe.

All it costs is my humanity.

I crouch down beside her, so close I could reach out and touch her hand, but I'm not afraid. The gut-wrenching agony she's in makes it impossible for her to concentrate on anything else.

"And remember this, Mariana. The body you're reborn into will not be immune. Nor will the next. And in a thousand years they won't even vaccinate babies as a precaution and you'll be utterly vulnerable to me, for eternity."

Air is hissing out of her mouth and I think she might be trying to form a word, but even as I lean closer her muscles contract and her neck bends so far back I swear I can hear her bones pop.

"Kill me."

The words are unmistakable even in her hissed whisper.

I wonder if Audra knew the poison would be this bad when she marked it in the textbook.

Probably.

"No," I say. "After everything you've done to me, to Rebecca, to Sonya, to Greta, to Lady Leona, I only had one act of mercy left in me. And I've already used it."

Hatred shines in her eyes an instant before they squeeze shut in a deathly grimace and silent sobs wrack her chest. It takes thirty more seconds for her movements to slow and her face to turn completely blue before she stops moving, stops breathing. But in those few seconds, every drop of human emotion drains from me.

I will walk the world forever, cursed to remember this

moment, lifetime after lifetime, until the skies burn and the seas boil and the stars fall from the heavens.

I am a monster.

I am Earthbound.

CHAPTER THIRTY-FOUR

Benson's arms around me are as agonizing as they are comforting.

"Dear Lord, Tave! What happened to you?" But examining me involves pushing me away from his chest and I'm having none of that.

"Just hold me. Gently!" I caution when he starts to squeeze. His hands are soft as butterflies on my back.

"They're dead," I say, choking on the sob in my throat. "I couldn't kill them forever, though. I couldn't sentence that many people to die."

"It's okay. You did the right thing."

I feel a complete emotional breakdown building up inside of me, but I can't fall to pieces yet. I gulp down my anguish and sniff and dab at my eyes, clawing for control. "We've still got to get back to your dad."

"We need to find Audra and Logan too," Benson says tightly.

"They're with Thomas," I say, glad to finally have some good news. "I saw them on the security screens in the other room. There are some controls in there, too, and I was able to open some doors, but I think everyone else in this whole building is dead. And I don't see any way to free Alanna."

Benson shakes his head. "What a nightmare."

I can't talk anymore. If I do I'm going to cry and if I start now, I'm never going to stop. "Let's go."

My body protests with every step I take. Benson sees me wincing and tries to help by ducking under my arm and pulling me snug against his side.

"Don't! My ribs," I gasp and he jumps back.

"Can I…carry you?"

I think of my new organs in my sadly punctured torso and that doesn't sound very pleasant. I shake my head. "I need a doctor. Some amateur has been trying to keep me alive with half-remembered facts from an anatomy book."

Benson gives me a puzzled look. "What? Who?"

"Me."

He smiles weakly. "What can I do?"

"Hold my hand and walk slowly."

"Deal," he says.

It takes us about fifteen minutes to get to the room where Alanna is still held captive. Thomas is clearly at the end of his rope and when we enter the room, his eyes widen like he's seeing a ghost.

Though, considering the state I'm in, that's pretty *apropos*.

"You're alive!" Logan jumps up and groans and Audra smacks him.

"Sit down. Three bullets in that hip," she says in explanation. "I can take them out but it would be better if you or Alanna…well, a Destroyer would be helpful," she finishes awkwardly.

"Are they dead?" Thomas asks, in his typical straightforward fashion.

It doesn't bristle today—I'm grateful for it. I nod, the knot forming in my throat again. "And so is—" But I catch Benson's eye and he gives a tiny shake of his head. We can talk about what Benson was forced to do later. "Everyone else," I finish.

Thomas stands in front of the grotesque apparatus still holding Alanna captive. "What do I do? The only people who could free her are dead. Not that they would have," he adds.

I didn't know before, but now I've brutally slaughtered two people and something has shifted in my brain. Solutions I could never have brought myself to even *consider* now seem entirely possible. I hate that I've started to think like them, but maybe this once it'll save a life. "I have an idea," I say slowly. "But you're really going to have to trust me."

"Of course," Thomas says without hesitation.

"No, you are really, *really* going to have to trust me."

Thomas eyes me suspiciously, but he says, "I do, Tavia."

"Okay. Benson, what kind of material can contain dimethylmercury safely?

"Glass, silver. *Maybe* stainless steel but I don't remember for sure. Stick with one of the other two."

"Okay. I know what to do then. But I need the three of us to work together and we have to be completely synchronized. First, Thomas, has she tried to wake up at all since I left?"

"Once. I created a bolus of diazepam under her skin," he says, haltingly. "She went out again." His voice is flat, like he doesn't have the energy reserves to feel anything anymore.

I understand completely. "Okay, I need you to give her something very, very strong. Something that will keep her asleep despite terrible pain."

He looks at me for a long time in silence.

"Let me do my job, Thomas." My voice is flat, devoid of emotion. I have to be that way for precision. It's why I can't tell him what I'm about to do—he'll be too scared.

"I hate this," he says at last.

"I know," I say, still in that lifeless voice. "But I need you focused. Entirely. On the now, not on the future."

He turns to Alanna, focusing on her outstretched arm, then breathes out a long and ragged sigh.

"Is it done?"

"Yes."

"Do I need to wait for it to take effect?"

He shakes his head. "I distributed it throughout her bloodstream."

"Good, I need you and Benson to stand by her arms, but don't touch her yet. On the count of three grab her and pull her out."

"Okay." His voice is barely more than a whisper, but it's there. He moves into place beside Alanna's left shoulder and Benson goes to her right. Logan is on his feet again, but carefully shifting the weight to his good hip, and Audra is sitting beside her EB Scanner, watching me with glittering eyes.

"One."

I can't do this.

"Two."

It's too awful.

"Three!"

In synchronized motion Thomas and Benson grab Alanna's shoulders and as their hands touch her, I encircle the sphere of dimethylmercury in a larger circle of solid silver. As they pull I transform gaps into all four of her limbs, severing her hands and feet from her body.

A stream of blood follows Alanna's limp form to where it slides to the floor at almost the same moment that the hiss and snap of the spring triggers engaging fills the small room. Each of the four capsules still trapping Alanna's hands and feet bubble and foam and, as Benson theorized, a corrosive acid spews out, drenching them and eating away the skin, converting it to acrid smoke.

I turn and gag, choking up bile from my empty stomach.

The next sensation I feel is the whipping sting of skin and Thomas standing over me shouting words that I can't quite make out.

Benson slams into his father, pinning him against the wall and I cradle my already broken cheekbone where Thomas backhanded me. I scuttle out of the way and over to Alanna. If I don't act quickly, Alanna is going to bleed to death. I take one bloody stump in my hands and close my eyes, remembering. When I open them, a new, perfect, unmarred hand is sitting in mine.

But creating a new body part—especially one as intricate as a hand—takes far more energy than simply fixing one. And I've already had to replace a goodly percentage of *myself* today.

I move to the other stump, my hands already slick and wet with Alanna's blood—and mine—and I focus again. A second hand. By the time I move to her feet I'm feeling the nausea that tells me I'm reaching my limit. But I can't stop—not even if it kills me.

One perfect foot. But that's all the longer Benson can hold Thomas back. Thomas gets a full-armed swing and catches Benson right in the jaw. Benson stumbles to his knees and Thomas is coming for me again, murder in his eyes. Logan and

Audra shout at him, but their voices sound like they're coming from very far away as I take that last severed leg in my hand and close my eyes. I feel the last appendage forming beneath my fingers when everything goes black.

CHAPTER THIRTY-FIVE

I awake to a barrage of conflicting sensations—brilliant beams of sunshine, prickles of cold on my cheeks, a cocoon of warmth, something very soft against my chin. It's hard to open my eyes and I let my lids flutter, trying to take in my surroundings. Everywhere I look all I can see is dazzling white.

Am I dead?

I wiggle my fingers and toes and am not immediately assaulted with burning pain. Maybe I *am* dead. Maybe I burned myself out. I always thought it was a possibility.

But after a few more blinks I realize that what I'm seeing is snow. Someone is holding a warm, soft blanket around me and I turn, expecting to see Benson, but it's Alanna's smiling face that greets me instead.

"Oh good," she says softly. "You woke up."

"*You* woke up," I retort, struggling upright.

"Careful," she says, pulling the soft blanket—that I realize now is some kind of fur—around my shoulders and gently nudging me back down against her chest. "You've lost a lot of blood. While the boys and I were searching the facility for anything useful, Audra and Thomas put you back together—though I insist on a follow-up once we're back in civilization. But Thomas said there's something special about your blood and Audra wasn't comfortable giving you a transfusion."

"I can do it," I mumble, but Alanna holds up a hand.

"Not yet. Please just rest."

I lay back against Alanna's chest, her arms around me, feeling—for the first time in over a year—safe.

It's a good feeling.

"What *is* this?" I ask, rubbing my face against the soft fur.

A low chuckle sounds in her throat. "Mink. My favorite. Except that Thomas creates it for me. So it's all the awesomeness, none of the death. Nice, huh?"

"Very." Seems like less death is the single most important thing the world needs right now.

She grins. "No animals were harmed in the making of this luscious fur blanket. Oh, Benson told Thomas some of your favorite foods and he made them for you."

I groan. "Please not a peanut butter chocolate milkshake."

"Benson thought trail mix and caramel macchiato might be more suitable in this weather."

She hands me a steaming thermos and I inhale the heavenly scent. "I love that boy," I whisper.

"I know."

My face flushes, but I hide it by taking a long sip of the

steamy drink that seems to warm me right down to my toes.

And gives me that now familiar buzz of sugar in my blood.

"Thomas is sorry," she says, stroking my cheek, which is tender, but not painful like before. They must have repaired my broken facial bones. "He'll tell you himself when he comes back, but he asked me to also let you know immediately if you woke up before they returned. He's devastated over what he did to you."

But I'm already shaking my head. "I'd have smacked me too. No really," I say when Alanna tries to protest. "There's nothing to forgive. I knew there would be consequences for not telling him beforehand. It was a terrible, terrible moment."

"It worked though."

I take a deep breath and let it out shakily. "He'd have never let me do it if I'd told him before what I had planned."

"Sometimes it's better to ask forgiveness than permission."

"I'm just glad it worked." I munch several handfuls of trail mix, hardly believing this day is actually over. "What are they doing?"

"Setting charges." Alanna shifts so I can see a veritable mountain of black duffel bags. "We've gone through and taken everything from the bunker that we think will be helpful. Enough documents and files to keep us busy for months. Years. Now they're getting ready to blow everything up."

"With all the bodies in there?"

"Partially because of all the bodies in there. Erase the evidence. But also so Daniel and Mariana can't come back here in their next life."

"Good point," I say ruefully, because regardless of the terrible way they perished, death is only a reset button for Earthbound.

I see movement between the rows of solar panels and Alanna sits up a little straighter. "Here they come."

The four of them are trudging along in their snowshoes—though happily without all the weapons this time—and when they crest a hill Benson sees me and begins to run. I get shakily to my feet and manage two steps in his direction. A huge grin breaks out on his face and when he's about three feet from me I launch myself into the air and tackle him backward into the powder-soft snow.

I laugh as he covers my face with kisses, but the laughter melts away when he finds my mouth, kissing me like I'm going to disappear at any moment. My arms twine around his neck and I don't feel the chill of the cold with his body pressed to mine; his lips delve, warming me even better than the macchiato.

"Do not ever, *ever* do anything like that again."

I let out a snort of laughter. "Oh Benson, you are barking up the wrong tree if you think life with me is going to be easy, or safe, or...or ..." He's kissing my neck again and I'm having trouble keeping track of my train of thought.

"A week then," he says close to my ear. "Take a week off and just be boring. With me," he adds.

"Deal," I say against his lips, pushing my fingers into his hair and pulling him tight against me.

"You're going to miss the show," Audra says dryly.

Benson pulls away and helps me sit up, brushing snow out of my hair. I laugh at his efforts, then look up and catch Logan's eye. He turns away instantly—trying to pretend he didn't get caught staring, I think—but there's a defeat in his expression that makes my heart ache.

"It's starting," Audra says as the ground begins to rumble.

I expected to see fire and smoke and such, but in the beginning, all I see is the field of solar panels collapsing into the ground below. Eventually there *are* flames, and smoke, but it's far less showy than I anticipated. Which is probably good.

The six of us stand together, huddled close for warmth, and watch the place where we all had to face our nightmares transform itself into a smoldering depression in the middle of a snowy field.

CHAPTER THIRTY-SIX

I give Benson the promised week. In part because Thomas and Alanna insist on it. They arrange for us to stay in a small cottage in North Carolina, just far enough from the beach that it escaped the flooding.

Alanna and Thomas, of course, go right back to liaising with the same government officials Dr. Martin has been working with for months. Alanna brought Kat to come see us for a day, but beyond that, she's not letting anyone have access to me. I'm grateful; I've needed it. I'll have to get back to making vaccine soon, but I try not to feel guilty about my days off. I need to take care of myself too, as Benson continually reminds me. We've got our work cut out for us—but at least no one will be actively undermining us anymore.

With its still-low fat reserves my body isn't up to swimming in the chilly Atlantic yet, but most days Benson and I walk down to the ocean and stroll along the sand, enjoying the sunshine. It reminds me of Brisbane.

The beach bungalows—the ones that haven't been washed away completely—are damaged; probably beyond repair.

"The news is saying that ocean levels are lower than anyone could have expected—almost normal," Benson says, picking up a doorknob from the sand and tossing it my way. I make it disappear. It's a game we've been playing. Pick up trash, make it go away. *Simple* magic. Helpful magic. "Now they're arguing over whether it's global warming to blame, or 'tectonic redistribution,' I think they're calling it. With all the land that vanished, the new island in the Atlantic hasn't made as much of a difference as feared. Of course, they don't know about you and Alanna, either."

"Close to normal is good enough for me," I say, though even if the ocean levels remain stable, I know what he's not mentioning—that the change in currents and ocean floor topography is influencing the environment in totally unpredictable and often dangerous ways. Even without Daniel and Mariana fighting us at every turn, Kat still expects it to take over a year to eradicate the virus, so I'll take whatever good news I can get. We might have another Earthbound death in the next eighteen months that *lowers* the levels of the ocean. Until things are truly settled, anywhere close to normal is probably the best we can hope for.

We're silent for several minutes before I broach a topic I've been trying to segue into for the last few days. "Did you tell Thomas about your mom?"

Benson stiffens for a moment, then leans down and grabs

what I think is a piece of a toy. He tosses it, and it disappears. "I decided not to."

"Why?"

He shrugs. "Thomas doesn't even think about her anymore. Hell, until last week I haven't thought about her more than fleetingly in months. Maybe that makes me a bad person, but you know what? She was a worse one."

"They made her a worse one."

"She let them." His tone is cold and I'm not sure how hard to poke him on this issue.

"She was still your mom and I'm sorry you had to be the one to kill her." I pause, then blurt out the words I've been wanting to tell him since the moment he pulled that trigger. "I would have done it for you."

"I know." He throws a rock into the waves, then turns to look at me. "That's why I did it instead. I saw in your eyes that you were going to take her out, and I knew that I could spend the rest of our lives trying to convince you I didn't resent you for it, and you'd never believe me. Not entirely." He shrugged. "Your happiness is more important to me than her life."

"But...but she's your family."

"You're my family. You and only you. Well," he adds with a grin, "kind of Thomas and Alanna too, I guess. But you're number one in my life."

"You were so upset." The truth is that I keep expecting to

see the emotional meltdown he had to hold back in that bunker. But I haven't.

"I was. But I realized while I was standing outside that wall, separated from you, that what I really lost when my mom died was the illusion that I could ever have my old family back. That hasn't really been possible since Thomas left us, and I knew it. But part of me always kind of hoped that maybe...well. It was never real. What was *real* was what I had with you. What I was so terrified I'd lost without ever being able to tell you."

"I want to be with you, Benson."

"And as incredible as that is, I'm still shocked every time you say it."

"I want to be with you forever."

"Our whole lives," Benson whispers, leaning forward to kiss me.

"What if...what if it could be longer?"

Benson pulls back, blinking in question.

"I...I haven't told anyone, Benson—although I think your dad suspects. When we were in the Curatoria headquarters, I discovered that I was immune. Your dad led me to that, actually. That's why I made the vaccine from my own DNA. But what I didn't tell him is that when I was Greta, three lives ago, Mariana and Daniel tried to kill me with the virus, but they failed. The virus mutated, or reacted strangely or...or something. And it changed my blood. That's when I became a

Transformist. And immortal. And so powerful. It's there in my blood, and that's what Daniel and Mariana wanted so badly. It wasn't just about stopping me from making the vaccine. It was about getting my blood."

"But they were already immune," Benson said, and he's standing so stiffly, I know he's aware that he's still missing a piece.

"My blood can change other Earthbound too, Benson. Make them like me. That's what Daniel and Mariana wanted."

Benson closes his eyes and lets out a low whistle. "Imagine them as powerful as you. The world wouldn't stand a chance."

"Right? And to be quite honest, the day might come when I have to use the virus on them and risk the loss of more human life if that's what it take to keep them from getting what they want." I wrap my arms around my waist. "Though I hope not."

Benson tosses another rock before I continue speaking.

"Benson, I'm pretty sure it works on humans too."

He freezes. "What works?" But I can tell he already knows the answer.

"My blood." I walk forward and slide my hand down his arm and lace my fingers through his. "I could change *you*."

Benson starts walking again, pulling me with him, and I sense that he needs a few minutes of silence, so I say nothing.

"Tave," he says finally, "few humans on Earth understand

the pull of an Earthbound's soul mate the way I do. I don't resent the fact that the only reason you're with me is because you don't remember all your lives with Logan. I don't." He turns to face me and tucks a strand of my hair—shoulder-length, at the moment—behind my ear, his fingers so soft on my face. "But in your next life, you won't choose me. You'll choose *him*."

"But—"

"I get it's hard to comprehend now, but I know it. I've *lived* it. And Tavia, *Logan* knows it. What would I be then? A bitter, unhappy immortal with powers beyond human comprehension, and nothing to do with his time but feel sorry for himself." He lifts my hands to his mouth and brushes kisses over the knuckles. "I've read all the comic books, Tave. Those are the kinds of conditions that turn a hero into a villain."

He snugs an arm around me and starts walking again, leaving me with bittersweet thoughts swirling in my head.

"I'm only human, Tavia," he says after a long silence. "I have only one life. And when it's gone, it's gone. If I can spend that life with you, then when I'm an old gray man, stumbling around with a cane and bad eyes"—he grins and I laugh at the thought—"then I'll die happy."

"And so will I," I promise him.

He pulls me close, our bodies pressed tightly together, and

kisses me long and gentle. I twine my arms around his neck and lose myself in the moment. He's right, really; one life is a long time. And I intend to make the most of it.

CHAPTER THIRTY-SEVEN

I climb the steps of the Torre Matilde in Viareggio, Italy, my heart pounding in my chest. It's been almost six months since I last saw Logan. By the time I returned to work after my week off with Benson, he was gone.

He did have the courtesy to leave a note. It said: *Don't look for me.*

Convincing Thomas to honor Logan's request hadn't been easy. He'd come to really respect Logan and the calm, well-considered decisions he made that had allowed Thomas to spend time with Alanna those last few weeks of our travels. But in the end, that's how I convinced him—I told him he had to trust Logan.

A week ago I got a letter. A roundabout letter. It was sent to Kat, who's now the Mayo Clinic Presidential Liaison—a hopefully temporary position created specifically to aid in the eradication of the Kentucky virus.

The letter was in an envelope, in another envelope. The outer one was addressed to Kat, the inner one to me. But for security reasons, that envelope was opened as well. He's lucky they decided to bring me the "blank" piece of paper at all.

Written in Earthscript, of course.

He asked me to meet him here. Today.

So here I am.

I'm assuming he's been following the news and knows how well the efforts against the virus are going. I'll make a couple warehouses of vaccine while we're here—maybe even hit Spain and France before we go back. Travel is easier now. We're still very careful, but with Daniel and Mariana gone the remaining Reduciata forces are in total disarray. Plus, Benson gave Kat directions to the Reduciata headquarters in New England, and she turned that info over to the government, who raided the compound looking for bioterrorists. I'm sure most of the actual Earthbound got away, but the raid separated the Reduciates from their labs as well as their command center. There haven't been any more city-wide plagues of the virus since.

Or blown-up planes.

Or bombed buildings.

They're not *gone*. Just like with humans, there will always be Earthbound who want at best, chaos, and at worse, suffering. But we crippled them.

So mostly I stay home now—well, in the United States, anyway. I still live mostly in hotels, but I'm not catching a new flight every other day. We mainly depend on the authorities to ship out the vaccine. Healthier for me, by far.

Still hard. I can't wait until I'm not sleeping eighteen hours a day and eating three to four times what I really should need. But that time is coming quickly. More quickly than I could have estimated since we've been able to streamline the process. Another six months or so, I think. Or, at least, I should be able to shift to part-time vaccine-making at that point. Creating a stockpile instead of saving lives in immediate danger. But we're doing well enough that when I said I was going to Italy, no one argued.

It took a little doing to get into the tall, crumbling tower. It's not open to the public, but of course that'll simply make our meeting more private. Human security poses no challenge to me.

This town awakens a niggling memory in my brain and I'm certain that Logan and I must have shared a life here. I don't know when, or for how long, but it has that sense of home that only places where Logan and I were together evokes.

I feel him before I see him, but even so, I can't stop a gasp from escaping my lips when I catch a glimpse of that golden blond hair. His back is to me, and he looks more Quinn-like than I've ever seen him before. His hair is shoulder-length, pulled into a low ponytail, and though he's wearing a leather jacket and cargoes rather than a dress-coat and breeches, the riding boots are Quinn's. He turns at the soft sound and I'm certain our brightening expressions are mirrors of one another.

I jump onto the top step and run to him; we meet in the middle, crashing together, arms wrapping around each other. I pull him tight against me—or maybe myself tight against him, I'm not sure—and time is meaningless as we hold on. My face is buried against his shoulder and I inhale his familiar scent. I've missed him so much. It was odd to suddenly have something I really wanted to tell him, and I'd sometimes turn, half-expecting him to be there to hear it.

But he wasn't.

After a long while Logan clears his throat and laughs awkwardly, raising his hand to swipe at his eyes. "Sorry," he says, and my insides melt at the sound of his voice. "I thought I was ready for this."

"Don't apologize," I say, tears making my own eyes burn. I slide my hands down his arms and twine our fingers. "I'm overjoyed to see you too."

"I'm glad." His smile is back, even if sadness lurks on the edges.

"Where've you been?" I ask, not bothering with meaningless small talk.

"Around," he says vaguely. "It's not a secret or anything," he adds when I narrow my eyes. "I plane-hopped. No pattern or logic really. Spent some time in Australia, Greece, France, Brazil. Couple other places." He shrugs. "I just traveled."

"Did you…have fun?" The air feels suddenly awkward and I don't know what else to ask.

"Not really. What have you been doing?"

I laugh wearily. "Making vaccine. I have *not* been traveling, though. In fact, this is the first trip I've made out of the country since—since you left."

"It seems to be working."

"Yeah. We have a good system."

"How about the others?"

I smile. "Audra's getting ready to take her MCATs…again, of course. She'll ace them. She wants to be able to practice medicine in *the real world*, as she calls it." I sober. "And she's looking for Sergei. Alanna convinced Kat to help her. With all the tech and data she has access to now as a government bigwig, I mean. Audra hopes to find him in his childhood so she can track his movements and keep him safe until he's older and…ready."

"What about Thomas and Alanna?"

"They're on Atlantis."

He laughs. "I can't believe they called it that."

"Well, that's what it is, isn't it? Thomas and Alanna figure it may be the last time they're ever going to be able to take part in settling an entirely new continent, and that as a mixed pair, they really *ought* to be there." I roll my eyes at that.

"Sounds like a convenient excuse for an adventure," Logan

says.

"Basically. But it also keeps them far away from the remaining Earthbound who might be loyal to either brotherhood."

"Probably a good idea."

Silence falls like a heavy blanket.

"And Benson?"

I had to know it was coming. "He's good. Wants to go back to school. When we're finished with the vaccine project."

"Still…together?"

I nod, not able to force the words from my throat.

"Still sure that's what you want?"

I have to verbalize it this time. "Yes."

Logan lets go of my hands and walks a few steps to the edge of the tower, leaning on the ledge and taking in the expanse of the city. "Are you happy?" he asks quietly.

"As happy as I can be." I join him, though I remain standing instead of leaning, like he is. "I've missed you. I always will. Which makes me feel guilty. Because it's not fair for me to want you around when it's got to be so hard for you."

"I thought it would get better with time," he replies, the light breeze carrying his voice to me. "That's why it I left."

"Did it?" But I already know the answer.

"No. It got worse." He's quiet for a long time. "I asked you to meet me so I could say goodbye. So you wouldn't have to wonder. Clean break." He turns to face me fully and his words are forceful, like he can pound them into me. "This is what I want—what I need—and I think it'll be better for both of us."

I swallow hard. "I understand." And I do, even though it's tearing me into pieces.

He stands now, facing me. "I hope you really mean that. I mean, *you* made your choice. And this is mine. I need you to respect that."

"I will," I say, a trickle of irritation bubbling up in my belly. "I'm not arguing with you."

"Just remember what I said, okay?"

"Okay."

"Promise?"

I scrunch my eyebrows together. He's being really weird about this. "I promise."

He nods, looking grim for a few seconds before he meets my eyes and smiles. "You look really great, by the way. I mean, you were always beautiful. But you've—I feel weird complimenting you by saying you've put on weight but—"

"Don't feel weird," I say, laughing. "It's true, I was too skinny last time you saw me, and I was way unhealthy. Actually, since you're, well, *you*, I'll confess that Audra taught me how to add, um, fat cells to my body. The good kind and in the right places."

He snickers. "Like reverse liposuction?"

"Pretty much."

He smiles and shakes his head, then sobers. "You do look better though. Stronger. I was worried."

"I *am* better." I sigh. "I was in bad physical shape before. I couldn't have kept it up much longer. Now that I'm healthy again, I can understand how far gone I really was."

He gestures to a bench and we walk over and sit down.

"I'm painting again." I haven't told anyone else that except Benson.

Logan's smile is warm and understanding. "That's excellent! I know how important art is to you."

"It's more than that, though. I…I create frames for them and I leave them in hotels that I stay at. Instead of the tacky art they hang there."

It takes him a second to understand. "You're making sure there are plenty of artifacts."

"Exactly."

"Thank you." His voice is a little shaky, and I'm glad I told him.

I hesitate, but the last six months have given me so much time to think, and to regret things I never told him. "I was never very honest with you before about…about my brain injury. And I think you need to know the truth."

"What truth?" He looks worried.

"I told you about the things that I don't remember, but there's something else Audra told me that I won't actually know until...until next time. Next *life*," I clarify. I wait for Logan to say something—a by-proxy way of procrastinating, maybe—but he doesn't, and I'm forced to continue. "She said there's something wrong with my memory process and that my brain might not be able to get this life into long-term storage."

Logan is staring at me, and when he asks, "Meaning what?" I think he already knows, and just needs me to say it.

"Meaning that next life I may not remember being Tavia at all," I whisper.

Logan laces his fingers and leans forward with his elbows on his knees.

"I won't remember being a Transformist, defeating Daniel and Mariana, the vaccine or the virus. None of it."

"I'll remind you," Logan says fiercely. "I'll tell you everything you need to know. I'll make sure you understand that *you saved the world*. I'll remember for you."

"I know you will," I say, tears escaping down my cheeks at his immediate support. "But it's more than that. When I...when I killed Mariana, I threatened her. I told her than no matter how much time passed, I would always know how to make the virus and I would use it on her if they tried to hunt me or kill all the humans again." I clench my teeth. "It was a bluff."

"*Might* be a bluff," Logan says. "We don't know that yet."

"I've done what I can. I gave extensive notes to Kat and Thomas and Alanna about the virus and vaccine. They've each put their copy somewhere secret for safekeeping. But even so, it's not a guarantee."

"You've done what you can. And I'll be there to help." He pauses, then grips my hand. "You have to know by now that together we can do just about anything."

I smile. "I do know that." My mouth goes dry as I try to work up the guts for my last confession. "One more thing."

His eyes widen almost imperceptibly and I see a hint of fear.

"Remember the big secret?"

He snorts. "Which one?"

I laugh too and it breaks up the tension a little. "Good point. The one about Daniel and Mariana jointly running the brotherhoods?"

"Ah, that one. Yes."

"When I was Rebecca and you were Quinn, we decided that I would keep that a secret even from you."

His lips are pressed into a tight line now, and he nods once.

"We were wrong."

He looks up at me and then lets out his breath in a long sigh. "I think we were, too."

"Logan, nothing good has ever come out of me not trusting

you. Nothing."

"And vice-versa," he said fervently.

"So I'm trusting you with an even bigger secret."

His face drains of color and he angles so he can face me. "Go ahead," he whispers.

There's no one around—and we're at least a hundred feet above anyone on the street—but still, I whisper. "My blood is what makes me a Transformist. It makes me immune and it's where we got the protein to make the vaccine. I think you know all of that."

A quick nod.

"But there's one more step. It's why Mariana and Daniel wanted me even after they had the vaccine." I pause. "My blood can turn anyone into what I am."

Air hisses between his teeth. "You know this for sure?"

"I did tests."

"Anyone?"

I nod.

I see his jaw clenching and for long seconds I don't think he's going to speak. "Did you change Benson?"

"No."

At that word he looks up at me, both shock and hope shining in his eyes.

"I offered," I confess. "But he turned me down."

"Good man," he murmurs.

"Smart, I think," I reply. "I didn't believe him at first, but over the last several months, I've thought about it a lot and I think that he's right. I'm giving him my present, Logan. I'm sorry for the pain I *know* that causes you. So, *so* sorry. But…my future still belongs to you." I smile sadly. "I might not even remember Benson next life."

"I'll remind you of him too," Logan says softly.

It's more than I deserve.

"Thank you for telling me," he whispers.

I lay my hand over his. "I trust you. With everything."

He smiles, though it doesn't reach his eyes. "I know."

"And Logan I want to—"

"Don't," he says and there's a river of pain in his voice so deep it makes me hurt. "Don't offer it to me in almost the same breath as you tell me you offered it to him."

My mouth claps shut and I remind myself I shouldn't be surprised he can read me so well.

But he forces a smile. "Let's talk about it the next time we're together."

"Next time?" I say softly, needing to be certain what he means.

"Next life," he says, and though it feels like a rock has just formed in my stomach, I nod. At least he's said it straight out.

"Oh," he says after a moment, "I owe you something. Two things, actually."

He slides his hand out from under mine, reaches into his pocket, and gives me a long, black velvet box. I smile and open it, even though I'm pretty sure I know what it's going to be.

But the box is empty.

"It's already on you," Logan whispers.

My fingers find the familiar silver and ruby pendant that I lost almost a year ago. The one Quinn made for Rebecca. The necklace that started this whole ordeal.

"Thank you." I could have made it myself. But he told me months ago that he'd do it, and I've been waiting.

"And this," Logan says, handing me a perfect, thornless, blood-red rose. "I told you once in the Curatoria headquarters that I'd give you flowers every day. I guess I haven't done very well at keeping that promise."

"You're forgiven," I say with a smile, reaching for the rose.

Logan glances up at the skyline, already turning orange. "Watch one last sunset with me? Then we'll go our separate ways."

"Of course," I say softly.

"I mean it, Tavia," he says, a sliver of desperation creeping into his voice. "We won't see each other again. I need you to not look for me. Not until you're ready to be mine again. *Completely* mine."

"I understand." The thought makes my chest hurt, but I owe him this. "I promise I won't."

"*My* choice," he says again, barely over a whisper.

"Deal," I say, forcing a smile.

He lays his arm across my shoulders and I lean against him, my eyes on the purpling sky. We don't say anything, and I enjoy a few minutes of silence in his quiet company, trying not to think about the separation that's coming.

But he deserves to have what he needs, and somehow, I'll find the strength to walk away. The sunlight disappears and the air takes on a sudden chill. More than I expected. I force back a shiver and wait, deciding that I'll let him tell me when our meeting is over.

But the sun disappears, and darkness begins to spread, and still Logan says nothing. Doesn't move. Doesn't even stir. I look up at him and his eyes are closed. I wonder if he's fallen asleep.

"Logan?" I say, nudging him. "Logan?"

But he slumps sideways onto his propped-up arm and in an instant, snatches of our conversation come back—racing through my head.

I asked you to meet me so I could say goodbye. So you wouldn't have to wonder. This is what I want—what I need.

Fear pounds in my temples and I put my fingers to his throat, even though I already know what I'm going to feel.

You made your choice. And this is mine. I need you to respect that.

My breath comes in loud gasps and I'm fighting to remain

calm.

I mean it, Tavia. We won't see each other again. I need you to not look for me. Not until you're ready to be mine again.

My choice.

My choice.

My choice.

I sit there for several more minutes, my hand on his throat, willing his heart to beat again. Even though I know it won't.

He's gone.

It feels like something is breaking inside me and everything in my body hurts as I hold his body against my chest, sobbing so deeply I can hardly draw breath.

Nearly an hour passes before my tears dry and a numb sort of acceptance comes over me. I rise from the little bench and look down at Logan's body, cooling in the evening chill. I was supposed to walk away at sunset. I've stayed too long already. He didn't want me to be unhappy.

I have to remember—our gift and our curse—death is not the end.

He's right, of course. As overwhelming as the grief is now, in my mind I can comprehend that one day it will lessen. And I understand that this is the feeling Logan has been living with for months—almost a year. He'd spend the remainder of his life feeling the same way I do at this moment. Maybe worse. He is Earthbound, after all.

I shouldn't resent his not wanting that. It gives me freedom as well—freedom from the guilt of making him suffer. Logan will live one more blissful, unawakened, unknowing life as a human while I grow old with Benson.

And after that…well, that's his plan. We'll be together then. When we're both ready.

It's a gift. A gift from Logan to both of us. All of us.

I kiss the red petals and leave the rose on his chest.

And I walk away.